ALL THAT SHE WANTS

"Leaving already?" Jennette stood in the moonlight looking everything like the angel she'd dressed to be tonight. She rubbed her arms as if to keep the cold wind away.

"Yes. I wouldn't wish to cause you any further distress tonight."

She lifted one black eyebrow. "Am I to assume the dance with Lucinda didn't go as I'd planned?"

He approached her slowly. She had matured into an exquisite beauty. She had delicate cheekbones and flawless ivory skin, a mouth too full to be perfect but just right for other things. The white gown outlined her slender body and slight fullness of her breasts. He shook his head to clear it of his sordid thoughts.

"No," he finally replied. "She determined my identity."

Jennette sighed, a delicate sound that brought his attention to her full, pink lips again. "I will have to do better at this matchmaking plan."

He moved a step closer to her, knowing they already stood far too close. "Unless you don't wish to do better?"

She looked up at him with a start. "What do you mean?"

"Perhaps you don't want to find me a bride."

"But . . . Oh, no," she said with a little smile and a shake of her head. "I will not marry you."

"Maybe," he whispered. "But don't you want to know what you will be missing?"

Her blue eyes sparkled with mischief. "Not particularly."

He stroked her cheek with his gloved hand until she trembled. "Haven't you ever wanted a scoundrel in your bed?"

"Like you?"

"Exactly like me."

BOOK YOUR PLACE ON OUR WEBSITE AND MAKE THE READING CONNECTION!

We've created a customized website just for our very special readers, where you can get the inside scoop on everything that's going on with Zebra, Pinnacle and Kensington books.

When you come online, you'll have the exciting opportunity to:

- View covers of upcoming books
- Read sample chapters
- Learn about our future publishing schedule (listed by publication month *and author*)
- Find out when your favorite authors will be visiting a city near you
- Search for and order backlist books from our online catalog
- Check out author bios and background information
- Send e-mail to your favorite authors
- Meet the Kensington staff online
- Join us in weekly chats with authors, readers and other guests
- Get writing guidelines
- AND MUCH MORE!

Visit our website at
http://www.kensingtonbooks.com

EVERY TIME
WE KISS

CHRISTIE KELLEY

ZEBRA BOOKS
Kensington Publishing Corp.

http://www.kensingtonbooks.com

To my biggest fan,
my mother,
JoAnn.
Thanks for all the loving support over the years.

Acknowledgments

This book would never have been completed without the help of all the workers at Panera and Atlanta Bread Company. Dealing with a home under complete reconstruction, I never would have finished this book without the hot, free refills of coffee spurring my creative juices. Thanks for giving me a warm place to write while my house had no heat.

Again, I must thank my critique partners, The Tarts. Kathy Love, Kate Poole, Kate Dolan, and Lisa, I can't thank you enough for reading through this so quickly for me.

I also must thank my editor, Peter Senftleben. Thanks for having patience with this one and helping me make it so much better. You're the best!

Lastly, to Mike, Stephen, and Tommy, I love you all so much. Thank you for understanding when I needed to get out of the house to write.

Chapter 1

"So this is really goodbye, then?" Vanessa stared up at him with watery blue eyes.

Matthew tried his best to be the coldhearted scoundrel his reputation demanded, but it never worked with her. Drawing her into his arms, he said with regret, "You know I can't afford your retainer any longer."

"I always thought . . ."

She didn't need to say another word. He knew exactly what she thought and maybe at one time it might have worked. As a second son, he could afford to be frivolous with his reputation, but not now. Two accidents and his life had changed in so many ways.

"It's not fair," she mumbled into his chest. "I know a mistress isn't supposed to fall in love with her protector, but. . ."

"Shh, Vanessa."

"How could you not have known the debts he incurred?"

He stroked her long, blonde hair, savoring the silky texture. He would miss her but the time had come to end this with her. She had become far too serious about loving him and becoming more than just a mistress.

"I thought that was David's responsibility. I had no idea that the two of them were so irresponsible with the estates and the money." Pausing for a moment, he finally added, "And I was no better than either of them."

"I could help you," she whispered.

"I'm afraid you know that would never work." Vanessa's love had been constant for a year. While he didn't return the feelings in the same manner, he never wanted to hurt her with the truth.

"I would be a good wife."

Matthew blew out a long breath wanting to end this quickly, but he felt unable to hurt her. She had been there for him when he needed her.

"Darling, you will make some man a wonderful wife. And as soon as I get myself out of this mess my father and brother left me in, I'll help you any way I can."

"But a wife, Matthew? Must you marry to save yourself?" She drew her fingers along the lapel of his jacket.

"You know as well as I, there is no other way out of this disaster." But he still wondered just what type of woman would want him *and* his reputation.

She pulled away and looked up at him. Her diminutive stature forced her neck back. "Do you honestly think you will be able to find a woman of your social rank?"

"Yes. I am the earl now. There are always fathers who want their daughters to be a countess."

"Until her father discovers your name. Then he'll make certain his little darling doesn't marry a killer."

His body tensed. "I *will* find a wife, Vanessa."

"It's all her fault, Matthew. You should make her pay for this. Go to her and let her family pay you for what you did for her."

"I don't believe they know what happened that day." At least that had been the plan. No one would ever know except them.

"Well, they should." She turned away and dropped to the sofa, crossing her arms over her chest. "She has spent the last five years doing as she pleased while you were the one in distress. You were the one scorned. Her reputation never suffered from her actions that day."

"This has nothing to do with her, Vanessa. Everything that happened is my father's fault. He should have known better than to gamble away his fortune. And David was no better. Besides, I need more than money. I need my reputation improved with the help of a woman of quality."

He only hoped that some man out there would be so desirous of a title for his daughter that he would willingly ignore the baggage that came with it. After five long years, he craved the friendship of his peers. Respectable peers. Not the scoundrels who befriended him once he'd destroyed his reputation.

"I should be leaving." He knelt down and clasped

her hands in his. "You will be all right, Vanessa. You're beautiful and will have another protector in days."

Vanessa looked away from him. "I don't want another protector, Matthew."

"It will never work out between us."

She stared wistfully down at their joined hands. "After you have married, if I'm available . . ." She paused, blinked hard and then continued, "Will you have me again?"

Matthew dropped his head to her lap. He'd always assumed someday in the far off future, he would fall in love and the woman wouldn't care about his reputation. But now? There was every likelihood the woman he married would only do so in order to be the next Countess of Blackburn. And he doubted he'd ever fall in love with a woman whose only concern was herself. At the same time, he knew his time with Vanessa was done.

"If I don't love her, then I might be tempted to take a mistress again," he said only to appease her.

He looked up to see a catlike grin cross her face as she said, "Then I will pray you don't fall in love."

He smiled back at her. He knew there was little chance of falling for a woman who only wanted his title.

"Perhaps I might think of a few women you should court," she said, absently twirling a lock of golden hair around her finger. "After all, I do know quite a few gentlemen with sisters."

"Oh?"

She rolled her blue eyes and smiled coyly. "I didn't mean I know them that way, Matthew. But I always have to keep my options open. There's no telling when a girl might find herself on the street."

"Like now, perhaps?"

"I'm hardly on the street. With the money you've generously given me over the past two years, I will be able to stay here for months."

He rose and straightened his gray jacket. "Wish me well?"

Vanessa pouted but stood and wrapped her arms around him. Leaning in close, she kissed him fully on the mouth. For once, her overt passion had no impact on him. He was done with her. Slowly, she drew away.

"I won't say good-bye, Matthew. You will return to me, begging me to take you back."

"Good-bye, Vanessa," he whispered.

"Come along," Somerton said, half dragging Matthew into the candlelit ballroom with him.

"I wasn't invited," Matthew insisted.

"Neither was I. But it's never stopped me." Somerton paused and watched the crowd on the dance floor. He glanced over at Matthew and shook his head. "You have a leaf in your hair."

"Well, if you hadn't insisted we jump the fence, I wouldn't have been snagged on that branch." Matthew quickly drew his hands through his hair. The last time he'd sneaked into a ball he'd been seventeen. Now, thirteen years later, he was still acting like an immature adolescent.

"I really don't think we should be here," he tried again.

Somerton shot him a quelling look. "Men with

reputations like ours don't get invited. If you wish to go through with this mad idea of marriage, you must be in the company of women. Preferably women of your rank."

"Very well."

Matthew had spent the past week and a half attempting to secure invitations to parties, balls, even musicales. Anything that would bring him back into the *ton*. Unfortunately, nothing had worked well so far. With the Season not in full swing for months, he had to make do with the few parties held in London in the fall.

His first musicale ended in disaster as no one would even sit near him. He hadn't needed to hear the women to know they were discussing his attendance behind their brightly colored fans.

"I'm off to the gaming room. Enjoy yourself, if that is possible," Somerton said, then walked away.

Enjoy himself? Hardly. Matthew scanned the room for anyone he might know who could make introductions if needed. The large dance floor appeared washed in colored silk as couples glided past with the variety of dance steps. Crystal chandeliers reflected the flickering candlelight diffusing a warm glow throughout the room.

He'd missed the sights and sounds of Society.

As he continued to look around, he noticed people had detected his appearance. A few fingers pointed his way, heads nodded in his direction, and fans rose to cover gossiping lips.

"What are *you* doing here?"

Matthew turned to see Nicholas Tenbury, the Marquess of Ancroft and the future Duke of Belford, standing next to him. Matthew needed to impart a casual tone when all he felt was tension stringing his muscles taut.

"I heard this was a ball for the scoundrels of the *ton*."

Ancroft laughed. "Well, when I throw a ball, no one knows for certain who will attend."

"I take it you won't have your footmen toss me out on the streets?"

"Why should I care if you are here? Your reputation doesn't bother me a bit. If people can't understand an accident when one happens then I pity them."

Matthew blinked. This was quite possibly the first time in five years that someone had defended him. What amazed him was the fact that it came from Ancroft. They were barely acquainted with each other. As a second son, Matthew had befriended the less lofty of the *ton*.

"Besides, I never believed that nonsense about you being in love with her. She isn't your type of woman."

"Thank you," he said softly even as heat crossed his cheeks. He wondered why Ancroft decided she wasn't Matthew's type. Five years ago, she'd been everything a man could want in a woman. He scanned the room . . . Was she here tonight?

He glanced over at Nicholas, who shook his head as if he could read his mind.

"She is not in attendance. They are still at the estate. Although, I believe they will return by week's end for her birthday ball."

Matthew gave him a sharp nod and released a breath. He'd forgotten her birthday was in October. But he needn't worry about that, for a few days

at least. Perhaps by the time she returned, he would
have a woman to court. Then he would have no
need to see her again.

"Come along and I'll introduce you to a few
people." Nicholas looked around the room. "With
whom did you slink in—Somerton?"

"Yes."

"Crafty scoundrel. He's always stealing into someone's party for a chance to play the gaming tables.
Damn man always wins, too."

For the first time in weeks, Matthew laughed.

As he walked the boundary of the dance floor,
the whispers followed him. Nicholas stopped beside
an older woman dressed in gold satin with a match-
ing turban wrapped snuggly around her head.

"Mrs. Layton, may I introduce Lord Blackburn."

Without a word, her eyes widened, and then she
pursed her lips and walked away. The cut was direct,
why was he surprised?

"Well, this may be harder than I assumed,"
Nicholas commented. "She's a haughty bitch and
her daughter no better. For a woman whose husband left her a fortune from illegal activities, I
would have thought she'd be more open to an introduction."

If that was the reaction from her, he could only
imagine the response from the others. After several more attempts at introductions, Mr. Seymour
allowed him to dance with his daughter. He walked
to the dance floor with the quaking Miss Sarah Seymour and thought the pale woman might just faint
dead away.

"Are you enjoying the ball?" he asked.

She could only nod with her big doe eyes blink-

ing madly. She continually glanced to the side of
the dance floor where two young ladies stood
watching their every move. They looked as if they
might beat him with their fans should he make one
improper move.

As they danced, he attempted a few more times
to get the mute Miss Sarah to speak. Nothing
worked. The poor girl with her watery brown eyes
and pale skin appeared scared to death of him.
When the dance ended, he quickly returned her to
her father without a word.

Tired of the music and overly loud whispers, he
headed to the garden. A beautiful full moon lit his
way as he avoided the secluded nooks taken by couples looking for a bit of privacy. The soft whispers
and moans of the couples only increased his frustration.

It wasn't supposed to be this difficult. He had
thought with inheriting the title the *ton* might have
forgotten his reputation. Damn them all. Here
he'd done the honorable thing for a friend and no
one even knew. Not that he was looking for acco-
lades on being a good friend and chivalrous man.

But could no one see the truth?

Other than the accident, he had been an upstanding citizen. He never seduced an innocent
young lady and rarely even chased the widows. He
much preferred the companionship of a steady
mistress.

He sat on an iron bench and stared out into the
dying garden. Soon all the leaves would be gone,
the flowers dead, and he'd still be in this damned
situation. After a long talk with his solicitor this
afternoon, he knew he had enough money to last

until the end of the year. Ten weeks at most. Then the property he legally could let go of would have to be sold. The tenants possibly put out on the street in the middle of winter.

He couldn't let that happen to them.

To him.

There had to be another way out of this mess. But he had no time. Even if he took a job (as if anyone would hire an earl), the money earned would never cover his expenses.

It was all her fault.

Vanessa's words haunted him. There was one woman who could fix his problems. And cause him untold others.

It was all her fault.

She should have accepted responsibility. Except, for all he knew, his words had caused her actions that day. He should have kept his mouth firmly shut.

Besides, it wasn't *all* her fault. He'd never given her the chance to take the blame. She had done only what he told her to do, play the frivolous lady with no cares, except of course the current fashion of the day.

He closed his eyes and pictured her raven-black hair, sparkling blue eyes that always held a hint of humor, and legs so long he'd wanted to kiss every inch of them. He wondered how much she might have changed.

Shaking his head, he attempted to rid his mind of these errant thoughts. He couldn't see her again. He'd promised to stay out of her life, leave her and her family alone as penance for his part in what happened that day.

And yet, now he had no choice but to reenter Society. Interact with her friends and, quite possibly, her. He'd paid his dues so now she would have to accept his presence at balls and whatever else he decided to attend. If he actually were invited to a ball, which at this point seemed very unlikely.

He still hadn't determined how he would integrate himself back into the same Society that shunned him years ago. The reactions so far had not given him any encouragement. Embers of anger flamed to a red heat again.

He had paid his reparations for his small part of what happened that day. And he didn't even know if his words had affected her. For all he knew, she might have scorned his heartfelt speech. She'd certainly rejected his kiss that morning. While he spent five years in purgatory for his action, she'd done nothing but go back to her prosperous life of shopping, painting, and socializing.

No one knew of her part in the destruction of his life.

Vanessa thought she knew the entire story, but she did not.

No one knew everything, except him.

Chapter 2

"Come along, it's your turn now," Sophie demanded.

Jennette stood by the refreshment table and looked over at Sophie. The fancy-dress ball was in full swing. Sophie had dressed like a gypsy in bright-colored skirts with her dark hair falling upon her back and a red mask covering half her face. Jennette had chosen the white gown of an angel to celebrate her twenty-fifth birthday.

"But my guests," Jennette protested.

"They will be fine without you for a few minutes."

"I promised Lansing a dance and Colby one after that," Jennette tried again.

"We need to do this now before the musicians take their break. Once that happens, I'll be too busy."

"But . . ."

"No more protests. You invited me to keep everyone entertained with my fortune-telling." Sophie grabbed Jennette's hand and tugged her toward the doorway, down the hallway to the salon. The small room had been set for Sophie to read people's fortunes, and she'd been doing a brisk business all evening.

"Yes, keep *them* entertained, not me. I don't even believe in such things as fortune-telling."

No one could predict the future, even if her friend was quite recognized for doing just that. Especially her matchmaking fortunes. The last thing Jennette desired was anyone telling her of her future. She didn't want to know, not when she'd tried so hard to forget her past.

"I know you don't believe in this, which is why I can't understand your vehement protests. It's just for fun. After all, it is your birthday."

Jennette had waited five long years for this day. After signing more legal papers than she'd ever imagined today, she was free. With the inheritance from her grandmother, she finally had the money to do what she should have done years ago.

"Besides, you will be leaving to study with that master in Florence soon. You should want to know if everything will go as expected."

Sophie motioned for Jennette to sit in the yellow damask chair while she took the seat across from her. "I will, of course, come visit you. But I shall miss you dreadfully."

Study with a master in Florence. The lie she'd told everyone from her mother to her best friends. No one knew the truth. No one could ever learn why she had to leave England. She had only waited so she could gain her inheritance and live comfortably. Now it was his turn to have a chance at happiness, even if it meant her misery.

With her gone, the memory of what happened that day would slowly leave the minds of the *ton*. He would be able to come back into Society, find a lovely woman, and marry. He was the type of man who would want a family and he deserved one, especially now that he held the title.

She had to leave now—for him. He had given her the past five years of peace. This was the least she could do for him.

"Now take off your mask and give me your hand," Sophie demanded.

Knowing it was useless to argue with her stubborn friend, Jennette did as commanded. In seven years of friendship, she had never let Sophie read her tea leaves, her palm, or any other thing the medium might want. But there seemed no dissuading Sophie tonight.

"Oh my," Sophie said, holding Jennette's hand with her eyes closed.

"What is it?"

"I sense a deep secret you are keeping from everyone."

She yanked her hand away only to have Sophie frown and grab it again. Jennette immediately thought of something to block Sophie's intrusive sensations: dresses. Jennette imagined herself inspecting every dress she owned, anything to keep Sophie from determining her secret. In her mind, she opened her linen-press and pulled out her violet silk gown. The dress needed some trim, perhaps lace.

Was this working?

She needed to think of something else, quickly. Shoes! She had more shoes than dresses.

What was wrong with her? Sophie was her friend.

But that did not matter, not even her friends could know her secret. What else could she think of?

"Stop fretting, Jennette. I can't guess your secret. But I am a little surprised you have told no one. It's not like you."

"Do you see anything else?" Jennette asked, attempting to get Sophie on another topic.

"A man," Sophie whispered. A deep frown marred her exotic beauty. "Perhaps it's your new painting instructor in Florence."

Since Jennette was only pretending to have a painting instructor, she highly doubted he was the man Sophie saw in her trance. After all, when she'd devised her plan to move to Florence, she had to create a valid reason for leaving. Enriching her artistic skills seemed the perfect solution.

"What does he look like?"

"I can't see him like a portrait, Jennette. I only get fleeting images."

"Images of what?"

"Just bits and pieces of things," she replied with a delicate shrug of her shoulders.

"But what do you see now?" Jennette's impatience rose.

"Darkness," Sophie whispered with her eyes still closed. "I see darkness surrounding this man like a shroud."

"Anything else?" Who could this man be? Some swarthy Italian who would sweep her off her feet? A man to help her forget her past and forge a brilliant future?

"His eyes are fascinating—light gray that lend a softness to him." Sophie sighed. "Such sad eyes."

Gray eyes.

Jennette swallowed. Surely, there were men in Florence who had gray eyes and chestnut hair—she pulled her hand out of Sophie's grip again and stood. Sophie never said the man had chestnut hair, so certainly she must be thinking of another.

It had to be someone else.

"I must get back to my guests now."

"Of course," Sophie replied with a strange little smile. "Just remember, Jennette, I was right about Avis and Banning."

Jennette walked to the door and paused at the threshold. Her brother and new sister-in-law had been happily married now for two months. And Sophie had helped make that match by scheming to get them together at a party. While Jennette doubted Sophie's plan had really made a big difference, she had known about them before they even knew themselves.

But Sophie couldn't be right about this one. Jennette had to believe that because the alternative was unimaginable. He'd promised to leave her alone after that fateful morning.

"What does he want from me, Sophie?" she whispered from the doorway.

"I cannot know for certain. But have a care, Jennette. With all the darkness surrounding him, I don't think anything he might want could be good."

She nodded sharply and left the room. With shaking hands, she retied her mask and readied herself to enter the ball again. Yet, when she reached the small ballroom of her brother's house, she wasn't ready to reenter the party. All the well-wishers and festivities could wait just a few minutes while she tried to compose herself. She turned and walked to the back terrace, hoping for some peace.

The cool wind made her shiver as she left the terrace for the dark garden. Hopefully, the chill in the air would keep the guests inside. Peering around, she noticed no one out here.

Thank God.

After taking a seat in the shadowy corner by a rose bush, she spread out her white satin gown and sighed. Unable to sit back due to the lace wings tied on her back, she leaned forward and placed her chin in her hands.

Sophie had to be wrong. He would never seek her out. He had promised John he would protect her name but there was no reason for him to speak with her.

She shook her head and inhaled the musty smell of dead leaves rotting on the ground. Even if he did approach her publicly, she could always give him the cut. No one would reproach her for that, they would commend her.

"Are you a fairy or an angel?" a low raspy voice sounded behind her.

Jennette sat up straight and looked around frantically. She'd been sure there had been no one out here. Her heart pounded in her chest erratically. This was ridiculous. She was at her brother's house in the middle of a party for *ton*. Only those invited could be here.

"Who's there?"

"Well, if you're an angel, I guess that makes me the devil. Can you resist the devil, Jennette?" the voice whispered.

Jennette stood and turned toward the voice. A

man dressed like a highwayman from the last century rose from his seat behind the dying rose bushes. His clothes appeared dirty and worn, and she wondered for a moment if perhaps he wasn't in costume. A black mask covered enough of his face to make her pause.

But as he stepped forward into the torch light, she could make out his eyes—icy gray as the morning frost. She would never forget those eyes. The way he had stared at her that morning from his seat, unable to move because of what she'd done.

He could not be here. Not at her brother's home. Not at her birthday ball.

He'd promised to leave her alone.

"Don't move," he commanded. "You are the reason I came to this party. I need to speak with you."

"I have nothing to say to you."

She lifted her skirts and ran toward the safety of the terrace and her family. The gravel crunched loudly under her feet. Couldn't someone hear her footsteps? As she reached the first step of the terrace and within shouting distance of the party, he pulled her against his chest. His large, gloved hand covered her mouth, silencing her.

Jennette attempted to twist out his strong grip as he dragged her back into the shadows of the garden. This couldn't be happening. Not now, when all her plans were almost complete. She had less than four weeks before her ship sailed, allowing her to leave him and this mess behind forever. He shoved her back against the pillar of the pergola and trapped her there with his arms. Fear shot through her like lightning.

"What do you want from me?" she asked.

His smile turned feral. Through the mask, she could just make out his eyes. She shivered from the cold stare he leveled at her.

"What have I always wanted from you?" his low voice rasped.

"Take off your mask," she whispered.

"Why? You know who I am."

"You're frightening me."

He leaned in closer and smiled. He drew a gloved finger along her cheek, making her tremble even more. "Good. You should be afraid of me, Jennette. You know what I could do to you and your family."

She closed her eyes and tried her best to breathe in deeply. "Please," she begged.

"Very well." He untied the mask and shoved it into his vest pocket. "Better?"

God, no, she thought. Seeing his face again after five years was not better. It was far worse. Chestnut hair, too long to be fashionable, lined his square face. His high cheekbones and stubborn jaw accented his rugged features. He'd always been a handsome man but the last few years had only made him more intriguing.

Her errant gaze moved to his lips. If she closed her eyes, she could remember the sensation of his mouth on hers. And that was what had caused all the problems.

"Matthew . . ."

"Are you still frightened of me, Jennette?"

She nodded. "What do you want from me?"

He laughed in such a soft tone it made her tremble again. "I had to see you."

"Why? You promised to stay away from me." She closed her eyes in thought. Anger surged when she realized the only reason he could be here. She glared up at him. "You only came to me because you need money, don't you?"

"Who doesn't?"

"No," she said. "You want to blackmail me, am I right?"

He leaned in closer until the scent of his sandalwood soap teased her nose. "Blackmail is such an ugly word."

"I heard about your father and brother's accident. And I know about your finances."

He glanced away from her for a moment. A hint of vulnerability crossed his face. "I didn't think anyone else knew about my situation," he whispered.

"Word of an earl's finances spreads swiftly through the gossipmongers."

"It really doesn't matter." His cold eyes stared into hers. "I didn't come to beg you for money."

If he didn't want money, what could he possibly want from her? She had nothing else she could offer him.

"What do you want from me?"

"Your hand in marriage, of course," he whispered nonchalantly.

Matthew watched as her brilliant blue eyes sparkled in the moonlight. What the devil had he just said to her? He'd only come to the party to see her, admire her from afar. Perhaps gather the courage to speak with her and tell her of his return to Society.

Not propose marriage!

When she'd stepped out into the garden, he knew he had to speak with her. But only to let her know that he was in town and what his plans were.

Not propose marriage.

Every time he was near her, he said the most foolish things. He couldn't take his gaze from her. The woman was still an "Incomparable" in the mind of the *ton* and with good reason. Her tall, slim body, black hair, and blue eyes made her a novelty amongst the petite blondes and brunettes. And the *ton* always loved something new. She had an alluring maturity now that seemed even more enticing. It was an absolute wonder she hadn't married by now.

"My what?" she finally blurted.

"Your hand in marriage," he repeated softly. He had no idea why he continued in this vein. He couldn't marry her. Even if it would solve most of his problems.

"To you?"

"Yes."

Her face contorted as if she were trying to determine the reason for his proposal. Finally, she looked up at him and simply said, "No."

Matthew almost smiled. "I don't believe you have thought this through, Jennette."

"There is nothing to think through, *my lord*," she answered in a condescending voice. "I have no plans to marry you or any other man."

"You have no choice in this matter."

"Oh my God, you mean to blackmail me into *marriage*!"

He hated how that sounded, no matter how true. The idea of blackmailing her into marriage sounded sweet in his mind. At least as far as the benefits marriage would bring him. Her sensual body had haunted him for years.

"Jennette, I've spent the past fortnight attempting to integrate myself back into the folds of the *ton*. Only to be rejected on every front. I *need* a wife."

"A wealthy wife," she added in a sarcastic tone.

Matthew clenched his fists against the columns. "Yes," he bit out. "I need a wealthy wife and a respectable wife. Someone who can elevate my reputation."

"Well, it won't be me." She ducked under his arm and moved toward the bench.

"I've tried everything I can think of. If I don't marry quickly my tenants will be removed from the land, my property sold, and I'll be even more ruined."

She bit her lip. "You ask too much," she whispered, staring at her hands.

"I know." Even that realization didn't stop him from pursuing her. "But you owe me this, Jennette."

"I know that, too." Her gaze remained locked on her hands. "I can't marry you, Matthew. I just couldn't live with the memories of what happened."

Matthew paced the small confines of the pergola. This was not going the way he'd expected. They were only supposed to talk and yet, now that he'd started this ridiculous conversation, he couldn't stop it. Marrying her had never crossed his mind until he blurted the words out.

"Marry me or I'll walk into that ballroom and tell everyone the truth."

He cringed seeing the expression of shock cross her face. He couldn't believe he had said that to her. What was it about her that brought out all the stupidity in him? The one glass of brandy he'd had before the ball couldn't be the culprit. The urge to flee this scene grew. He should leave her alone, find another way to solve his problems. That was for the best.

But he couldn't let go.

"You wouldn't really do that, would you? If you did, there would be another inquest. You can't possibly want that." She moved slightly as if to run once more. Instead, she held her ground and stared at him. "What would John think of you?"

"John's dead, Jennette."

"I know that," she hissed.

"But do you really want everyone in the ballroom to know *you* killed him?"

Chapter 3

Jennette gasped and stared at the cad in front of her. No one would believe him, she reasoned. Matthew had admitted to accidentally killing John. By doing so, he had protected her name and her family's reputation. And he'd lost his. He left Society and became an outcast . . . all for her.

But if he suddenly changed his story, no one would trust him. They would think he was trying to place the blame on her to clear his name.

Yet, even as she tried to rationalize things, her guilt assailed her. The reason he could not find a bride had nothing to do with his finances and everything to do with a reputation he didn't deserve. A reputation she had given him by letting John beg him to save her name.

If she had only stood up for herself back then. She knew now that if she'd taken the responsibility, the most likely outcome would have been sympathy for what had happened. Eventually, her reputation would have healed.

But now?

If people believed his story, she would be far more ruined than he ever was because everyone would hate her for not stepping forward five years ago. And worse, her actions would reflect poorly on her mother's name, and Avis and Banning's, too. All because of her.

This was all her fault. She never should have let him take the blame for her.

She had to find a way to help him. Marrying him was out of the question. His father and brother had gambled the family fortune away. No matter how much guilt she felt over what happened that day, she would never marry a fortune hunter and a gambler. Marrying Matthew would give him full control over her money so he could spend it all at the gaming hells. She would never let that happen.

Still, the guilt she felt over what she had done to both men would never leave her. There had to be some way she could assist him without marrying him.

A bride.

A wealthy bride was all he was after. There was no reason it had to be her.

Finally, she looked up at him. "I cannot marry you, Matthew. But perhaps I can help you in another way."

"I won't take your money. I need a wife who will correct my position with the *ton*. I need an heir to carry on my name, inherit the title and the money *I* will ensure is plentiful."

As he walked to the far side of the pergola, she thought about running back to the house and calling a footman to toss him out on the street. But when he turned back toward her, the desperation etched on his face stopped her. She and John had caused his ruination. She had no choice but to help him if she could.

"I have an idea," she said quickly.

He stopped in front of her and tilted his head. A lock of chestnut hair fell upon his forehead. "Oh?"

"I will find you a bride. A woman wealthy enough to suit you and willing to be your countess." A woman with a diligent father to watch over his daughter's husband to ensure he didn't gamble the money away.

A sharp laugh escaped him. "And how do you propose to do such a thing when I'm not even invited to a simple musicale?"

He made a good point. But she had connections and by pleading his case, she might obtain the coveted invitations for him. She could be quite convincing when necessary.

"Leave that all to me," she replied softly. "I might be a spinster but I do have my ways."

A half-smile curved his lips upward. "I have no doubt about that, Jennette. But I don't trust you."

Taken aback, she glared up at him. "I beg your pardon?"

"Why would I trust a woman who has never defended me to her friends?"

"I was supposed to defend you when you claimed to have killed my fiancé?"

"*Accidentally.* You could have at least reiterated that piece of information to them," he said harshly.

"You know how that would have looked to them." She looked away so he wouldn't see the guilt written on her face. He was right. She should have supported him.

"Yes, it would have looked as if you were protecting a friend. God knows there are so few people in this world capable of doing such a thing."

"You were the one who told me to go back to my life, forget what had happened. Pretend as if nothing happened that day."

That damned guilt for treating him so poorly washed over her again. There was no possible way he would understand how hard it was for her to pretend she was the eccentric spinster who'd had her heart broken by her betrothed's untimely death. To pretend she was the harmed party in the situation.

"I'm sorry," she whispered, staring downward.

He walked back and forth across the lawn, looking more like a caged tiger than a man searching for a wife. Suddenly he stopped.

"How exactly would you find me a wife?"

"Well," she stalled, "I would talk about you at all the social occasions."

"That would take too long. I need a wife now."

"All right, then," Jennette sighed. She had no real ideas about how she could manage this task. "I have a few friends who are getting rather desperate to marry before they are considered permanently on the shelf."

"Go on," he urged, crossing his arms over his chest.

"I will speak kindly about you to them. I shall tell them what an honorable man you are."

He laughed scornfully. "And how will you succeed at that when the most honorable thing I ever did was what stuck me with this damned reputation?"

Jennette frowned. "Surely you have done other honorable things in your lifetime."

"Such as . . . ?" he asked with one chestnut brow raised.

"You donate to charities?"

He shook his head. "Unless you consider my mistress a charity."

"No," she said with a pause. A smile formed upon her lips. "Although, I'm quite certain we could say you assist needy unmarried women."

This time his laugh sounded completely real. "I rather like that. What else?"

"If you could give five pounds to a home for orphaned children my friend operates, I could say you are generous to the poor orphans."

"Done."

"Over the next day or so, I will find other brilliant things to say about you."

He approached her slowly until he stood directly in front of her. She strained her neck to look up at him. Most men of her acquaintance barely matched her height, but not Matthew. As he bent down to her level, she gasped at his nearness. It had nothing to do with his perfectly molded lips, she told herself.

She couldn't still be attracted to him. It had been five years. No, the nervous feeling in her belly stemmed purely from the fact that he could ruin her.

"You have one month," he whispered.

Jennette blinked. "Pardon?"

"One month to find me a bride. If after one month you don't have me well-matched, I will have a special license with both our names on it."

She pressed her lips together and swallowed the lump of fear down. She could do this. All she had to do was find the most desperate spinster she knew and throw her at him. Besides, her ship to Florence departed in less than a month. If she failed, at least she would be gone before he could marry her.

But she would not disappoint him—her guilt wouldn't allow it. He deserved some happiness in his life after all that she'd put him through.

"Very well."

He stared at her with those cold gray eyes burning into her soul. "If you try to dupe me, I'll make sure everyone in Christendom knows who killed John."

"I understand."

"Now," he said as he straightened to his full height. He reached behind her and fixed her crooked wings. "Put a smile on your face and get back to your party. And happy birthday, Jennette."

"Thank you," she said.

He smirked. "Save me a dance."

"You're coming inside?"

"There is no better time to start your plan than now, don't you agree?"

Matthew didn't wait for her reply. After tying on his mask, he strode for the terrace, leaving Jennette behind. As he entered the ball, a footman walked by with glasses of wine. Matthew pilfered a glass and drank the fruity liquid down in two gulps.

His talk in the garden had not gone as he'd hoped. Somehow, that woman had twisted things around until he was threatening her with marriage. He'd only intended to speak with her. Inform her that he would be reentering Society. But his damned emotions had taken over.

Walking to the refreshment table, he pondered his predicament. He highly doubted Jennette's ability to find him a willing bride in such a short time frame. She probably had some information on a few people and planned to use it to blackmail one of them into marrying him.

Not that he didn't appreciate that bit of irony.

But at the same time, he didn't trust her. He would give her one week to show him what type of woman she could offer him. If he didn't approve of them or they wouldn't have anything to do with him, Jennette was fair game.

He was being reasonable. And he knew the only way she'd agree to marry him was a public compromising. He hadn't the heart to tell the world, or even the *ton*, what had really happened on the field that day. When he had given his promise to John to protect her name, he meant it.

No one would ever discover the truth from him.

Except Vanessa.

That one drunken bitter night when he'd spilled the truth to her. But that was what mistresses were for, after all. Secrets and passion. Subjects too sensitive for anyone else. Vanessa had given him her word never to reveal his secrets, and he'd paid her well for that service.

Looking over at the terrace door, he watched Jennette slip through the open doorway and back inside the room. Her pink cheeks gave away her flustered state. Immediately a crowd of women appeared at her side. She smiled at them, but he knew she was paying no attention to them. Her gaze locked with his for a long moment.

He felt like a cad for doing this to her. But his

options had run out. It seemed odd that he was hanging his only hope on her. Perhaps he should have taken her money. Yet money wasn't all he needed or wanted. He'd spoken the truth when he said he needed a wife and child. More importantly, he wanted to regain his respectability. No longer hiding on the outskirts of the *ton*.

He picked up a glass of wine from the table and lifted it in salute to her. Quickly, she looked away from him. Before he could turn and walk toward the gaming room to watch the playing, a man stepped in front of him. Even with a mask, Matthew immediately recognized the angry blue eyes behind the disguise.

"What are you doing here?" Lord Selby asked in a cold voice. "Uninvited, I might add."

"I'm afraid I don't know what you are talking about," Matthew replied and started to inch away. "You must have me confused with another."

Selby clenched his hand around Matthew's bicep and led him to a corner for privacy. "I know exactly who you are, Blackburn. And don't think I didn't see the little salute you gave my sister. I want you out of here."

"As you wish." Matthew placed the wine on the table and turned only to face Jennette.

"It is our dance, is it not?"

The melodic sound of her voice floated over him, caressing him. She stepped closer to both men.

"Jennette," her brother warned. "I don't think you know who this is."

"Banning, I believe you are mistaken." She

hooked her arm around Matthew's and said, "Our waltz is starting."

"Yes, my lady." Matthew started to lead her to the dance floor but stopped upon hearing Selby's voice.

"Jennette," her brother hissed.

"Leave me be, Ban."

"I hope you know what you are doing," Selby replied.

She turned and looked at her brother. "I know exactly what I'm doing."

Matthew blew out a breath and walked her to the dance floor. If he'd had a sister, he would have reacted the same way as Selby. "Perhaps your brother is right. I am the last person you should be dancing with tonight."

"I promised you a dance and I refuse to let you wheedle your way out of it."

He pulled her close as the dance began. "I never said I didn't want to dance with you."

He couldn't think of a thing he wanted more than her in his arms. Unless, she was naked and in his bed.

She smiled up at him as twin dimples lined her cheeks. "Good."

Her body almost touched his and he barely resisted the urge to drag her completely against him. He'd always attempted to think of her solely as John's betrothed. But just like five years ago, it never seemed to work. It must have been her alluring scent of exotic spices. A combination of fragrances that floated around them, intoxicating him.

"Are you still frightened of me?" he whispered when he felt her tremble.

"Always," she answered softly. "You have the ability to ruin me . . . and my family."

"So when do I meet this first lady?"

"Tonight. I shall speak to her as soon as our dance is finished."

He leaned in closer just to inhale her sweet scent again. "Is she beautiful?"

"She is quite fetching." Jennette drew away from him. "But you never told me beauty was a requirement."

"I shouldn't wish to be married to someone I dread making love to at night." Matthew smiled as her cheeks reddened.

"If you speak like that to all the innocent ladies they will run away from you," she finally replied.

"And yet, you haven't run away," he whispered in her ear.

"Cad."

"So everyone believes." He glanced away from her deliberately. "Personally, I have always preferred blondes. And petite, too. Will this be a problem?"

"I should think someone in your situation cannot be too particular."

"Yes, but you will find me the perfect wife, or so you said," he answered. The only perfect thing about a wife who met his description was that she wouldn't remind him of Jennette.

"Yes, I will," she said with more force than necessary.

As the music ended, Matthew reluctantly led her back to her brother. Selby stared coldly at him.

"Thank you for the dance, Lady Jennette. I quite

enjoyed it." He bowed over her hand, then left her to be chastised by her brother.

Banning led her away from the crowded ballroom. "Have you completely lost your mind?"

At this point, Jennette wasn't certain. Insanity might be preferable to what she'd gotten herself into tonight.

"Why is he even here?" Banning asked as they reached the salon where only an hour before Sophie had foretold her future, with far too much accuracy.

"He is looking for a wife, Ban. I'm sure you realize that his reputation is ruined and most families won't invite him to even a musicale."

"Well, then he shouldn't have impaled his best friend with a sword."

Jennette closed her eyes and pressed her lips together. The image of standing over John as he fell to the grassy field was too much for her. She could still smell the repugnant odor of blood. The red liquid flowed from his body like a river rushing to the ocean. For as long as she lived, she would never forget the look of shock on his face. Or his last gasp for breath with a rapier impaled in his lung.

Suddenly, Banning pulled her into his arms. "I'm sorry, Jen."

"He was such a good man." And *she* had killed him.

"I know. He didn't deserve to die so young."

A tear fell down her cheek. Matthew was a good man, too. And he didn't deserve this, either. If her attention had been on John and not elsewhere, Matthew would never have been put in this position.

"I have to help him find a wife, Banning."

Her brother drew away and stared down at her. "What?"

"It was an accident. He never would have hurt John. The grass was damp, his foot slipped and John couldn't react in time." Every time she told that damning lie, her heart raced with the fear of being discovered.

"They were grown men who should have known better than to practice with swords on wet grass," Banning said.

Jennette nodded, remembering Matthew's words of caution to her that morning. "And I suppose you never have made a mistake?"

"That bastard will say anything to clear his name."

"I was there. I know what happened."

"I don't want you anywhere near him," he said in a ferocious tone.

"It is not your business." Jennette usually loved a good quarrel with her brother but not tonight. After her encounter with Matthew, her nerves were on edge. "The man's name has been bruised enough. He needs a wealthy wife to save him from his father and brother's gambling debts. And I will do my best to find him one."

Banning crossed his arms over his chest. His blue eyes sparkled with anger as he stared at her. "Just as long as it isn't you."

Her lips curved upward. "I have no intention of marrying him."

"Good."

She walked toward the door and paused to gather herself.

"What are you going to do?" he asked.

"Find him a bride."

She just wasn't certain which of her friends to try first. Elizabeth, while the daughter of a duke, had strangely been left out of her father's will. With only her allowance, Jennette didn't believe Elizabeth would be wife material for Matthew.

Then there was Sophie. As the bastard daughter of an actress and some nameless earl, she had plenty of money from her father, but no real respectability. Matthew needed a woman with both.

With Avis married to Banning, that left Victoria. Jennette frowned in thought. Something about Victoria created doubt in Jennette. She was the daughter of a vicar who supposedly had given her enough money to buy a home, which she converted into an orphanage. However, Victoria was always seeking donations to keep the orphanage open.

Not that she could envision any of them marrying Matthew. Or more specifically, she couldn't imagine having to watch them with him. Seeing one of her friends come to love and desire him would be far more than she could bear.

As Jennette walked down the hallway, she realized this plan would be much more difficult than she'd impulsively thought. She needed to match him with an acquaintance, not someone with whom she was too close. Entering the ballroom, she scanned the area for anyone she could convince to dance with him. She smiled. No one needed to know who he was tonight.

Miss Lucinda Bartlett stood by the edge of the dance floor longingly watching the quadrille. The daughter of a viscount who reportedly had plenty of money, she might be just the thing. While she wasn't the most beautiful woman in the room, Lucinda had a quiet sort of beauty that many men respected.

"Lucinda, what are you doing standing on the edge of the dance floor when you could be dancing?" Jennette asked with a smile.

Lucinda's face fell. "No one has asked me to dance tonight. Apparently, after obtaining the age of six and twenty, I'm no longer in demand."

"I have a friend here tonight who I know would love to dance with you." Jennette glanced around for the scoundrel highwayman. After catching his eye, she nodded toward Lucinda.

"Who?"

Jennette laughed at her enthusiasm. "This is a masked ball, Lucinda. I cannot tell you his name."

Her dull brown eyes lit with excitement. "Where is he?"

"Right here, my dear." The sound of his deep voice rolled down Jennette's back until she shivered.

"Oh my," Lucinda whispered. She leaned forward and said, "Please tell me who he is, Jennette."

"Not yet," she replied.

Matthew held out his arm for Lucinda and Jennette watched the pair head for the dance floor. She wondered briefly at the little stab of envy that had pricked her heart, but she quickly brushed aside the feeling.

She had known even five years ago that she and Matthew were never meant to be.

* * *

"Did you hear the rumor circulating tonight?" Lucinda asked in a voice barely above a whisper. "It's quite scandalous."

"Oh?" Matthew leaned forward as if to listen better. Not that he cared about any gossipmonger's tale. He'd been on the wrong side of the gossips' tongues for far too long.

"Someone said they were certain Lord Blackburn was here tonight." Her eyes widened. "Can you believe he would have the gall to come to Lady Jennette's ball?"

"Perhaps," Matthew said tightly. "Just perhaps, the gossips are wrong."

Her brows knit into a cavernous frown. "Indeed. They have been known to be incorrect at times."

"Many times."

"Even still, I should never want to meet that man after what he did to poor Jennette. Can you imagine? The man impaled her betrothed."

Matthew tried to relax his taut muscles and enjoy the dance. There was no possibility of that with Lucinda defaming him to his face. "Do you think there's a chance that everything we know about Blackburn is all a falsehood?"

Lucinda looked up at him with confusion. "Whatever do you mean?"

"Maybe things aren't as they appear with him."

She shook her head. "The man is a killer. There is nothing more to know about him."

"I believe you know nothing about the man."

She glanced around the room and then back at him. She stiffened her back and said, "I am not feeling well. Please return me to my mother."

"Figured it out, did you?"

"How dare you come here? Jennette will have the vapors just knowing she sent me to the dance floor with the likes of you."

Matthew hurried to escort her off the dance floor and back to her mother. He should have known this would be the response from any decent woman among the *ton*. Any woman . . . except Jennette, his mind countered. Jennette hadn't run from him. She had even defended him to her brother.

As they reached Lady Bartlett's position in the matrons' corner, he attempted to bow over Lucinda's hand only to have her draw it away.

"Good evening, sir," she huffed and walked off.

There was no use in staying here any longer. No doubt, the word of his presence would blow about the ballroom with the strength of a gale-force wind. While he should at least thank Jennette for trying, he didn't wish to bring any gossip down on her. He would sneak out the terrace door, exactly as he'd entered.

Feeling the burning gaze of a hundred guests upon his back, he walked to the door. He made his escape quickly and silently. Or so he'd thought.

"Leaving already?" Jennette stood in the moonlight looking everything like the angel she'd dressed to be tonight. She rubbed her arms as if to keep the cold wind away.

"Yes. I wouldn't wish to cause you any further distress tonight."

She lifted one black eyebrow. "Am I to assume the dance with Lucinda didn't go as I'd planned?"

He approached her slowly. She had matured into an exquisite beauty. She had delicate cheekbones and flawless ivory skin, a mouth too full to be perfect but just right for other things. The white gown outlined her slender body and slight fullness of her breasts. He shook his head to clear it of his sordid thoughts.

"No," he finally replied. "She determined my identity."

Jennette sighed, a delicate sound that brought his attention to her full, pink lips again. "I will have to do better at this matchmaking plan."

He moved a step closer to her, knowing they already stood far too close. "Unless you don't wish to do better?"

She looked up at him with a start. "What do you mean?"

"Perhaps you don't want to find me a bride."

"But . . . oh, no," she said with a little smile and a shake of her head. "I will not marry you."

"Maybe," he whispered. "But don't you want to know what you will be missing?"

Her blue eyes sparkled with mischief. "Not particularly."

He stroked her cheek with his gloved hand until she trembled. "Haven't you ever wanted a scoundrel in your bed?"

"Like you?"

"Exactly like me."

Her eyes darkened to the shade of sapphires as her face went somber. "But we both know you really aren't a scoundrel."

"If you say so." He moved away from her, tipped his hat, and walked off the terrace. Before he was too far away, he turned and said, "Please let me know when I should expect another prospective bride."

"Very well," she answered. "I will send a note."

"Or you could call on me in person."

"You really are a devil, Blackburn."

"You have no idea, Jennette." He gave her an exaggerated bow and then walked to the back of the garden. He hopped the stone fence and headed for his crumbling home.

He'd thought this insane attraction to her would have ended after not seeing her for so long. Never had he imagined the draw would be stronger, deeper in an agonizing manner. His body never reacted in such an immediate way with any other woman.

Should he end up married to her, the attraction would make marriage so much more interesting. What was he thinking? He shouldn't marry her after all they'd been through. The marriage idea was only a threat to get her to help him.

He could never marry her.

After all, she might even find him a suitable bride. Then he wouldn't have to worry about his own guilt at finding John's former fiancée the most attractive and desirable woman he'd ever met.

Chapter 4

"What is going on, Jennette?" Elizabeth asked as she sat down in the salon. "I have been hearing rumors all day that Lord Blackburn attended your party last night. Was he there? I never noticed him."

"I have also heard the rumor," Avis added, pouring tea for everyone. "I have a very good source who says he knows for certain Blackburn attended. And you danced with him."

Jennette closed her eyes and rubbed her temples. "My brother doesn't know everything, Avis."

"As his wife, I realize that, Jennette. But I also know how much he cares for you. He would never want someone to hurt you again as Blackburn has in the past."

Jennette looked around at her roomful of friends. Avis, her dearest friend and now sister-in-law, handed tea to Sophie, who sat on the sofa with a small grin on her face. Of course, Sophie most likely had concluded that Matthew had gray eyes. Victoria sat primly in the chair by the window, looking completely uncomfortable with the conversation. While

Elizabeth's green eyes took everything in with eagerness.

"Mat—Blackburn and I talked for a few minutes. I did dance with him only to get him away from Banning's overbearing attitude."

Elizabeth twisted her lips. "But why was he there in the first place? Surely, you didn't invite him."

"No. He sneaked inside after we talked in the garden." Jennette clamped her hand over her lips when she realized how scandalizing that sounded.

"Does Banning know about that?" Avis whispered as if he might appear at any moment.

"Of course not," Jennette said. "It was completely innocent." And frightening. And somewhat sensual, especially when he trapped her against the column with his body. Or that brief instance on the terrace when his head leaned in as if he were going to kiss her.

"Jennette, you know better—"

"Elizabeth, you are not my mother," Jennette retorted, then sighed. "He needs a wife."

"Blackburn?" Elizabeth asked. "But he's an earl. How difficult is it for him to secure a bride?"

"With his reputation, 'difficult' would be easy." Jennette sipped her tea in hopes the liquid would help her headache.

"But why would he come to you?" Victoria finally spoke up. "He didn't think you would marry him, did he?"

Well, she couldn't tell them that awful truth. And she still didn't quite understand his threat of marriage. With all that was between them, marriage would be dreadful.

"No. He wants my help."

"Why would you help him after what he did?" Avis demanded.

"It was an accident," Jennette said softly, staring at the folds of her blue silk gown. "We had been friends. He never meant for that to happen. He's still distraught over John's death."

"As he should be," Victoria said, crossing her arms over her chest. "He took a man's life, accident or not."

Jennette pressed her lips together. They would never understand what happened that day, nor could she ever tell them. If no one could believe Matthew's killing of John was accidental, who would believe her?

It would look even more sordid in the gossips' minds—the way she let Matthew take the blame to protect her. Everyone would assume he did it out of love for her. It hadn't been love. Lust, maybe, but not love. And while she never loved Matthew either, she certainly had felt something with him that she'd never felt with John.

"Jennette, why did he come to *you*?" Sophie asked softly.

"He thought if I showed support for him then perhaps others might see him for who he really is and not just his reputation."

"And did you agree to help him?" Sophie said with a knowing look in her eyes.

"Yes. I offered to help him find a bride."

"Then maybe we can all assist you." Sophie looked around at the women in the room. "There must be some woman among the quality who would marry Blackburn, reputation and all."

"She must have money," Jennette added. "His

father and brother gambled their way into a huge debt. And she must have a sterling reputation. Anything less will not help him."

"Very well," Sophie said with a smile. "We need a wealthy woman with an impeccable reputation."

"And not hard on the eyes for him," Jennette said softly. He did deserve a pretty woman.

"That goes without saying." Sophie looked at them. "Well? Any ideas?"

"Not Lucinda Bartlett," Elizabeth said with a small giggle. "She is still causing such a fuss because she unknowingly danced with him last night."

"Yes, she wasn't my best idea." Jennette leaned back against the chair feeling a little better now that her friends were helping her.

"You know," Elizabeth said with a big grin. "My sister is having a fall country party commencing this weekend. I will get her to invite him. There will be plenty of unmarried women and a week to find him someone perfect."

Avis laughed. "You must have something you're holding over her head if you can get her to invite him."

"I am her sister," Elizabeth said with a big smile. "Of course I have information she would never want her husband to learn."

"Excellent," Jennette said. "I believe we should compile a list of names as there will be some who will reject him outright because of his reputation. Any other thoughts?"

"What about Susan Whitmore?" Sophie asked. "Her mother insists her daughter get a title since Mrs. Whitmore did not."

Jennette pondered that idea. "She does have a large dowry. She is quite pretty."

"But how will she feel about his reputation?" Victoria asked.

"I suppose we could inquire." Elizabeth leaned forward. "Jennette, how well do you know her?"

"Not well at all."

"I say we should call on her tomorrow afternoon. But first, I think we should get him invited to Lady Sheldon's musicale. She has five daughters to marry off."

Jennette smirked. "And how do we do that?"

Elizabeth shook her head. "Leave that all to me."

"Very well. So tomorrow night Lady Sheldon's musicale and what do we do about Miss Whitmore?"

Elizabeth smiled brightly and said, "Avis could host a literary . . ." Her voice trailed away as she looked at Avis.

Jennette shook her head. While Avis loved hosting literary salons and talking about her own book, which hopefully would be published soon, she was now married to Banning. That would never work.

"No, Avis can't do it. Well, I haven't hosted a literary salon since before my father died." Elizabeth turned toward Avis and said, "Surely you can assist me with this?"

Jennette turned toward Avis. "You cannot tell Banning about this. If he knew how involved I was in Blackburn's life, he'd kill me."

She felt dreadful asking Avis to keep something from her new husband. But Jennette knew her brother far better than Avis did. Banning would lock Jennette in her room to keep Matthew away from her.

"Of course, I shall help you, Elizabeth. And Jennette, it's our secret," Avis said, making a cross over her heart. "Banning will not hear about this from me. Although I still wonder why you are helping Blackburn."

Jennette looked away, knowing she couldn't keep the guilt from sweeping over her face. Since marrying Matthew was out of the question, assisting him might be the only way to help her forgive herself.

A few hours later, Elizabeth and Jennette sat in the salon of Miss Susan Whitmore, waiting for the younger woman to join them. Nervous energy filled Jennette as the time dragged. She tapped her foot on the floor, keeping time with the clock.

"What is the matter?" Elizabeth asked. "You're as jumpy as a toad."

"You haven't told me how we will get them together."

Elizabeth waved a hand at her. "At the literary salon. It won't be a large gathering so we shall introduce them and hopefully they will sit next to each other."

"But what if she doesn't agree?"

"Then we will find someone else. Why are you so concerned?"

Jennette looked away from her friend's prying eyes. "I feel rather sorry for him."

Elizabeth shook her head. "Why would you feel anything save contempt for the man?"

"What happened that day was a complete accident."

Before Elizabeth could meddle any further, Mrs. Whitmore sailed into the room with Susan following directly behind her.

"Lady Elizabeth, I'm honored to have you here."

Mrs. Whitmore glanced over at Jennette and smiled tightly. "Good afternoon, Lady Jennette."

Damn. She hadn't counted on Mrs. Whitmore to be with them. Elizabeth flashed Jennette a cautious look.

Mrs. Whitmore and her daughter sat together on the sofa. Susan graciously poured tea into delicate china cups, then handed them to everyone. At twenty-one, Susan had a refined beauty. How was it that she had not married yet? She'd been out for three Seasons and was quite well-liked.

"Susan, we came on a delicate matter," Elizabeth, the more decorous of them, spoke first.

"Oh?" both Susan and her mother said and then looked at each other.

"It's nothing dreadful."

Both Susan and her mother sighed and leaned back in the sofa. Jennette watched every move they made while Elizabeth talked. Susan's hands trembled as she lifted her teacup to her mouth. Perhaps she was shy and that was the reason for her lack of a husband.

"I know a man whose reputation isn't the best but he would like an introduction," Elizabeth said. "He is an earl and looking for a wife. Preferably, one with an excellent reputation."

Susan's eyes grew large as she glanced over at her mother. Her mother patted her daughter's hand.

"Exactly whom are we discussing?" Mrs. Whitmore asked before taking a bite of her biscuit.

"Lord Blackburn."

The silence in the room almost made Jennette laugh. It wasn't as if they were trying to introduce Susan to the devil. The Whitmores exchanged odd looks as if having a private conversation without words.

Finally, Mrs. Whitmore smiled and said, "I think my daughter would be most pleased to be introduced to such a fine gentleman."

Jennette almost dropped her teacup. What the bloody hell was going on? No one had that reaction to him. Even Elizabeth sent her a curious look.

"Very well," Elizabeth said, still looking puzzled. "I will be hosting a literary salon Thursday evening. He will be in attendance."

"Then so shall we," Mrs. Whitmore replied with a very satisfied look on her face.

A sudden chill crossed Jennette's arm, raising gooseflesh. She had the singular feeling that this meeting was a very bad idea.

"Come along, Jennette," Elizabeth said as she stood.

"Good day," Mrs. Whitmore said with a positively evil grin.

What had she gotten Matthew into? She walked with Elizabeth in silence through the hallway. But as soon as the door shut behind them, she put her hand on Elizabeth's arm.

"What were they about?"

Elizabeth frowned. "I am not certain. Their reaction to the introduction was not what I expected."

"Something is very wrong." Jennette walked down the steps and then into their carriage. Once Elizabeth had settled herself inside, Jennette gasped.

"What?"

"Have you heard any rumors about Susan lately?" Jennette whispered. "Scandalous rumors?"

"None whatsoever."

"I have the oddest sensation that they plan to trap him," Jennette remarked as her indignation rose.

"Why would they need to do that?" Elizabeth asked, pulling at her white gloves. "She is wealthy, and beautiful, and . . ."

"And what if she's with child?"

This time, Elizabeth gasped. "Jennette, what a dreadful thing to say about her."

"But what if it's the truth?"

Elizabeth tapped her finger against her lip. "Then Blackburn must be warned so he can be on guard. If you are right, Susan will try to get him into a compromising position to force the issue as quickly as possible. Maybe even at the salon."

Jennette sat back against the velvet squabs and crossed her arms over her chest. "I shall make certain that doesn't happen."

Matthew entered Lady Sheldon's impressive home on George Street at exactly seven in the evening. When he'd agreed to Jennette's plan, he had doubted she would be able to secure him invitations to any functions. But now he had the musicale tonight and Lady Elizabeth's literary salon Thursday. He knew Lady Elizabeth and Jennette were good friends so Jennette had, no doubt, coerced her friend into inviting him.

Nevertheless, it mattered not how he came about the invitations as long as they continued to appear at his house every day. He looked forward to starting his new life. Respectability had been too far out of his reach for so long. Now, it was there, just a little beyond his grasp, not such an impossible feat.

While he followed the footman down the hall, he smiled. As soon as he entered the music room, his smile disappeared. The audible gasp of at least five women sounded when he crossed the threshold, followed quickly by the lifting of fans over their lips.

Not a single friendly face greeted him. Lady Sheldon's granite expression told him without words that she was only allowing his appearance because of Jennette. Glancing around the room, he noticed she hadn't attended tonight, leaving him stranded in a sea of frowns. He walked toward the seats in the back and sat down, hoping the chair would swallow him completely.

A commotion at the door forced him to look over just in time to see Jennette enter the room with a swish of violet silk. Several women formed a circle around her, whispering to her.

"I really don't see why it is a problem," she answered loud enough for him to hear.

After a few more vehement protests from the ladies surrounding her, Jennette broke from the group and walked directly toward him. "Good evening, Lord Blackburn."

Damn, she had pluck to greet him in front of everyone. "Good evening, Lady Jennette."

"I do hope you enjoy the musicale this evening. Lady Sheldon's daughters have quite the talent for both singing and the pianoforte."

He couldn't stop the pleased smile from forming. "I am certain I shall enjoy myself immensely."

She nodded and then gave the ladies a sardonic look. "I think you shall at that." She glanced about the room as if looking for someone in particular. After blowing out a delicate breath, she said, "But you do need someone to sit beside you, my lord. You shouldn't be alone."

"You could do me the honor," he said just loud enough for her to hear.

Her black eyebrows rose and her lips twitched as if she found the idea perfectly amusing. "I have just the person."

She walked away before he could stop her. His preference would have been Jennette, not someone who would sit quaking in the chair next to him. Nonetheless, he couldn't stop himself from watching her work her magic on some poor young girl whose face suddenly blanched as Jennette spoke with her. After a quick nod, Jennette led her toward him.

"Miss Amelia Sheldon, may I introduce Lord Blackburn," Jennette said with a smile to them both.

Matthew stood and bowed over Miss Sheldon's quivering hand. "It is a pleasure to meet you, Miss Sheldon."

"Th—Thank you, my lord."

"I would be truly honored if you joined me." He had to keep from rolling his eyes back into his head. The girl couldn't be more than eighteen and appeared scared even to let him bow over her hand. Perhaps he should set an age limit with Jennette. No women under twenty-one. He had no idea why she chose the youngest of the Sheldon women, unless Jennette assumed Amelia would be the easiest to manipulate.

Miss Sheldon sat in the seat next to him and pulled out her fan. Staring straight ahead, she made no attempt to draw him into conversation. Matthew's attention skipped to Jennette. She'd taken a chair three rows in front of him but to the right. He could just make out her profile and delicate, long neck.

After a quick shake of his head to clear his errant thoughts, he tried to get Miss Sheldon to speak to him.

"Are you looking forward to the Season?" he asked gently.

Her eyes widened with either fear or surprise that he had the audacity to speak with her.

"Yes," she said in such a soft voice that he had to strain to hear her. She glanced around the room as people turned to stare at them.

"Will this be your first Season?"

She shook her head. "No, my second."

Well, at least he received a three-word answer instead of one. "Did you enjoy your last Season?"

"No."

"No?" he queried.

"With four older sisters out, my mother would prefer I don't draw too much attention to myself."

And it appeared Amelia had done a fine job of that until tonight. By sitting next to him, she'd gained the attention of the entire room. Every few moments, someone looked back at her as if to make certain she was still alive. As people continued to watch, he noticed a gleam of pleasure enter her eyes.

"I see," he finally said. Well, he didn't really but he couldn't say that to her. "Will you be performing tonight?"

"No, again too much attention with aging sisters," she said.

Lady Sheldon stood and walked to the front of

the room. She introduced her eldest daughter, Beatrice, to start the night off with a sonata. As Beatrice took her seat at the pianoforte, Matthew let his gaze settle on Jennette again.

He'd noticed her glancing back at them before the music started, but now her head faced the pianoforte. What was it about her? Was it the way a few hairs had escaped her pins only to fall against the soft skin of her neck? A neck so perfect his lips wanted to touch that sensitive place where her shoulder met her neck.

Dear God, he was insane!

He should not feel attracted to Jennette. This was madness. There had to be something he didn't like about her.

Her shopping habits, he decided. The woman was known for her fashion sense and style. And he didn't like it. She was most likely driving her brother into huge debt over clothing.

Although, the violet silk gown she wore tonight deserved applause. The color suited her perfectly. And then there was that curving neckline framed with a hint of fine lace, drawing attention to the gentle outline of her breasts.

Before he knew it, the sound of clapping alerted him to the fact that the eldest Miss Sheldon had completed her music for the evening. Lady Sheldon next introduced her two middle daughters, who would sing a selection of songs for them.

Matthew forced his concentration on the two young women. It was then that he realized they must be twins. He couldn't tell the two apart. Both had light brown hair, dull hazel eyes, and freckles over the bridge of their noses. His gaze slid to the

woman next to him. He now understood why Lady
Sheldon insisted Amelia do nothing to call notice
to herself. Amelia Sheldon was the only beautiful
lady of the Sheldon family.

She was exactly what he'd told Jennette he was
looking for in a woman: petite, blond, quite pretty,
and from a fine family. With no sons to inherit,
Lord Sheldon had been quite vocal about the small
fortune he would give in dowry for the women.

So why didn't he feel drawn to her? After her initial nervousness, he'd noticed that she relaxed
when the music started. She'd even glanced over at
him a few times with a shy smile.

He should court her. Put all his efforts into
making her want to marry him. After all, he only
had a few weeks before he either married or faced
selling off his properties. Amelia Sheldon would do.

When the musicale finally finished with a violin
solo by the fourth Miss Sheldon, he turned toward
Amelia. "May I get you some lemonade?"

Her thin pink lips turned upward. "I would
like that."

The refreshments were in the dining room and
this could be his opportunity to converse with her.
"Would you accompany me?"

"Thank you, my lord." She rose with the grace
of a swan then hooked her arm with his.

He watched her as she looked around the room
with a smug smile on her face. Blowing out a small
breath, he understood exactly what she was doing.

"Are you enjoying the attention?" he whispered.

"Yes, I am," she replied just as quietly. "I do hope
you don't mind. It is very rare that anyone notices

me when my mother is constantly pushing her older daughters on any man she can."

"I see."

She glanced up at him with sympathy. "I know what you are about, my lord."

"Oh?"

"You think to marry a wealthy woman. The gossips have spoken of nothing else for days." She looked forward but continued in a hushed tone, "But it won't be me, my lord. I have my sights set on another."

"Indeed?"

"Yes."

While he should have been disappointed, it was relief that washed over him. For some inexplicable reason, he had no desire to have her as his wife. So as they walked into the dining room, she using him to draw attention to her, and he using her to help gain some respectability, he smiled.

Chapter 5

Jennette shoved her pins into her reticule, thrust some money inside, too, and then strode from her bedroom. She had to do something with this anger eating her from inside and there was only one thing that would soothe her frustration: shopping.

The image of Matthew's face as he entered the dining room with a smiling Amelia Sheldon on his arm had kept Jennette up all night. She should be ecstatic that they both seemed so pleased with each other. Happy, even. The last thing she should be was overwhelmed with tension and frustration.

"Are you ready, miss?" Molly asked as Jennette entered the salon.

"Yes," she answered back harshly.

Hopefully, her maid would understand that she had no desire for conversation today. Jennette climbed into the carriage, then sat back and waited for the usual calm that settled over her when she shopped. Picking at the fingertips of her gloves, she wondered just how long it would take peace to come to her.

This annoyance was illogical. He had done exactly what she'd wanted him to last night. Amelia's reaction to Matthew, however, had surprised Jennette. She thought of Miss Sheldon as shy and retiring, not alluring with that secret smile of hers. And she was the epitome of what Matthew had said he desired in a woman.

Curiosity picked at Jennette's inquiring mind. Did Matthew call on Amelia today? For all Jennette knew he could be at the Sheldons' home right now having tea and biscuits, making polite conversation while he courted her.

Therefore, Jennette should be pleased with herself, not about to rip off the tips of her gloves. She did not love the man. She never had.

But there was something about him.

Something tempting that made her think wicked thoughts she shouldn't about him. Lurid thoughts about what he looked like without his shirt. Was he as muscular as he appeared? Or had he taken to padding the shoulders of his jacket, as did so many men? She highly doubted he had.

Closing her eyes, she pictured his chestnut hair and thought about what it would feel like to her fingers. Soft and silky? Thick and coarse? And his lips . . . would they feel as wicked against hers as they had that morning? How could the memory of that ever-so-brief kiss have stayed with her all these years?

Thankfully, the carriage slowed to a stop on Bond Street before her mind went further down that disquieting road. She and her maid walked down to the draper's with a footman following closely behind them. She put Matthew out of her mind and concentrated on what she'd come for today.

A little bell rang as she entered the shop. Bolts of cloth lined the small room.

"Lady Jennette, how wonderful to see you again," Mrs. Greenwood announced.

"Good afternoon, Mrs. Greenwood. Did you get the fabric I wanted?" She had no time for polite conversation with the amount of items she needed today.

"Of course, wait here." Mrs. Greenwood went to the back of the store and returned carrying a bolt of forest green velvet.

Jennette removed her gloves and caressed the soft fabric. "This is beautiful."

"It will make a lovely gown for you."

"I will take it all."

Mrs. Greenwood's mouth dropped. "All of it, my lady?"

"Yes." She would need all that fabric for what she had in mind.

While Mrs. Greenwood wrapped the cloth in paper to keep it clean, Jennette wandered the room looking at all the fabrics. She would miss Mrs. Greenwood's shop. The woman could find any fabric Jennette ever wanted. Mrs. Greenwood handed the bolt to the footman, who hefted the cloth over his shoulder.

"Good day, Mrs. Greenwood," Jennette called as they departed for the next shop.

After a trip to the cobbler's and then a stop for gloves, hats, and stockings, Jennette had finished. With the footman and Molly weighed down, she carried four of the boxes herself. Just able to peer over the top of the teetering boxes, she walked down the street toward the carriage. Several people smiled or laughed as the group ambled forward.

Approaching the carriage, she noticed a man standing nearby. As she tried to get a better look, her hat blew in the wind, half-covering her eyes.

"Allow me," the deep voice said.

One by one, the man lifted the boxes out of her arms until she could finally move the offending hat out of her eyes. And then she saw him.

"Busy day, Lady Jennette?" Matthew inquired with one brown eyebrow raised.

"Yes."

He watched with disdain in his gray eyes as the footman placed all the boxes into the carriage. "I'd always heard the rumors of your shopping but thought they were largely overstated. I can see I was wrong."

"I think you are vastly mistaken, my lord."

He turned toward her and bowed. "I can see that I am not. Good day, Lady Jennette." And then he was gone, striding down the street as if she'd done something wrong.

"Mat—" Jennette quickly covered her mouth realizing how that might sound if she were overheard using his Christian name. "Lord Blackburn!"

But he never turned back. *Bloody stupid man,* she thought. She'd been known to shop in excess for herself but what harm did that cause? Banning had been more than generous with her allowance and now with her grandmother's inheritance, she need not worry about money. She could never spend it all if she tried.

Besides, she only used shopping as a method of

calming herself at times. Of course, her bad habit had started almost exactly five years ago. After what she'd done to John and then hearing the rumors about Matthew, she'd needed something to do. Painting and shopping were her only options.

As she sat in the carriage, she realized just how much she missed painting. When she and her mother moved into Avis's former house after Banning's wedding, Jennette had never unpacked her canvases and paint pots. She'd told her mother there wasn't enough light in any of the rooms. When in truth, there seemed no point as she would be leaving for Florence in three months. And now her departure was only weeks away. Once she arrived and settled in, she would take up painting again.

This restless energy was driving her mad. The image of Matthew's scornful face as he helped her with her packages just wouldn't go away. She needed to talk to someone.

After getting the attention of her driver, she said, "Please take me to Miss Reynard's home."

Sophie would understand Jennette's need to have a friend listen without solving her problems, as Avis and Elizabeth would attempt.

Sophie's lips twitched but she quickly gained control over her desire to smile. Things were progressing nicely so far. Jennette's reaction to Blackburn was exactly as Sophie had hoped when she'd seen the vision of him.

"He wouldn't even let me explain," Jennette complained for the second time. "He just stormed off."

"Well, the man is having financial difficulties,

Jennette. Surely you can understand that he might be envious watching you spend money without a care."

Jennette slammed her teacup down. "It most certainly wasn't without a care."

"I realize that but he only knows what he hears about you from others. And you do have a reputation for fashion."

"Of course I do. But I am not much different from most of the other ladies of the *ton*. And at least I am now spending my personal money, not that of my father, or brother or husband."

Sophie desperately wanted to laugh. Poor Jennette looked so put out by all this. "What are your plans for tonight?"

"Lady Cantwell is having a dinner party. I'll deliver everything after Elizabeth's literary salon tomorrow night."

Lady Cantwell was due here for a tea reading in an hour. Sophie smiled. The tea leaf reading was bound to tell her that Lord Blackburn must be invited to dinner or something dreadful might happen.

"You are welcome to join us tomorrow night for the salon," Jennette added with a smile. "You know we love your company."

"Perhaps, but not all of Society agrees with that sentiment. I am quite the thing as long as I stay in my place and don't venture into your world."

"Regardless, come along," Jennette pleaded. "I could use the support. I have a very strange feeling about introducing Susan Whitmore to him."

"Why are you introducing him to Miss Whitmore if you believe he might be happy with Miss Sheldon?" Sophie watched Jennette's reaction with a smile. Her friend's face tightened, her hands fisted, and a deep frown brought her eyebrows downward.

"Because there is always the possibility that he and Miss Sheldon won't suit. Or her father might decide not to let Blackburn court his daughter."

"Very well, then. What has you so concerned about Miss Whitmore?" Sophie asked softly.

"She and her mother were too agreeable. They know all about him and were willing to put aside his reputation for an introduction." Jennette frowned. "It makes no sense."

"Hmm, I haven't heard of any rumors regarding the girl. Perhaps after three Seasons, they feel Blackburn would be their best option before she's on the shelf."

"I just cannot believe that, Sophie." Jennette reached for her teacup. "He is not received and therefore anyone he marries takes the chance that she will be scorned unless her reputation is sterling."

"What do you think is the reason, then?"

Jennette looked away. "I fear she might be with child and trying to trap any man she can."

"Very well, then. I will attend and I'll try to perform a reading on her."

Sophie picked up her teacup and sipped as she thought. Getting Jennette and Blackburn together might be more difficult than she'd imagined. She needed an accomplice in this mission. Someone who knew them both. And as much as he would hate her for asking again, there was only one perfect man for this mission.

"I can usually sense a pregnancy. May I bring a guest with me tomorrow?"

Jennette's black eyebrows rose in question. "Of course. Anyone I might know?"

Sophie smiled. "Yes, but just a dear friend of mine."

Matthew couldn't help the frown from forming on his face as he picked up a glass of sherry from the refreshment table. Lady Cantwell's invitation to dinner shocked and pleased him. He had no idea how Jennette managed to wrangle an invitation out of the oldest and most eccentric matron in the *ton*. But he supposed he would have to thank Jennette for it.

After seeing the truth of her shopping habits thrown in his face this morning, he had no desire even to speak with her. John had told him that her father and brother spoiled her. Her actions today only confirmed his assumption that she was frivolous and spoiled.

He watched her as she spoke with Lady Cantwell. Jennette's blue eyes flashed with what looked like anger but she smiled at the older lady. Lady Cantwell glanced over at him and then back at Jennette. Finally, Jennette nodded.

Lady Cantwell moved away from Jennette and ambled toward him. The older woman pressed heavily on her cane as she walked. He had no idea how old she was, but he would guess somewhere in her mid-eighties.

"There you are, my boy," she said as she reached his position. "I wanted to welcome you to my little party."

Little party? There had to be at least fifty people

here tonight. His own dining room wouldn't seat half these people.

"Thank you, my lady," he replied and then bowed over her ancient hand.

She tilted her head and sized him up. "Perhaps the gossips have been wrong about you."

"Oh?"

"I see nothing that would make you unwelcome amongst us. In fact, I believe somewhere beneath that scoundrel mask is a gentleman." Lady Cantwell made her declaration and moved on toward another guest, her cane tapping a slow rhythm as she left.

"She *is* a widow. Perhaps you can charm her in the next two weeks."

Matthew slowly fisted his hands. "Good evening, Lady Jennette."

"Lord Blackburn," she replied with a nod. "However did you get invited here?"

He whipped around to face her directly. "What do you mean? You arranged this, not me."

Her eyebrows rose. "No, I had nothing to do with your being here."

"Then . . . how?"

She shrugged and smiled as if trying not to laugh. "Maybe Lady Cantwell is after another husband."

"Do be quiet," he whispered. He glanced at her burgundy-velvet gown and wondered if it was part of the collection she had bought today. "Fetching dress, by the way."

"Thank you. I do hope no one notices that it is last year's style."

"I'm quite certain no one but you would notice

such a thing." Try as he did, he couldn't keep the bitter tone out of his voice.

"Then you really do not understand women, my lord."

"Of course I do." He took a sip of his sherry before continuing, "God forbid you wear a gown more than once. Heavens, someone might remark about it!"

Her eyes narrowed on him. "You pompous, arrogant . . . man."

"Spoiled, little b—"

"Well now," Lady Selby came up to them both. "I do believe I need to speak with you, Jennette."

Jennette's eyes flashed at him. "Avis, I think we can talk later. You are interrupting my conversation with Lord Blackburn."

Lady Selby smiled at both of them as she hooked her arm with Jennette. "Yes, I am, before you two cause a bigger scene than you already have."

"Oh, please, Avis. How many times did I break you and Banning apart from your arguments?"

Lady Selby's lips twitched in obvious humor. "Yes, you did, many times. And see how we ended."

Lady Selby looked over at Matthew with a little smirk. *Oh dear God,* he thought. The woman probably thinks he and Jennette were arguing because of deep-seated desire for each other. Complete and utter nonsense, he thought. After seeing Jennette's true colors today, he would squash down any ardent feeling he might have for her.

The only thing he needed Jennette to do was find him a bride. Any woman would be a better option than the frivolous, self-absorbed woman walking away from him.

* * *

Jennette stood next to the potted palm with her arms over her chest in what she knew was a very unladylike posture. And she did not care. She wasn't spoiled.

"Lady Jennette, please at least try to look like you are enjoying my party."

"I apologize, Lady Cantwell."

The older woman leaned on her cane and then scanned the room until her gaze landed on Matthew. "He is a—"

"Pompous, overbearing, arrogant—"

Lady Cantwell's cackle interrupted her tirade. "I was about to say a handsome devil. Handsome not in a pretty way, but with an air of danger about him. He reminds me a little of my third husband. Now he was a man. . . ,"

"Lord Blackburn? Hardly. His hair is highly unfashionable. He could almost put it in a queue. His clothes are wrinkled and at least two years out of date."

"Lady Jennette," Lady Cantwell started, "I do believe Lord Blackburn should escort you into the dining room."

Jennette's mouth gaped open. "I—I—"

"I am the hostess of this little gathering."

"But, Lady Cantwell, he is the man who killed my betrothed," she argued.

"Accidentally, if my old memory serves." Lady Cantwell's brown eyes flashed with something akin to humor. "It is far past time for that incident to be buried."

How could Lady Cantwell find anything about

this situation amusing? "Yes, it was an accident. Still, most people don't understand that and—"

"And you shall do exactly as this old lady tells you, miss." Lady Cantwell smiled and patted Jennette's hand. "Stop worrying about what other people think of you. Life is far more enjoyable that way."

"Yes, ma'am." Jennette closed her eyes as Lady Cantwell slowly walked away.

"I was told in no uncertain terms that I am to escort you into dinner."

She opened her eyes to see Matthew staring down at her with contempt in his eyes. "Yes. She informed me, too."

"Shall we?" He held out his arm to her.

She nodded and linked her arm with his. Inhaling the tangy smell of sandalwood, she shivered.

"Are you cold?"

Unable to tell him that his nearness caused such tumultuous feelings in her belly, she nodded. "It is a chilly night."

"Yes, it has been a dreadful year for weather."

At least the weather was a safer topic of conversation than her shopping habits, or his overly long, chestnut hair. She had to get her traitorous desires under control. Why couldn't she have felt this way about John? He at least had loved her. Matthew didn't even like her. He thought she was nothing more than a spoiled brat. At least she hoped he'd been about to say brat and not the other "b" word.

"So I hear there is to be a literary salon at Lady Elizabeth's home tomorrow night," he said while they walked down the hall to the dining room.

"Yes."

"Very good."

"Is it?" Jennette asked with a strained tone to her voice.

"What do you mean?"

"You seemed quite pleased with Miss Sheldon last evening. Did you call on her today? Do you plan to court her?"

He glanced over at her with a strange little smile and her cheeks burned. She sounded like a jealous shrew.

"So many questions."

"You could try to answer one of them," she replied tightly.

"Then the answer is no."

"No, you didn't call on her? Or no, you don't plan to court her?"

"No, to both questions."

"You are the most frustrating man I have ever met," she mumbled.

They reached the dining room and strolled around the table until they found their name cards. Right next to each other. Matthew pulled out her chair and waited for her to take her seat.

He moved to the chair on her right. She greeted the others near her, attempting to ignore his masculine scent. Several people glanced down the long table at them. Most of them had pity in their eyes at her plight.

She did her best to keep her conversation with Lady Caroline, who sat to Jennette's left. But with every bite she took, her gaze slid to him. She couldn't help but notice everything, from his long fingers gripping the fork to the smile he gave Miss Colbert.

A shiver raced down her arm when he accidentally brushed up against her shoulder. She hated these feelings she had for Matthew. Why couldn't she control her reaction to him? No man before him had ever made her feel so off-centered.

Not even the man she was supposed to marry.

Chapter 6

The invitation to Lady Elizabeth's impromptu literary salon had been a pleasant surprise. He knew she was one of Jennette's friends. He assumed either Jennette was holding something over her head or Lady Elizabeth knew of his problem.

He actually hoped it was the former and not the latter. The last thing he needed was all of Jennette's friends knowing his business. Clenching his fists in frustration, he felt the carriage roll to a stop. Someday this would all be over, his name returned to its proper position, his debts paid and his tenants safe. Then he could rebuild his wealth.

The image of Jennette with all those boxes almost teetering out of her arms refused to leave his mind. He couldn't imagine how much money she must have spent yesterday. Far more than he could ever afford, he ruefully thought.

So the last thing he needed or wanted was a frivolous woman to spend money he didn't have. He would ignore the rush of desire that overcame him every time she neared him. Overlooking her shouldn't be a huge problem.

Except, he couldn't take his gaze off her at Lady Cantwell's dinner. She'd entertained all the people around them, drawing them into polite conversation. At times, he even thought he saw her glance toward him.

Inhaling deeply, he walked up the steps, pushed Jennette out of his mind, and wondered what type of reception he would receive tonight. An aging butler answered the door and held out his hand for a card. Matthew handed him the newly embossed card with his title.

"Come in, my lord. Lady Elizabeth is expecting you." The wizened man opened the door and waved him in. "They are in the conservatory."

Matthew followed the servant, admiring the white marble floor and paintings on the wall. Once his finances were in order he could restore his homes to their formal glory. One particular oil landscape was so alluring he halted his stride to take a better look at it. The scene of a river flowing through a hamlet was skillfully painted. He looked for the artist's signature but only the initials "JMT" marked it.

Hearing conversation ahead, he knew they had reached the room. He stopped as the butler announced him at the threshold.

"The Earl of Blackburn."

No matter how many times he heard it, he would never get accustomed to hearing that esteemed name used to announce him. The scoundrel, the black sheep of the family, and the man who had ruined the family name.

Lady Elizabeth turned and smiled at him.

"Lord Blackburn, welcome to my salon."

"Thank you, my lady. I am very pleased to be here." He bowed over her hand.

He scanned the room until he found Jennette sitting near a large orange tree. Her maroon gown accented her pale skin and dark hair, but it was her hair that held his attention. Tonight her raven tresses piled high on her head had white pearls woven throughout. His fingers itched to remove every hairpin and every pearl until her hair flowed down her back. He shook his head to clear his maddening thoughts.

Damn. He was attracted to the frivolous woman and every time he saw her, the draw worsened. This insane desire had to stop.

Sophie Reynard sat beside her, holding her hand and whispering. Could Miss Reynard be the woman he was supposed to meet tonight? While oftimes she was seen in the company of Lady Elizabeth, Lady Selby, and Jennette, as the rumored bastard daughter of some unknown earl she would hardly set his reputation straight.

He tore his gaze off the two women and looked around the room. Only about twenty people attended and he was acquainted with most of them. While no one had approached him yet, at least here he didn't feel as if all were talking about him behind their fans.

His gaze fell upon Lord Somerton, who stood leaning against the wall, watching him. A smirk formed on Somerton's lips as Matthew ambled toward him.

"Now, I'm quite certain I have seen it all,"

Matthew said with a grin. "A literary salon? There is no gaming here."

"I only attended as a favor to a friend," Somerton replied in a quiet tone.

"That must be some favor," Matthew said.

"You have no idea," Somerton muttered.

Before Matthew could reply, a soft cough from behind him stopped him.

"Lord Blackburn, may I introduce Mrs. Whitmore and her daughter, Susan."

Matthew turned to see Lady Elizabeth with two other women in tow. He sketched a bow over each of the ladies' hands. "It is my pleasure to meet you both."

"Perhaps you would do us the honor of escorting us to our seats," Susan said, only to receive a slight elbow nudge from her mother.

"I would be honored indeed." He held out his arm and Mrs. Whitmore clutched it like a lifeline. After leading them the short distance to their chairs, he bowed.

"Would you do us the honor of sitting with us, my lord?" Mrs. Whitmore asked.

Matthew glanced around the room until he found Jennette. She frowned but gave him a quick nod in confirmation that Miss Whitmore was indeed the woman. Obviously, Matthew thought, *Jennette must not know of Miss Whitmore's reputation with certain men.*

"That would be lovely, Mrs. Whitmore."

He took the chair next to Susan and blew out a breath. While he never minded a good musicale, literary salons tended to bore him to tears. Sitting there, his attention followed Jennette as she took her seat near the front. Not once did she glance at him.

Why did he care?

He did not.

He should be lavishing his interest on Miss Susan Whitmore. But Miss Whitmore, with her light brown hair and amber eyes, didn't appeal to him. It wasn't her looks. He'd heard three men boast about how she fell directly into their arms with very little encouragement. When he married, he wanted a woman who would remain faithful.

As the first author rose to speak about a poem, he felt Miss Whitmore's leg brush against his. The cloying scent of her perfume circled around him like a vise, choking the breath out of him. He desperately wanted to move to a different seat. Instead, he sat trapped with her for the evening. While he couldn't be choosy about who would be his wife, he and Miss Whitmore would never suit.

The program dragged through the evening and as each author spoke, Miss Whitmore's advances bordered on scandalous. She *accidentally* skimmed her hand up the side of his thigh. Luckily, no one noticed as her skirts blocked their sight.

When the program finally came to end, he rose to excuse himself.

"Lord Blackburn, would you like to take a turn on the terrace with me?" Miss Whitmore asked with a flirtatious smile. "Several other couples will be doing the same."

"I'm sorry, but I must speak with someone." He bowed and walked away. He had no need to talk with anyone, but he did desire a moment alone with no nauseating perfume.

He slipped out of the room and found the billiard room just down the hall. Closing the door behind him, he breathed in the clean scent of the room. A seat by the lit fireplace beckoned him. He leaned back into the soft leather and let his eyes shut. He really shouldn't be alone in this room. Miss Whitmore didn't seem the type of woman who would have any qualms about coming in here.

The sound of the door opening slowly forced his lids upward. Expecting to see Miss Whitmore, he released a frustrated sigh.

"Am I disturbing you?"

"Well, this is a surprise," he replied.

"I had to warn you before . . ." She hadn't moved from her position against the door.

"Warn me about what?"

"Miss Whitmore." She took two steps closer. "I fear I made a huge error with her."

"Oh? And why is that, Jennette?"

She gnawed at her bottom lip. "I can't tell you for certain. But I think she was a little too eager to meet you."

He raised a brow in question. "So you don't believe a woman might actually *want* to meet me?"

"It's not like that," she protested, wringing her hands. "I—I do not trust her. I followed you in here because I thought she might attempt to find you alone and try to compromise herself with you."

Which had already crossed his mind. "And why would that be so dreadful? It would get me off your hands rather nicely, wouldn't you agree?"

"No."

He rose and strode across the room until only a billiard table stood between them. Leaning over the table, he whispered, "Why do you care whom I marry as long as it isn't you?"

She closed her beautiful blue eyes. "You deserve better," she answered softly.

No one had cared about him in so long that he had no idea how to react. "Pardon?"

"I promised to find you a bride. But I do believe you at least should have a decent woman. A woman who isn't already with child."

So the rumors of Miss Whitmore were true. Another reason he needed to tread more carefully when searching for a bride. The most eager of women likely had a cause for a rushed wedding.

He strolled along the edge of the billiard table, slowly coming closer to her. In her distracted state, she apparently hadn't taken notice of his position. After the cloying odor of Miss Whitmore's perfume, the slight scent of jasmine that Jennette wore smelled like a breath of summer air.

"Precisely how did you determine Miss Whitmore is with child?" he asked. "I doubt she volunteered the news."

"As I told you, she acted extremely eager to meet you. She and her mother kept giving each other odd looks when I spoke with them."

Matthew suppressed a chuckle. "And from that you decided the only logical explanation had to be pregnancy?"

"No," she answered in a hesitant tone. "I asked Sophie to attend tonight because she can usually sense these things. She spoke with Miss Whitmore and held her hand. From that she determined her condition."

Matthew groaned out of frustration with her

illogical thoughts. But there was also the possibility that she was correct about Miss Whitmore. Perhaps the only women who would have anything to do with him all had something to hide. Except Jennette. She had the most to keep secret . . . and *she* didn't want him either.

"So far you have made me dance with a woman so disgusted with me she could scarcely move. Another woman, barely out of the nursery, who was in love with another man—"

"Miss Sheldon?" she gasped. "I had no idea."

"And now you set me up with a woman who might be carrying another man's child." He stepped closer to her as his anger surged until he had her trapped between his body and the billiard table. He leaned in closer, inhaling the tempting scent of her perfume. *Ignore the clawing desire,* he told himself.

"You had best have a care, Jennette," he whispered near her ear.

"Wh—Why?" she stammered.

"You're starting to look like my only hope."

"You're mad!"

"Hardly," he said with a small grin. "You have yet to protest my close contact, either."

Deliberately, he traced the delicate line of her jaw with his finger. God, he was a fool to want her as he did. She was everything he didn't need in a woman. The last thing he should do was bait her. Or stand so close that her breasts almost scraped against his jacket.

He should back away . . . but his feet wouldn't move. The urge to retreat flew out of his mind only to be replaced by a much stronger yearning.

No. He looked away from her. He should do what he intended and ignore her.

Jennette shoved at his chest, embarrassed by the accuracy of his statement. Three times, he'd pinned her body between him and another object and not once had she protested. Instead, she only savored the scent of him and the strength of his hard, lean body all but touching her. God help her.

"I believe you are quite wrong on that matter," she said resolutely.

"Are you trying to convince me or yourself?" he asked with a grin.

"You are the most annoying man I have ever met."

He leaned nonchalantly against the billiard table, crossing his arms over his chest. "Tell me, Jennette, would it be so horrid if we had to marry? Would you be unable to tolerate my kisses?"

She turned toward him as embarrassed heat crossed her cheeks. "How dare you insult me with such a question?"

"I apologize," he said softly.

"I would find it unbearable," she lied. She could never let him know how much he affected her senses.

"Unbearable?" he said with a low chuckle. "You can't possibly believe that."

Jennette stood her ground, crossing her arms over her chest as he had. "Utterly unbearable."

Anger flared in his gray eyes. "Liar," he bit out. "You have done nothing to find me a *proper* bride, thus allowing you to absolve your conscience when you find yourself married to me."

"That makes no sense at all," she replied, throwing her arms up in frustration.

"Indeed?" He moved closer to her again. "You can tell yourself that you did your duty—you found me several eligible young ladies. Only you will never admit the truth, that you deliberately interfered with the process so you could marry me without guilt."

"You have completely lost your mind!" She'd never thought that intriguing idea.

"Do you think I don't feel the same guilt?" he asked.

"You have nothing to feel guilty for. I am the one who impaled my betrothed."

"Prove it to me," he whispered. "To *yourself*."

"What do you mean? Prove what?"

"Kiss me, Jennette." He stepped directly in front of her. "Show me how repulsive it would be if you were forced to kiss me."

"Never. We have kissed before and it meant nothing," she lied frantically to avoid his proposition.

"That kiss could only be considered a peck on the lips. I am speaking of a real kiss, Jennette."

"I have nothing to prove to you." And she had nothing to prove to herself either. She'd dreamed of exactly what his kisses would really feel like—repulsive and unbearable were not even close. But she had no need to experience it firsthand. She had the memory of that one kiss no matter how brief the contact.

She turned to storm out of the room before this ridiculous conversation became more intimate than it already had. As she stepped past him, his arm reached out and caught her. Dragging her closer to him, his feral grin suddenly had her quivering.

For an impossibly long moment, they stared at each other. Neither saying a word.

"What—"

He cut her question off with his lips. Hard lips that hoped to punish her for her lies. She should push him away from her. Yell at him for his arrogance and gall. The last thing she should do was bring her arms up to wrap around his neck, drawing him closer.

His lips softened and he deepened the kiss, sending her into an abyss of heavenly sensations. As his velvety tongue skimmed across hers, she gasped. No man had kissed her like this in five years. Tentatively, she let her tongue touch his and discover the secrets of his mouth. Fire burned inside her belly as they explored each other so intimately.

She shivered and moaned as he pressed her even closer to his hard body. She'd wanted his kisses for so many years. His hands roamed down her back, cupping her derrière and squeezing softly. Even knowing she should put a halt to their kiss, she did nothing but return the heat of his passion.

While she had kissed numerous times before, never had she felt such a lightning shock of sensual desire. She had the strangest urge to unravel his cravat, unbutton his shirt, and let her fingers roam his broad, naked chest.

Unthinkable!

She pushed him away and turned so he would not see the bright red color tinting her cheeks. How could she have let this go so far? The man didn't want her. Not after what she'd done to him.

"And?" he whispered.

And? She twirled around to him with a frown. The man wanted a critique of his kisses?

"It was utterly unbearable," she whispered, then raced from the room.

Matthew released a long breath as the door closed behind her. What had he done? Kissing Jennette had not been on his agenda for the evening. And yet, every time she came near him, he found his physical attraction to her growing. Not that it mattered.

There had to be another woman he could wed.

A woman who wouldn't bring out his guilt for what he'd done. A woman who wouldn't look at him with guilt in her eyes.

He needed to solidify his reasons for not wanting to wed her. She was a wastrel like his brother and father. While they gambled their money away, she wasted it on clothing she did not even need.

Anger for his stupidity surged within him. Even Miss Whitmore was a better option than Jennette. He walked to the door and reached for the brass knob. But the last thing he wanted to do was raise another man's bastard as his own. His heir would be his progeny, not another's. Nor did he want a woman who would be unfaithful to him. So perhaps not Miss Whitmore as a wife, but almost any other woman would be a superior choice.

But no matter whom he was forced to marry, it would not be Jennette.

Pausing, he closed his eyes and the image of her face came to him again. The look of shock and desire flashing in her blue eyes imprinted on his mind forever. Just as the sensation of her kiss would never leave him. He should have known how it would feel to taste her sweet lips again.

John had told him about her passionate nature and that alone should keep Matthew away from her. He didn't need a woman who gave herself so freely to a man, even if that man had been her fiancé at the time. Jennette should have insisted on a quick wedding and not taken risks by prolonging the engagement for six months.

Shaking his head, he realized none of these insane thoughts mattered. He wouldn't be marrying Jennette when there had to be at least one other woman who would have him. Walking down the hall, he heard the sound of angry voices and stopped.

"Why do you want me to do this?"

Matthew had never been one to eavesdrop, but Somerton sounded truly vexed, and in all the years Matthew had known him, that never happened.

"You have asked me for more favors than I have ever given another. This is the least you can do for me."

He tilted his head in thought. The woman's voice sounded vaguely familiar but he could not place it. He heard what sounded like a glass slamming down on the table.

"Very well," Somerton said harshly. "But after I do this for you it will be time for you to tell me the truth. I want her name."

"And you shall get it when the time is right," the woman responded lightly as if she had no fear of Somerton's wrath.

"No, Sophie. The time will be right after I do this for you."

Sophie? Sophie Reynard? Jennette's friend and the current medium taking the *ton* by storm? It made no sense that Somerton would have anything to do with her. Unless they were lovers . . .

"Anthony," she replied softly but firmly. "I make this decision, not you."

"Bitch," he said roughly.

"Yes, I am. And just like you, I'm not one to cross."

Hearing footsteps, Matthew continued down the hall before someone caught him listening in on what sounded like a very private conversation. He walked toward the gallery where people had congregated.

"Blackburn, hold up for a moment."

He turned to see Somerton treading toward him with a smile. No sense of frustration appeared on his features, his stride relaxed, and his shoulders not tense. Nothing to make a person think he'd just been arguing with a woman. And losing the argument, from what Matthew had heard.

"Did you need me?" Matthew replied.

"I have two favors to ask of you."

"Oh?"

Somerton smiled with his usual ease. "Accompany me on an errand, would you?"

"At this hour?"

"Yes."

Matthew shrugged but wondered if this had anything to do with the conversation Somerton had with Miss Reynard. With his curiosity roused, he said, "Very well, I have nothing to get home to."

"Excellent."

"And the other favor?"

Somerton gave him a half smile. "I need you to save me from myself."

"Is that even possible?" Matthew asked with a chuckle.

"Of course not. But I'll be at Norton's tonight and losing a tremendous amount of money—"

"But I thought you always win?"

Somerton shook his head. "I do. But tonight I shall appear to be deeply in my cups and losing money. I need you to stop me and drag me out of the building before I accuse someone of cheating."

"Why?"

"Just a little something I'm working on. I need to gauge a man's reaction to my outburst," Somerton replied lightly.

"Very well, I will help you with both favors. But remind me again why I should assist you?"

"Because I am helping you with your quest to find a bride."

Matthew barely suppressed his laugh. The idea of a profligate scoundrel like Somerton assisting him with finding a bride seemed highly unlikely.

Chapter 7

Matthew leaned against the lamppost, again wondering why they were standing on Maddox Street at almost midnight. Nothing seemed out of place. Inside the stately houses, servants slowly snuffed out the candles, leaving darkness in their place. Except the brothel across the street. He assumed the prostitutes must have something to do with why they were here.

"So you can't tell me why we are here?"

"I wish I knew," Somerton muttered. "I was told to be here and stay until something happened."

"Until what happens?" Matthew asked.

"I don't know—something."

"Who the devil would tell you that?"

"No one you need to know about." The usual answer Somerton gave to anything the least bit intrusive in his life.

Matthew should be angry, but, knowing the type of work Somerton had done in the past, he decided not to press the conversation further.

"How long did you work for the Home Office?"

Somerton narrowed his eyes. "Whoever said I worked for them?"

"Just a rumor I'd heard," Matthew said nonchalantly.

"And a rumor is all it is."

Matthew sighed and watched several men walking out of Lady Whitely's brothel. Everyone knew she wasn't really a lady, but she did run the cleanest establishment in town. With a frown on his face, Somerton continued to glance over at the house.

The sound of a carriage rolling to a stop down the street drew his attention. He and Somerton watched as a groomsman opened the door and a woman wearing a hooded black cloak emerged.

"Is she involved in your business tonight?" Matthew whispered to Somerton.

"I am not certain," he replied slowly.

The woman pulled out several packages from the nondescript carriage. The groomsman did the same until they were both struggling to walk down the dimly lit street. Something about the woman looked familiar but he couldn't determine why. They placed the packages on the doorstep of the home next to the brothel. The servant hurried back to the carriage and returned with even more parcels.

Matthew watched as the woman arranged them by the door and turned to walk down the steps. Seeing her fully, he gasped.

"Well, now I believe we have determined our purpose here," Somerton said with a chuckle.

"What the bloody hell is she doing over there?" he asked but didn't wait for an answer. Racing across the street, he reached her just as she grasped the carriage door.

He swung her around to face him.

"No," Jennette whispered. "Not here, not now! You will ruin everything."

She clambered into the carriage and he followed. Ignoring him, she continued to glance out the window. Matthew turned and watched as the grooms-man banged on the door of the house and then raced for the carriage. Just as he swung himself up, the door to the house opened, revealing a petite, blond woman.

"Get this carriage moving!" Jennette shouted as she sat back against the cushions.

"Who was that woman?"

"My friend, Victoria," she replied and then pulled the curtain back to look out the window.

Victoria? Of course, Miss Seaton. The woman who cared for the orphaned children.

Why would she hide from her friend?

He continued to watch as Miss Seaton slowly picked up the packages and surveyed the carriage rolling away. Realization finally dawned on him. Those packages were the same he'd seen Jennette carrying from the stores yesterday. They were not for her but for the orphans.

The orphans.

Not her.

God, he felt like an idiot.

He'd spent the past two days criticizing her behavior when all she had done was buy clothing for some orphan children. Yes, he was definitely a fool, he decided.

* * *

Jennette finally relaxed against the black velvet squabs and sighed. She had no idea what to do with the man who sat across from her. In all the years she had been supplying Victoria's orphans with clothing for Christmas, no one, save Sophie, had discovered her. Nor had she ever wanted anyone to find out what she did for the children. Buying clothing for the children made her feel good, but she didn't need admiration for the charity. She preferred to stay anonymous.

Victoria was proud of the work she did with the orphans. While Jennette knew she struggled with money at times, Victoria hated to take money from her friends. Even though it was a month earlier than Jennette normally left the packages, Victoria would know they were for Christmas.

"I believe I owe you an apology," Matthew said softly.

"Oh?"

"You refuse to make this easy on me." He leaned forward and clasped her hands.

"And for what do you apologize? Believing the worst of me? Calling me spoiled? Or kissing me without my permission?"

His sensual smile made her heart pound wildly in her chest. "I will never apologize for kissing you, Jennette."

She could only stare at his face. The shadows in the carriage made it difficult but she could close her eyes and remember every detail. She would love to sketch him, or better, paint his portrait. Charcoal would never do justice to the strands of red in his dark brown hair. Nor would it capture his eyes—the color of a stormy day.

"But I do owe you an apology for thinking the worst of you. I had no idea you were buying all those items for the orphans."

"You never asked. You just assumed I was buying for myself."

He looked down at the floor of the carriage. "I made a dreadful error. Please accept my sincerest apologies."

A part of her wanted to mock him further, but he did look sincere. "Apology accepted."

"Why didn't you just tell me what you were doing?" he asked softly.

"I do not buy the children clothing so everyone can congratulate me on being such an upstanding lady."

"Then why do you do it?"

"Because the children should have decent clothes to wear. Because Victoria is a dear friend but won't take money from me out of pride." She paused then whispered, "Because it is the right thing to do and I have the means to do it."

He nodded. "And you don't care what people think of you."

If only he knew the inaccuracy of his statement. "If they wish to believe I'm a frivolous spendthrift, then let them. I know the truth."

"And now, so do I."

"Not because I chose to tell you," she reminded him.

"I shouldn't be here," he whispered.

And he shouldn't. But she did not want him to leave her just yet. "We could drive for a short while. My mother knows where I am and if it takes a bit longer than usual she won't worry overmuch."

"Someone might see us." He squeezed her hands slightly.

"True, but it is very dark."

"The servants might gossip," he whispered.

"Never."

"Indeed. But why would you want to spend even a minute longer than needed in my company after what I said about you?"

Jennette bit down on her lip to keep from blurting out that she actually enjoyed his companionship. At least when he didn't believe the worst of her. The raspy tone of his voice soothed her and made her feel secure.

The man who could ruin her and her family made her feel protected. What a ridiculous notion!

Ignoring his question, she asked, "Did you enjoy the literary salon?"

He released her hands and leaned back with a smile. "Not at all. Between Miss Whitmore's suffocating perfume and her scandalous advances—"

"She made advances in front of everyone?"

"Very furtively. I doubt anyone would have noticed."

"You did!" she said as outrage filled her. She should have known better than to follow through with their meeting once Sophie had confirmed Miss Whitmore's secret.

"It was hard to miss her hand sliding up my leg."

"She did that? Where anyone might notice?"

"Oh yes. Her skirts hid her hand's gentle caress," he added in a husky tone.

"And I suppose you did nothing to stop her?" She folded her arms across her chest.

"If I had, people might have noticed."

Why did the idea of Miss Whitmore touching Matthew make her heart sink deep into her chest? She didn't want Miss Whitmore to lay a hand on him in any manner.

"Of course," she replied.

"Now that we know Miss Whitmore won't suit, who is next?" he asked lightly.

Next? She hadn't even thought of whom else she could ask. She'd pinned her hopes on Miss Sheldon and Miss Whitmore. "I will let you know soon," she finally answered.

A soft chuckle erupted from him. "You do not have any ideas of who will be next, do you?"

"No." She released a pent-up sigh. "I thought more women would be interested in your title than your reputation."

"And now I believe you fully understand my predicament."

"I always did," she mumbled softly. There had never been one doubt about society's reaction to John's death. And she had been such a bloody coward to let Matthew take the responsibility.

He glanced out the window quickly. "I shall take my leave now," he said, knocking on the carriage to gain the driver's attention. As the vehicle rolled to a stop, he reached for the handle. "Please let me know if you have any other women for me to meet. Or the date you would like to be wed."

Before she could sputter an answer, he jumped down and closed the door behind him. Bloody arrogant man! She would show him. She would find him the most perfect woman.

Watching him, she wondered what he was about at this hour. He walked into an establishment and her heart sank. A gaming hell. He really was a gambler like his father.

The next morning Jennette sat at her desk in her bedroom compiling a list of possible brides for him. After much consideration, she'd decided on three more women. Each lady met his specific requirements and she hoped they would acquiesce to a meeting.

Having completed her list, she picked up her charcoal and let her imagination run free. Her hand deftly formed the image in her mind. Lips, hard and yet velvety soft, not too full but not too thin. A jaw that showed stubbornness and compassion.

"Interesting drawing, my dear girl."

Jennette started and looked up to see her mother staring at the sketch that consisted of only lips and a jaw. "Mother, what are you about this morning sneaking in and give me a fright?"

Her mother pulled up a chair closer to Jennette and looked at her with one eyebrow raised. Oh dear, she knew that expression.

"I am a tad worried about you, Jennette."

"Oh?"

"Yes, you haven't been your usual self. You seem distracted lately, as if you have something on your mind and can't speak of it." She glanced down at the paper again. "Perhaps you are considering a man?"

"No, Mother." Jennette swept the paper under her pile and placed her folded hands on top. "I believe you are mistaken. I have been preoccupied with a favor to a friend, that is all."

"So I have heard."

Jennette's eyes widened. "You have?"

"Banning told me all about the uninvited guest at your birthday ball. Would those lips you have concealed be his, perhaps?" Her mother gave her a knowing look.

"No," Jennette replied far too quickly.

"There are far worse men in the *ton* than Lord Blackburn," her mother said softly. "Far worse."

Jennette knew she had to pretend outrage or no one would ever believe her. She scraped back the chair and stood. "I cannot believe you think I might have an affection toward that man. It is nothing of the sort."

"Sit down, Jennette," her mother ordered. "I of all people know not to believe that feigned anger. You, John, and Blackburn were very close. While you chose John, that doesn't mean you couldn't have felt something—"

"Mother, I did not have feelings for Blackburn."

Her mother eyed her carefully before tilting her head in a quick nod. "Very well."

Slowly, she returned to her seat and stared at the papers on her desk. "Mama, when did you know you had fallen in love with Papa?"

"Oh dear," her mother whispered. "Well, most people wouldn't believe it, but I knew almost from the start. It made no sense. Then again, when does love ever make sense? He was so much older than I. And yet, I knew the first time I danced with him that I would be his wife."

"Were you a—attracted to him physically?" Jennette whispered.

"Very much so."

She looked up into eyes as blue as hers. "Do you

think you can be physically attracted to a man without loving him?"

Her mother patted her hand softly. "Unfortunately, I do think it is very possible. But it doesn't mean we must act on those feelings, my dear."

"I understand that, Mother. I'm just so confused where he is concerned. I do not love him. I don't. But . . . ," her voice trailed off as she stared out the window seeing nothing but the image of Matthew in her head. The look of desperation in his eyes when he talked about his finances. The look of desire when he kissed her.

"But when he looks at you your insides turn to mush. You feel a certain stab of something undefined in your belly."

"Yes!"

Her mother shook her head. "Lust," she whispered.

Jennette leaned in closer to her. "Lust? I thought only men had those feelings."

"Unfortunately, no. And that is why so many widows have their reputations ruined."

"I don't want to be lusting after him."

"We don't always get much choice in the matter. It all comes down to how we act."

Jennette's eyes shot open. "You don't believe I would act upon these feelings, do you?"

Her mother smiled at her. "No, my dear. You never did so with John, why would you now?"

Jennette nodded. But the only reason she had never followed through on her feelings for John was that she never had these strange sensations with him. His kisses were sweet, not hot with passion. Even then, her thoughts had been on how Matthew's kisses would feel. But telling her mother that would only cause her to worry needlessly.

Jennette had no intention of acting upon her feelings for Matthew. Even if his kisses created sensations she'd only previously encountered in her dreams. She would find him a wife and then she would be free of her past and could live in Florence.

Only every time she thought of Florence her heart sank. She truly never wished to leave. But she couldn't stay. Matthew had given her five years of peace to enjoy life and gain her inheritance. He'd left Society for her. It was his turn to be happy.

At least that had been her plan. Seeing how Society scorned him, she doubted if her leaving would have any impact unless she told everyone the truth before she left. Doing that would mean never returning because there would certainly be another inquest. And she'd lied during the first one.

"Jennette?"

She glanced over to see her mother staring at her with a frown. "I'm sorry. I was woolgathering."

"So I noticed. I called your name three times."

"Oh," Jennette replied as heat crossed her cheeks.

"I was wondering if you think Blackburn is using this marriage idea as an attempt to court you."

"Court me? For what purpose?"

One dark eyebrow rose. "Shall I count the reasons? Money, status, reputation, not to mention you are a beautiful woman."

Jennette waved a hand in dismissal at her mother. The idea of Matthew coming to call on her was the stuff of dreams. Maybe five years ago, he could have courted her. But not now.

"You're being absurd, Mother. After all the rumors of him k—killing John because he actually loved me? The gossips would cut him dead."

"Perhaps," her mother drawled. "Still, remember what I said, there are far worse men who might have an interest in you."

Matthew finished packing the few items he would need for a weeklong trip to Lord Aston's estate in Surrey. As he placed a cravat into his bag, he wondered exactly how Jennette had managed this coup. Lord Aston was a very high-ranking member of Society. If everything went well this week, Matthew's reputation would be raised a notch or two just for attending.

He supposed Jennette would have a group of women to introduce to him. While that had been his desire only days ago, since kissing her he now doubted any other woman would satisfy him.

He wanted her.

But every time he thought about how much he desired her, his guilt slammed into him again. If only he'd never told her how he felt that morning. If only he hadn't kissed her that morning. If only John had kept his damned cock out of every other woman. Matthew would never have spoken to Jennette if he'd thought John could make her happy.

Damn. He was in a bloody mess. Marrying her was out of the question. She would never have him as a husband. There would always be John's death between them, an invisible wedge driving them apart.

"Bloody hell man, aren't you ready yet?"

Matthew turned to see Somerton standing at the

threshold to his bedroom. "I had to let my valet go so I'm stuck packing things up."

"So I see. I take it you let the butler go, too? I let myself in. Anyone might walk in and steal from you."

Matthew laughed harshly. "What exactly would they take?" he asked, sweeping his arm throughout the stark room.

"Hmm, I see your point."

"Welcome to the world of the poor nobility," Matthew said sarcastically.

"Not for long." A slow grin raised Somerton's lips upward. "I have a feeling this week something special is about to happen."

"Maybe for you, but I doubt anything interesting is in store for me."

"Oh, it will be interesting for me. Lady Mary Greenly will be attending. That is a widow who truly misses her husband. Or at least one part of him."

"Well, enjoy."

Somerton shook his head. "You only have a few weeks left. This week will bring you something fortuitous."

"We shall see."

"Shall we depart?"

Matthew nodded, thankful for Somerton's offer to ride with him. Only Somerton knew the true extent of the appalling state of his finances. The gambling debts had forced Matthew to sell all but one of his horses and let go of all the servants except one cook.

"Has Lady Jennette created a list of eligible ladies attending this party?" Somerton asked as he grabbed the valise on the bed.

"I haven't spoken to her in two days. The only

word I received was to make certain I attended this function."

Somerton chuckled. "Have you rendered her speechless? I didn't think that was possible."

Matthew suppressed a laugh. "No one would be able to manage that feat. She will express her opinion no matter what the consequence."

"And yet, it saves one the necessity of attempting to discover what lies in a woman's mind."

Matthew grabbed the handrail as they walked down the cracked marble stairs. Reaching the bottom, he wiped his hands on a handkerchief to remove the dust.

"You haven't told me how exactly you were invited to this soiree. Or have you decided to sneak in as you usually do?" Matthew remarked as he locked the door behind him.

"Quite odd, indeed. Two days ago, the invitation arrived at my doorstep. Perhaps Lady Jennette thought you might want some disreputable company."

Matthew frowned. "But how did she arrange such a thing?"

Somerton laughed as the coach door closed behind them. "Lady Elizabeth, of course."

"Oh?"

"Lady Aston is Lady Elizabeth's sister."

Now everything made sense. Yet, he still wondered why Jennette hadn't added Lady Elizabeth to the list of eligible ladies. She was the daughter of a duke so it stood to reason she had a large dowry. Even with her flaming red hair and freckles sprinkling her nose, she was an attractive woman.

Perhaps he should ask Jennette about her.

* * *

"Have you heard anything more about Blackburn?" Vanessa stroked her lover's chest with her long fingernails. Baron Huntley was a handsome devil, but not the brightest. He would make the perfect pawn should she need him.

"I saw him at Lady Elizabeth's literary salon." Huntley skimmed his hand up her bare back.

"Oh?"

"Hmm," he said, nipping her shoulder. "Miss Whitmore was all but climbing on his lap, making a complete spectacle of herself. But I know for fact what a little strumpet that gal is."

"Do you now." Vanessa shrugged her shoulder to get him to remove his wet lips.

"Never met an easier girl." He looked up at her with his hazel eyes flashing. "I had her at the Easton's ball. Right in the butler's pantry. Definitely wasn't the first man in that girl either."

Perfect, Vanessa thought with a smile. Once little Miss Whitmore married Matthew, he would discover exactly what he'd wedded and come running back to her. While she wouldn't get marriage, Matthew would keep her in gowns and a nice house. It wasn't what she wanted but Vanessa had always been a logical woman. Getting him back into her bed would have to do.

"Quite sure Blackburn saw right through her," Huntley continued.

Vanessa stiffened. "Oh? Why would you say that?"

"Couldn't help but notice him go into the billiard room and Lady Jennette follow him a few moments later." Huntley lowered his head toward her breast, but she pushed him off.

"Lady Jennette Selby?"

"Yes. The earl's sister."

"I know exactly who she is. What I want to know is why did she enter the billiard room when Blackburn was there?"

Huntley shrugged and then slobbered a kiss on her neck. "Don't know. Heard a rumor she's helping him with something. Starting to cause some talk after what he did to her betrothed and all."

Panic flickered through her. Matthew had loved Lady Jennette whether he admitted it or not. He'd told her of his attraction to Jennette but Vanessa knew he'd loved Lady Jennette.

There was only one thing Lady Jennette could be helping Matthew with—marriage. Vanessa's mind whirled with the possibilities. Why would Matthew let Jennette help him? Perhaps it was her idea. A way to keep him from revealing the truth about her.

But Jennette was the type of woman who could make any man fall in love with her. And Vanessa would never let Matthew fall for Jennette's charms again. Vanessa could accept Matthew marrying, but she knew he would never return to her if he loved his wife. And he would love Jennette.

There had to be a way to stop them.

Vanessa pulled Huntley closer until his chest brushed against her taut nipples. He groaned as her hand reached for his erection.

"Huntley darling," she whispered, drawing her fingernails up his shaft.

"What?" he growled.

"I have a favor to ask of you." Vanessa circled her hand around the head of his penis, then stroked downward.

"Anything you want," he panted.

"I want you to seduce a woman."

Chapter 8

Jennette let out a sigh of pain as her feet finally touched the ground again. After spending most of the day in the coach, her limbs ached, her bottom throbbed, and her head pounded. All she wanted was a warm bath, a cup of tea, and some peace. She'd been stuck in the carriage with her mother, and Banning and Avis. The trip seemed endless.

Poor Avis couldn't travel without being sick. But watching the newly wedded couple holding hands and whispering secrets to each other made Jennette's stomach roil. Every time they were required to stop for Avis, Banning was there for her, comforting her.

They were so much in love.

Jennette wanted that so desperately for herself it pierced her heart with agony.

"Come along, Jennette," her mother said in an impatient tone. "Lady Aston is expecting us."

"Well, I require a bath before we greet her," Jennette commented. "I am covered in dust."

"Of course. But we can still make our initial greetings."

"Yes, Mother."

Jennette followed behind the group. Footsteps crunched on the gravel drive. The large wood double doors of the manor house opened wide as they approached. A butler in full livery and powdered wig stood sentry. Banning held out his card and the man nodded slightly before moving away to let them inside.

She had never been to Lady Aston's house. In fact, she barely knew the woman. Jane was ten years older than Elizabeth and well out of the house by time Jennette came to call on her friend.

"Lord and Lady Selby, welcome to our home."

Jennette glanced up the sweeping staircase to see a woman in her mid-thirties looking down at them in a haughty manner. Her mother stiffened slightly and Jennette wondered briefly if it was because she was now the dowager Lady Selby. Wanting to give her mother a bit of comfort, Jennette clasped her hand. Her mother patted it in understanding.

"And of course, the dowager Lady Selby and Lady Jennette, welcome to my home," Lady Aston said, slowly walking down the steps. She glanced over at Jennette with an upturned lip.

"Thank you for inviting us," her mother replied in a soft tone so unlike her.

"I have put you two together," Lady Aston said, motioning for a footman. "I assumed you would want to watch over your daughter."

Jennette's mouth gaped. She started to give the woman a proper upbraiding but her mother squeezed her hand forcefully.

"Thank you, Lady Aston. I appreciate your looking out for my daughter's welfare."

Lady Aston smiled tightly. "We mothers must watch over our children."

Jennette could not believe the nerve of this woman. She had no idea why Lady Aston appeared to dislike her so. That question would have to wait until she could question her mother in private.

Following the footman, Jennette walked up the stairs and down the opulent hallway. To her, the house was overdone. Massive gilt picture frames hung on the walls. Heavy velvet curtains covered the large windows, blocking out most of the daylight. And the colors were dreadful. The footman opened the door to their room.

"Your maid will be up presently with your trunks," he said then disappeared as he closed the door.

Jennette shook her head. "This room is oppressive."

Her mother gave her an angry look. "Don't even start refurbishing that woman's house."

"Why is she so distasteful?" Jennette plopped down on the bed closer to the window. "What does she think I will do whilst I'm here? Be found in a compromising position? Use the wrong fork with dinner? That woman was dreadful to both of us."

Her mother removed her bonnet and tossed it on the bed. "This has nothing to do with you, my dear."

"Indeed? Whatever did you do to anger the lady?"

Her mother's mouth pinched and her dark eyebrows rose. "She had an infatuation with your brother when she was one and twenty. He was only eighteen and far from ready to marry. But she decided to attempt to compromise herself in order to force the issue."

Jennette covered her mouth to keep from laughing. "What happened?"

"I overheard her talking about her plan with her best friend. She intended for her friend to walk in on them. I sent Lord Aston in Banning's stead."

"Mother!"

Her mother only waved a hand at her. "When you have children, you will understand that a mother will do anything to protect them."

Except Jennette doubted she would ever have children at this point in her life. She was already on the shelf by most people's estimation. By the time she had settled into her new life in Florence, she would be in her late-twenties. How many men wanted a woman that old? They all wanted young and fertile ladies for brides.

There were days she wished she had allowed John a few more intimacies than he had taken. She wondered if it was too late for her now. Would she die an innocent spinster?

And why did that thought suddenly make her think of Matthew? Worse, she couldn't help but remember the velvety texture of his tongue as it caressed hers. The feel of his large hands cupping her derrière, pressing her hips closer to his manhood.

She had to stop these dreadful thoughts. She could never have Matthew. He was a gambler who would go through her money like water.

Matthew lay back against the soft bed thankful for the private room. After a few hours in the carriage with Somerton, he needed to be alone. Not that anyone would call Somerton a chatty fellow—just the opposite, in fact. The stony silence in the carriage had felt strangling and uncomfortable.

But it had given him time to think and wonder about whom Jennette would introduce him to this week. He would give any lady his complete attention, no wandering erotic thoughts about Jennette.

She was out of the question.

She would always be John's woman. While they had all been friends, Matthew had always known she preferred John. He'd had the title and someday would have inherited the lands and money. Matthew had been a second son with no prospects. John had the blond hair and blue eyes. She had loved him. They'd desired each other and just like five years ago, Matthew was the odd man out.

He'd been terribly envious of John's relationship with her. And he'd known John wasn't the perfect man for Jennette. Still, Matthew had lost two friends that day.

A knock pulled him out of his musing. "Yes?"

Matthew sat up and waited for the door to open. Instead, a slip of paper slid under the door. He walked to the note and read it quickly.

I need to speak with you in private. Meet me in the gardens in five minutes.

J

It was time to discover whom she planned to introduce him to this evening. Matthew dragged himself to the mirror. Brushing back his hair with his hands, he realized how badly he needed a haircut.

His valet used to perform that duty. One more thing gone because of his father's gaming.

After straightening his cravat and jacket, he headed to the gardens. A harsh November wind blustered, making him wish he'd brought his great-coat with him. Dried leaves crunched under the weight of his boots. Wandering through the dead flowers and fallen leaves, he searched for her. He looked toward a small boxwood holly to see her sitting on a bench with her black, wool cloak wrapped around her.

She appeared innocent and, as she looked up at him, lonely. Her brilliant blue eyes held a haunting appearance.

"What is wrong, Jennette?"

She frowned and then smiled. "Nothing. It's quite cold out here."

"Why did you need to meet with me?"

"There are three ladies I think might approve of you."

Approve of him? "Who?"

"Lady Anna Grange, Miss Mary Marston, and Miss Olivia Smithe-Taylor."

"What about Lady Elizabeth?"

Her head darted upward. "Lady Elizabeth?"

"Yes. Your friend, I believe." He crossed his arms over his chest as he stared down at her. "And un-married."

Her face paled in the dappled sunlight. "I do not believe she is the right woman for you."

Anger surged through him. "So it is perfectly acceptable to toss me at some unsuspecting lady, as long as she isn't a friend of yours."

She rose and placed her hands on her hips. "How dare you suggest such an outrageous thing?"

"Then why?"

"I am not at liberty to say," she replied slowly.

"Has she specifically told you she doesn't want me to court her?" he demanded.

"No . . ." Her shoulders sagged. "It's not what you think, Matthew."

"Oh?"

"Promise me you shall tell no one what I'm about to say to you." She looked up at him with pleading eyes and he knew he would have agreed to anything.

"Very well."

"Her father left her out of his will," she whispered, staring at the ground.

"Why?"

She shrugged and shook her head. "She has never told any of us. I know she has a dowry but I believe it is not substantial."

"The duke had a huge fortune and I can't believe it was all entailed," Matthew commented.

"I know. He was involved in some business transaction with Banning. My brother told me just those deals would have left Elizabeth with more than enough money to last her entire life. Instead, she has only a small allowance."

Matthew sat on the bench she had occupied. "Do you know how much?"

"Excuse me?"

"Jennette, the facts are quite simple. Enough money for me would be very different than enough money for you."

"Exactly."

Watching her face, he realized she didn't understand his meaning. "I mean, you would require more."

"I cannot believe you said that."

He tilted his head and stared at her. "Indeed. What you spent on those orphans would have been enough to clear a large portion of my debts."

"I highly doubt that."

"You are used to a much higher standard than I, especially now. All I need is a woman who can help me clear my father's debts and keep my tenants from being tossed out. Hopefully, next year will be far more productive for them and they can pay their rents again."

"They haven't been paying their rents?"

"How could I take food out of their mouths?"

Jennette stared down at him in wonder. Most men in Matthew's position would have forced the tenants to pay or tossed them out. With the harsh weather this year, many crops had failed and even Banning's tenants had asked for more time to pay their rents. Her brother had extended them credit to assist them, but he could afford it. Matthew hadn't the money to be so generous.

"I'm sorry. I misjudged you." It seemed that she misjudged him more than anyone.

"It's not your fault. Perhaps I should have tossed my tenants out and leased the land to others." He shook his head.

"But you could not do that," she whispered. Again, he was far more of an honorable person than she.

"No, I couldn't."

He cleared his throat then asked, "Which of the three ladies do you think would be the most likely candidate?"

"Miss Mary Marston," Jennette replied without a pause. "Her parents have decided that they need to up their station in life. Mary is very well received, better than her parents even, but she hasn't caught the eye of a titled gentleman yet. Her sister recently became betrothed to Viscount Ellory."

"Would you consider her reputation better than mine?" he asked softly.

Jennette tilted her head and nodded. "Her mother was the daughter of a viscount. She married for love but beneath herself." And Mary's father was the type of man who would make certain Matthew didn't gamble Mary's fortune away.

Nonetheless, it was a sad day indeed when an earl was held in lower esteem than the daughter of a banker.

"Very well, then. I should like to meet Miss Marston this evening."

"I will arrange an introduction."

She glanced up to see him staring at her, his gray eyes unfathomable. Without trying, she could lose herself in the haunting depths of his eyes.

"Jennette, we have very little time left."

Her brows furrowed down. "I thought you said we had a month?"

"The first week is done and I still have no one to court. I expect it will take more than a quick introduction to procure a wife."

"I suppose it will." She smiled at him. "But you never know when a wife will just fall into your lap."

He raised a chestnut brow. "I wouldn't count on that happening. Time is running out."

"It won't be me, Matthew." It could never be her because even if he wasn't a gambler, he had honor for what he did for her five years ago. She would never be worthy of such an honorable man.

She often wondered if she was worthy of any man after what she'd done. Perhaps when she settled in Florence she would take a lover. But that idea left a dry, unpleasant taste in her mouth. There was only one man she wanted.

"Time will tell, Jennette." He dipped his head and then turned to leave. Just before he reached the end of the garden, he glanced back at her.

If only her life was different.

Jennette left her room and closed the door with a sigh. As she walked down the hall, her shoes barely made a sound on the Persian carpet. Everything was set, Mary would accept an introduction and because her parents wouldn't arrive until Monday night, she and Matthew would have plenty of time to get to know each other. There might even be an engagement to announce by the time Mary's parents arrived.

Jennette's heart constricted. This was for the best. She had to get him married before she left for the Continent. Even if her heart wasn't in it.

Mary would make Matthew a good wife.

"Lady Jennette?"

Jennette turned to determined who had called her. Seeing Mary Marston, she attempted to smile at the young woman.

"Yes?"

Mary quickened her step to reach Jennette. "Could we walk into the salon together? I fear I'm not as confident as I should be. My aunt is feeling unwell and decided to have dinner in her room."

"Of course." With her aunt feeling ill, Mary would have no one to condemn her for speaking with Matthew. Hopefully, Elizabeth performed her part and placed them next to each other at dinner.

The petite blonde linked arms with her and they started for the salon. "Lady Jennette, doesn't all the bustle of Society wear you down? You always look fresh and happy and, well, confident."

If only that were true. She had never felt so inept in all her life. "It does get easier. Each Season you will gain more confidence and composure. And once you marry you will be all the rage."

"I hope so. Do you really think Lord Blackburn is a good man?"

Jennette pressed her lips together. He was such a good man. Too good, at least for her. "Yes. I think you shall find that the gossips have been far too hard on him."

"I hope my parents will be pleased with the introduction."

"They should be, indeed. He is an earl."

After walking down the steps, they entered the salon and glanced about the room. A footman walked by with sherry and Jennette quickly grabbed two glasses. She handed one to Mary and then sipped hers.

"I don't drink spirits, Lady Jennette," she whispered, holding out the glass as if the devil himself were in it.

"If you want to be a success, you need to learn to drink a few sips. I promise you will not get foxed and lose your innocence."

Mary giggled softly. "Very well."

Jennette watched as the woman slowly drew the glass toward her puckered lips. Mary winced as she took a sip smaller than a mouse would have.

"I don't think I like it," she said, leaning in closer. "Must I drink this?"

"Not if you don't wish to," Jennette replied, shaking her head slightly. She lifted the glass to her lips and sipped at her sherry, wishing it were brandy. A nice stiff brandy and a good book by the fireplace would be a lovely thing right now. Instead, she smiled through the boredom as her mother had taught her and looked for Matthew.

She found him leaning against the wall in conversation with Somerton. She ignored the tightening in her stomach as she admired the angles of Matthew's face. Angles she would love to draw, or better yet, kiss.

"Is that him?" Mary asked. "The man near the wall with the short, light brown hair?"

Oh God, now she's admiring Somerton. "No. That would be Lord Somerton and he is a man you would not want to know."

"Why?" Mary's innocent tone grated on her nerves.

"He's the worst sort of scoundrel. It is rumored he's killed a dozen men. I'm quite surprised he was even invited to this party."

"Oh."

The insipid girl sounded disappointed that she

wouldn't be meeting the worst of the *ton's* scoundrels, only the second worst.

"We shall wait for them to quit their conversation before I introduce you."

Jennette finished her sherry as they waited. She finally caught Matthew's eye and nodded toward Mary. He inclined his head and left Somerton. Jennette watched his strong legs as he sauntered toward them. The black cotton fabric stretched across his muscled thighs with each extension of his legs.

"Oh my, he is coming," Mary said in a very excited voice.

"Stay calm and remember he is used to women—"

"I know. Women who are more sophisticated than I," Mary interrupted.

"Lady Jennette, how lovely you look tonight," Matthew said as he reached their position. He quickly bowed over her hand.

She tried to ignore the spark that leapt up her arm with the brief contact. "Good evening, Lord Blackburn."

Jennette turned to Mary. "I don't believe you have met Miss Marston. Mary, may I introduce Lord Blackburn."

"It is a pleasure, my dear," Matthew replied and bowed over her hand.

As he rose, Jennette couldn't help but notice the gleam of appreciation in his eyes as he took in Mary's appearance. She was everything he'd requested and more. A full bosom, slender waist and hips, plus blond hair and she barely reached his shoulders.

And she had no scandals in her background.

The roiling in her stomach told her that Mary was perfect for him.

Chapter 9

Matthew smiled at the young woman looking up at him. Mary Marston had every quality he'd asked Jennette for except possibly the right age. She couldn't be more than nineteen. Her innocence radiated from her like a beam from a lighthouse. Perhaps she was just the woman who could help him.

"Are you enjoying the party?" he asked.

She nodded with wide eyes. "Oh yes."

"It's almost time for dinner," Jennette commented. "Lord Blackburn, perhaps you would like to accompany Miss Marston to the dining room?"

"It would be my pleasure." He held out his arm for Miss Marston.

Miss Marston sent him a shaky smile then linked arms with him. There was no spark of energy as there was with Jennette. Instead, the light contact felt comforting, warm, and far more like that of a sister than a potential bride.

As they walked into the room, he said, "Tell me more about yourself, Miss Marston."

She giggled slightly. "There is nothing much to

tell. I'm eighteen and completed my first Season this past year."

"What type of hobbies do you enjoy?"

"Hobbies?" she asked with a frown.

They reached their seats, conveniently located next to each other. He pulled out the heavy mahogany chair for her. After they had taken their seats and greeted the others around them, he attempted to discover more about her again.

"I believe we were discussing hobbies. Do you paint? Perhaps a musical instrument is your passion?"

"I have to admit to not having an ounce of talent when it comes to painting. I can carry a tune but that seems to be the extent of my talents."

Remembering his mother's love of books, he thought that might be where her interests lie. "Do you enjoy reading?"

A slight blush tinted her cheeks. "Some."

"Oh?" He leaned slightly toward her. "What type of books do you enjoy?"

"Nothing of any literary importance."

Then he understood what she meant. She enjoyed the inexpensive novels of the day.

"Where are your parents?"

"They had another commitment with my older sister, Anne. They will arrive in two days. My aunt brought me here but she was feeling ill so she requested a tray in her room."

Matthew breathed a sigh of relief. So far, Miss Marston had no qualms about him. Maybe after two days, they would be so enamored of each other her parents would gladly consent to marriage. Although, in truth, he doubted he would be utterly in love with her. She seemed likable enough and he supposed marriage would be tolerable, but it wasn't what he'd hoped for in a union. But he couldn't be particular.

And perhaps if he continued to tell himself this, he would start to believe it. Miss Mary Marston would do for him. She would have to because his options were running out.

A footman placed a plateful of food in front of him. Once the footmen served everyone, Matthew attacked the ham. The meat seared his tongue with the most delectable flavors. While he'd kept his cook, there wasn't much money to buy anything decent. His gaze roamed to Jennette. He watched as a forkful of potatoes gratin entered her mouth. She chewed her food slowly as if savoring the bite.

She turned toward her brother and laughed softly at something he'd said. Her blue eyes sparkled in the candlelight. The woman was beyond lovely. The sapphire gown she wore matched her eyes perfectly. The low-cut bodice showed just a hint of her small, rounded breasts.

He closed his eyes briefly and imagined himself lowering the sleeves of her gown, tugging down the bodice over her breasts, and untying the laces of her stays. Then he could scrape the cotton of her shift over her rosy nipples, exposing them to his hungry gaze.

"Lord Blackburn?"

Matthew's eyes blinked open at the sound of Miss Marston's voice.

"Yes?"

"Are you all right? You had your eyes closed for several minutes."

"I am quite well, thank you. I was just thinking about someone—something," he corrected himself quickly.

He glanced back down the table at Jennette for a moment. He had to get past this mad infatuation with her. Miss Marston was everything he needed in a wife.

And yet, Jennette was everything he wanted.

He looked happy. The thought should have made Jennette glad, not burning with an emotion she refused to name. She'd done her duty and found him a woman he could marry. The last thing she should have been doing was blatantly staring at him, craving his kisses and his touch.

"You look perfectly miserable."

Jennette tore her gaze away from the card table where Matthew and Mary sat playing whist. She looked up to see Nicholas, Banning's dearest friend, smiling down at her.

"When did you get here?"

"Only a few minutes ago. I even missed dinner."

"I'm sure Lady Aston won't mind as long as she can crow about the Marquess of Ancroft, or should I say the future Duke of Belford, attending her country ball," Jennette said with a laugh.

"Yes, my cousin does love to boast about having a future duke in the family. I've already had five mothers stop me to tell me about their daughters."

Jennette chuckled, happy to have an old friend to chat with. "Want to steal some brandy and talk?"

"Nothing would please me more."

"Meet me on the terrace in ten minutes," she whispered.

"If someone catches us you'll be forced to marry me," he said, teasing her with a positively evil grin.

"Somehow I doubt Banning would force that," she said with a laugh.

"He knows better than that."

"I'll get the brandy."

Before he could reply, she walked to her mother and explained what she was doing.

Her mother's brows furrowed with concern. "Be careful, Jennette. I know I have nothing to fear with Nicholas but not everyone would understand your friendship."

"I understand."

"Go along, then."

Jennette strolled down the hallway until she found the earl's study. She peeked inside the room. Seeing no one, she pilfered the brandy and the snifters before continuing on to the terrace.

The cool day had turned into a cold night. She wrapped her shawl around her knowing it wouldn't keep the blustery wind from her.

"Would you like my coat?"

Jennette nodded. "Do you mind?"

Nicholas shook his head. "Not at all. Banning would have my head if I let you freeze out here."

"Please sit with me." Jennette patted the seat on the bench next to her.

"It's one thing if someone catches us out here and I'm over here. It's another if we're caught sitting together."

"Hang them all. I want to sit next to my friend

and if people cannot understand that they can go to the devil," she replied.

He laughed softly. "I've always admired your spirit, Jennette."

If only she felt as if she had some spirit left in her. "Nick, I'm so glad you're here."

"What's wrong?" he asked, taking the seat to her right.

"I'm so confused."

"And you haven't spoken to your friends about the matter?" he asked with a frown. "That's not like you."

Jennette shook her head. "I couldn't."

"Does this concern a man?"

"Yes."

"Who?" he asked softly as if to encourage her.

She leaned her head back and sighed. "Blackburn."

"I had a feeling."

She whipped her head toward him. "Why in the world would you assume him?"

His smile deepened before he took a long drink of brandy. After putting his glass down, he answered her. "I couldn't help but notice where your gaze was focused tonight."

"I—I—"

"Stop sputtering, Jennette. Banning came to me and asked me about Blackburn. Your brother told me what you were up to."

"It doesn't matter any longer. I think I found him the perfect woman." A woman who met his every desire. A woman who was nothing like herself.

"Well then," he drawled, "that should make you very happy."

Jennette nodded and lifted the brandy snifter to her lips. She swallowed down too much and coughed. After taking another smaller sip, she answered him.

"I'm very happy for him. I just hope her parents will agree to a marriage."

"Liar," he whispered harshly. "It's eating you up inside to see him with another woman."

Jennette refused to take the bait. Nicholas could infuriate her as quickly as Banning. After spending most summers and holidays with her family when Nick was young, they grew up like brother and sister. A very annoying brother.

"Admit it, Jen."

"No. I do not want him." She paused, staring out into the dark garden. "I cannot want him," she whispered.

"Why?" he insisted softly.

"I just cannot."

Jennette finished her brandy and poured herself more. How she wished the brandy would go to her head so she could blame this conversation on intoxication.

"You know he didn't kill John on purpose. So why can't you want him?" Nick questioned again.

"What would people think?"

"Why do you care? People will talk whether someone is in the right or not."

"I can't damage my family's reputation. Banning did enough harm with his courtship of Avis and the duel that ensued."

Nicholas laughed. "It's been over two months since that happened and no one seems to care."

"I care. My mother cares."

"Why?"

Jennette drained her second glass of brandy. "Because I promised my father I would never do anything to hurt my family's name. Or marry a gambler or a fortune hunter."

He blew out a long sigh then pulled her close. "So you made this promise at his deathbed?"

She nodded as tears welled in her eyes. "Nick, it was only a month after the accident with John. My father begged me to be more careful. He didn't want my mother's name ruined because of something I did. He didn't want me to make a mistake with another man."

"Your father would have only wanted your happiness," he whispered.

Jennette blinked, trying to keep from crying. "How can you know what my father would have wanted?"

He squeezed her shoulder. "Your father was a great man, Jennette. He raised me more than my own father did. And you forget that I have a daughter. I would only want her to be happy. Scandal be damned as long as I knew Emma would find contentment with a good man."

"Thank you."

But Jennette knew that she couldn't stop Matthew and Mary. They were both good people, even if Mary might be a little young. She would mature. They would make a lovely couple and have beautiful children. And Jennette would do as she had promised herself—leave him in peace.

"More brandy?" he asked.

"One more, I'm finally getting warm."

"I've always admired your ability to drink, Jen.

Not many women could manage three glasses of brandy."

The slight buzzing in her mind told her that she probably should have refused the third snifter. But tonight she didn't care. She had no plans to return to the party so no one would know if she was a bit tipsy.

She sipped her brandy as contentment spread throughout her. Nick still had his arm around her, keeping her warm and safe. It was a damned shame she didn't feel anything but sisterly affection for him. He would make some woman a wonderful husband.

The sound of someone clearing his throat broke them apart.

"Matthew!"

Nicholas chuckled softly beside her. "I believe we've been caught."

"Do be quiet," she replied.

"Ancroft, you should know better than to take a woman of quality out on a deserted terrace. Anyone might have come upon you."

"Like you, perhaps," Nick replied with a chuckle.

The sound of his laugh made her giggle, or perhaps it was the brandy.

"Should I get your brother, Lady Jennette?" Matthew asked stiffly.

Jennette's irritation grew with his pompous behavior. "There is no reason for that."

Nicholas stood up and removed his coat from her shoulders. She knew how damning this looked but didn't care. Nick was her friend and no one would disparage him in front of her.

"Good night, Jen." He leaned in close to her ear and whispered, "Don't do anything I wouldn't."

She slapped his shoulder. "Good night, Nicky."

He winked at her and left her on the terrace alone with the man she desired. She was quite tipsy. This was more than trouble. She should leave now before anyone discovered them out here.

"What the devil were you doing out here with him, Jennette?"

"Drinking brandy," she said, noting her words only slightly slurred.

"Good God, you're drunk!"

"Not terribly," she commented flatly.

"Not terribly? You let that scoundrel bring you out here alone and get you drunk. Anything might have happened if I hadn't come upon you both."

Jennette leaned back and looked up at him. "With Nicky?"

"The man has a bastard."

She rose in a quick motion, then grabbed the balustrade for support. "He has a daughter. She is a beautiful little girl whom he is raising because her mother wanted nothing to do with her."

"That has nothing to do with this," he growled.

She watched as his face changed, the look of anger replaced with acceptance.

"He's the reason you refused to marry me, isn't he?"

"Nicholas? Of course not."

"Indeed? I saw the look on both your faces. You love each other."

Jennette blinked, trying to muddle through his logic. "Of course we do."

"Very well, then. Good night." He turned on his

heel and strode from the terrace before she could explain.

"Oh, bloody stupid man."

Matthew walked to his room and then slammed the door behind him. He wanted to throw something to ease his anger, but everything in the room looked too expensive to replace. Instead, he dropped to his bed.

Anger and jealousy raged through him.

He should have realized that she rejected his proposal because of another man. It had nothing to do with guilty feelings over John. Once again, she loved another man. Nothing would ever change.

She would never love *him*.

It all made sense now. So why hadn't she married Ancroft yet? Perhaps Selby felt Ancroft's past wasn't acceptable for his sister.

Closing his eyes, he could picture them together on the terrace. Ancroft's arm around her shoulder as if he had the right to touch her. Matthew's fists clenched. The man had no right to touch her, to comfort her.

Then again, neither did he. No matter how much he desired to be there for her, to have his arm around her. He yanked off his jacket and flung it across the room. This line of thought was mad.

He would focus all his attention on Mary Marston.

Suddenly the door to his room swung open. Jennette stumbled over the threshold and slammed the door shut.

"So that's it?" she demanded.

"What the bloody hell are you doing in my room?" The woman had no sense at all. "First you're out on the terrace alone with Ancroft and now you stumble into my room drunk. Do you have any idea how you look?"

Unfortunately for him, he'd taken full notice of exactly how she'd looked—ready for a man to strip off her clothes and make love to her all night. His cock thickened as he thought about how he longed to do that. He wanted to lay her down on the soft bed and plunge into her sweet depths. Watch her as she shook with passion. Kiss every part of her body.

"I don't give a damn about how I look," she cried. "You have no right to play my protector."

"Isn't that exactly what I've been for the past five years?" he muttered.

She blanched. "You know nothing about my relationship with Nicholas."

"Nor do I need to." He stood and crossed his arms over his chest. "Go to bed, Jennette."

She closed her eyes and nodded. "I don't even know why I came here. I should have let Elizabeth do the introductions. Then I wouldn't have had to watch."

He knew she was mumbling in her drunken stupor but something made him question her. "Watch what?"

"You."

He stopped mid-stride. She was watching him . . . and Miss Marston? "Why were you watching me, Jennette?" he whispered as he stepped closer to her.

"I can't ever seem to stop myself," she said, staring at the floor. Her eyes widened as if she realized how much she had revealed. She turned and grabbed for the doorknob.

His hand covered hers, stopping her from opening the door and letting anyone see them together. A powerful spark skipped up his arm. He knew he should let her go.

But he couldn't.

Turning her back to face him, he brought his lips down on hers. The instant her tongue caressed his, he was lost. He couldn't remember a woman ever affecting him as she did. The minute she was near, he wanted her in every wicked way possible. On the bed, up against the wall, anywhere he could drown in the sensual desire rushing through him.

She wrapped her arms around his neck and wove her fingers through his hair. He brought his hand up to her breast and scraped his thumb over her silk covered nipple. As she gasped, he deepened the kiss, demanding everything she had to give him.

He wanted to rip every shred of clothing off her. Throbbing with unfulfilled need, he moved his lips to her neck. He found the soft spot where her pulse hammered against her throat. As she moaned softly, erotically, he moved back to her lips and tongue.

She tasted like honey and brandy. And he wanted to drown in the sensations.

Brandy.

The alcohol caused this reaction in her. She was in love with Ancroft, not him. Just as she'd been in love with John. He suddenly felt as if someone had dumped a bucket of cold water over him. Grasping her shoulders, he pushed her away.

She had admitted she was in love with another man.

Again.

Chapter 10

As Jennette drank her tea the next morning, nursing a pounding headache, she thought about what she'd done the previous night. While she had done some impulsive things in the past, walking into an unmarried man's bedchamber, more than a little drunk, was unconscionable. But it didn't explain why he kissed her . . . again.

And that second kiss was even more delicious than the first. Tingling, warm sensations had spread throughout her body as his mouth devoured hers. Every part of her had seemed over-sensitized. When he pressed his hand to her breast, she thought she might faint from the pleasure. Just remembering it sent moist heat to a region she shouldn't be thinking about now.

But she couldn't stop her mind from wondering what it would be like to make love with him. To have his thick shaft enter her, filling her, sending her over the edge of desire. She shifted in her seat, thankful most of the party had gone hunting. Her mind wandered back to the image of his hand stroking her and his mouth sucking her nipples.

She pressed her legs tightly together hoping the urge to touch there would go away. The throbbing only worsened. She wanted him there, touching her, stroking her.

"Jennette, are you unwell?"

Jennette blinked her eyes open to see Avis staring at her. Heat scorched her cheeks as her friend and sister-in-law took a seat in the morning room.

"I—I'm all right."

"You don't look all right. In fact, you look very flustered, as if I caught you doing something you shouldn't be doing." Avis smiled. "So what naughty thing were you thinking about?"

"Naughty?"

Avis smirked and nodded. "Judging from the look on your face . . . very naughty."

"N—nothing," she mumbled. "I was thinking about . . . the ball tomorrow night. And what I shall wear."

"Of course," Avis said, picking up a teacup. "I'm certain gowns were definitely on your mind."

"It's true!"

"Jennette, I have known you for far too long. The look on your face was positively . . . oh my," Avis said wide-eyed. "Who is it?"

"Who is what?"

"The man you were thinking of?"

"I was not thinking about any man!" She scraped back her chair and stood.

"Sit down, Jennette." Avis motioned for her to sit. "It's not like I haven't been in your situation."

"It's not the same, Avis."

Avis only chuckled. "Of course not. It's you so it is different."

"Stop that," Jennette complained. "You are imagining everything. Just because you fell into bed with my brother doesn't mean everyone else does the same."

"Perhaps not. However, there is nothing to say you can't have feelings for a—Oh my God, it's Blackburn, isn't it?"

"Of course not!" she lied frantically. The last thing she needed was her sister-in-law going to Banning with this news.

Avis sat back and tilted her head. "Oh, it is."

Jennette dropped her head into her hands. "Avis, you cannot tell Banning."

Avis was quickly there next to her, pulling her up. "We can't discuss anything this private in the morning room. Let's go to the greenhouse."

They walked down the hall until they came to the door. Stealthily, they left the house and raced for the greenhouse. After a quick check to make sure no servants were about, Avis pushed Jennette onto an iron bench by the orange trees.

"Now tell me," her friend demanded.

"I can't make you keep secrets from Banning."

"Jennette, you were my friend long before I married your brother. I will always keep your secrets safe."

Jennette closed her eyes. "I can't stop thinking about him."

"Thinking about him in what manner?"

Jennette blinked and stared at her friend. "How do you think?"

"Oh my," Avis whispered. "I have been in that situation. It's most frustrating."

"But you did something about it. I most certainly cannot take him as my lover."

Avis paced the pathway with her finger over her lips. "No, I don't suppose you can. However, you could take another man—"

"Avis! I could *never* do such a thing."

"No?" she replied coyly. "That is very telling, Jennette. If Blackburn killed John *accidentally,* what is stopping you from being with him?"

Jennette stared down at her jonquil morning dress. She longed to tell Avis the truth. Finally free herself of this overwhelming burden. But she couldn't. The truth was far too ugly.

There had to be a good reason she couldn't take him as a lover, other than the obvious, that it was against her upraising.

"I am leaving for Florence in a few weeks. It would be dreadfully wrong to make such a decision knowing I will be gone soon."

Avis chuckled. "Indeed. Seems like the perfect time as long as you don't wish to marry him."

"You don't believe me, do you?"

"No. I think you want him no matter what your past history and no other man will do. If you don't do this, you will wonder for the rest of your life what it would have been like."

Jennette shook her head. "I can't believe you, Avis. You had the same virtuous upbringing I did and yet you stand before me all but daring me to have an affair with a man who killed my betrothed."

"Sophie told you he was coming back into your

life. There has to be a better reason than simply he wanted your help in finding a bride."

"Sophie foresaw his coming," Jennette replied. "That is all. She never said we would fall in love or become lovers or anything to do with love. Only that he was returning to my life."

Avis laughed again. "Trust me, Sophie only tells people what she thinks they can handle at the time."

Jennette stood and walked over to the small lime trees. She stroked a green leaf and whispered, "He's kissed me twice."

Avis halted by the row of orange trees. "And?"

"It was amazing. Like no kiss I've ever had before in my life. I didn't want it to end."

"I think you had better decide quickly if you plan to seduce him."

There was nothing to think about regarding that idea. She knew she could never be with Matthew that way. Mary would be the perfect wife for him, Jennette couldn't. She had promised her father she would never marry a gambler or fortune hunter, and Matthew was both. Mary would warm his bed every night. Jennette's heart suddenly felt like someone stuck a knife into it.

"I will never be with him that way, Avis."

Miss Marston wrapped her arm with Matthew's as they walked through the dying garden. The wind whipped around them, chilling him and most likely her as well. They should have stayed inside by the fire and played cards.

"Tell me about your estates," she said, tying her

bonnet a little tighter. She glanced back and smiled at her maid who'd accompanied them.

"I have only two, plus the house in town."

"Are they large?"

"Good sized, though not as large as other peers'."

"Excellent," she said. "Do you have many servants?"

Matthew blew out a breath trying to determine the best answer for that question. "The estates are made to each have about twenty servants and fewer than ten in town."

He looked over to see her frown in concentration. She was the daughter of a banker and perhaps she'd never imagined managing such a large household. He would expect her to be able to assist him in hiring the servants. Jennette would know exactly what he needed to run several estates, which made her perfectly suited to marry a future duke. Nicholas would treat her well.

Why couldn't he get her out of his mind?

Damned lust.

Miss Marston had all the qualifications he needed for a wife. And anything she didn't know she could learn from either him or a friend. He sighed as they reached the dying rose garden. If only he felt a spark of attraction for her. Not that it mattered. She was pretty enough. He'd manage to do his duty and produce an heir.

Not that the feelings would be the same as with Jennette—the rush of excitement that raced up his limbs when she was near.

As they turned the corner, the object of his incessant desire sat on a bench with a sketch pad on her lap and a charcoal stick in her hands. She looked up as they approached. He couldn't determine the flash that sparkled in her blue eyes. At first, he thought she appeared quite displeased but then her full lips tilted upward. Quickly she shuffled the papers on her lap.

"Miss Marston and Lord Blackburn, what a pleasant surprise," she said. Hastily she placed a blank page in front of her drawing.

"Oh Lady Jennette, are you sketching?" Miss Marston asked quickly. "I love to draw but am horrid at it. I have heard you have quite the artistic talent."

"Greatly exaggerated, I'm certain."

Matthew doubted that. He'd also heard of her talent but had never seen any of her work. "Might we take a look at what you've been drawing?"

Her cheeks tinted pink. "No. It's not completed and I never show anyone my work until I'm finished."

"Please," Miss Marston begged prettily.

"No," Jennette replied in a harsher tone. "If you would like I could sketch you both."

Matthew cleared his throat and smiled. "I think you are being a bit premature."

"Oh?" she said with a devious grin.

God, he wanted to kiss that grin off her face. "But a drawing of Miss Marston would be lovely."

"Really!" Miss Marston exclaimed.

"I would be happy to do so." Jennette picked up her pad and looked around. "I think you would look best by the holly bush over there," she said, pointing to a small bench by the bush.

Miss Marston raced to the bench, untied her bonnet, and let it fall to her back. Tendrils of blond hair whipped around her face. "How is this?"

"Perfect," Matthew said before Jennette could refuse her.

"Why don't you go over there?" Jennette said as she inclined her head to another bench.

"I prefer to be here," he whispered, "*watching you.*"

Her hands shook as she picked up her charcoal stick and glanced over at Miss Marston. Keeping her voice low, she said, "I must apologize."

"Indeed?"

"I should never have entered your room last night."

"No, you shouldn't have. Although, I suppose I should have been more polite and invited you to stay."

Her head turned toward him with a blush of embarrassment coloring her high cheeks. "I beg your pardon?"

"You heard me," he replied in a husky tone. "I should have invited you to stay. Although, I don't usually seduce intoxicated women."

"I most certainly was not drunk," she exclaimed.

"How is your head feeling this afternoon?" Watching the color on her face brighten, he smiled.

"Do be quiet so I can concentrate."

She turned her attention back to Miss Marston. Her charcoal pencil skipped across the page with amazing results. As he watched, Miss Marston's features appeared on the paper, first her round eyes then the upward-tilted nose and thin lips.

"If you want me, you know the price."

Her hand stopped sketching the strands of Miss Marston's hair. "I didn't realize you were for hire, Blackburn."

Matthew chuckled softly. "Only for you."

"Why?"

"You know why. We've kissed twice and both times were amazing."

Jennette shrugged. "I wouldn't say that. Besides, I thought you determined I was in love with Ancroft."

"Are you?" he whispered, not really wanting to know the answer.

"I have loved Nicholas for years."

Why couldn't he let this go? She'd admitted her love for Ancroft. He should stop this conversation. And yet, he couldn't help but ask, "Why haven't you married him, then?"

"Perhaps he never asked me."

"Are you done yet, Lady Jennette?" Miss Marston shouted from her bench.

"Almost," Jennette answered. Her hand returned to the duty of sketching.

"Did you love him when you agreed to marry John?"

"Yes," she confessed without hesitation.

"So you garnered the attention of three men but only ever loved one." He looked over to Mary. "Miss Marston, I believe we should return to the house," he said stiffly.

"Is it finished?" Miss Marston stood and walked toward them.

"Yes, this is *finished*," Jennette replied, staring at Matthew.

Miss Marston walked quickly to them. Jennette handed the paper to Miss Marston.

Miss Marston stared with her mouth open. "I—I can't believe how you made me appear."

Matthew grabbed the paper out of her hand.

He glanced down at the sketch. Jennette had captured Miss Marston's quiet beauty in a remarkable manner.

"It is so lovely, Lady Jennette. I can't thank you enough," Miss Marston said.

"Perhaps you should give it to Lord Blackburn as a keepsake," Jennette commented.

Miss Marston leaned in closer to Jennette. "It seems a little forward to me."

"Nonsense."

Miss Marston turned toward him with a shy smile. "Would you like to keep it, my lord?"

Matthew felt a mix of emotions warring through his head. While he wanted to keep it as a memento of Jennette's talent, he knew he *should* want it as a sketch of the woman who just might become his bride.

"I would love to keep it," he muttered.

Miss Marston shivered as she tied her bonnet under her chin. "My goodness, it is becoming quite cool."

"We should return to the house. Lady Aston has a luncheon planned once everyone gets back from the hunt." Matthew pulled his greatcoat closer.

"Lady Jennette, will you accompany us?" Miss Marston asked.

Jennette let out a small sigh as she looked down at her dirty hands. "I suppose I should change before the luncheon."

"Lord Blackburn, you must help Lady Jennette with her things."

Matthew nodded. "Of course."

"I do not need any assistance," Jennette said hurriedly. She shuffled her papers and placed her charcoal pencil into a small box. "You two should go on. I will be along in a moment."

Miss Marston started to walk the garden path but something held Matthew immobile.

"Go on," Jennette insisted.

"Let me help you."

He reached for her stack of papers but she held them tightly against her chest.

"N—no," she stammered. "Go ahead without me."

He had no idea what could be making her appear so nervous. It finally dawned on him. She must be expecting Ancroft and wanted to be alone with him.

She leaned down to pick up her pencil case as a swift gust of wind whipped around them. Several of the papers she'd been holding blew out of her grasp. "Oh no," she exclaimed, doing her best to step on them before they were picked up again by the wind.

"Here," he said, reaching for some.

"No! Don't touch them!"

Ignoring her, he grabbed the closest papers. Turning them over, he gasped.

"Oh God," she whispered.

He stared down at the sketch of his face looking back at him. "When did you . . . ?"

"Give it back to me," she nearly shouted.

Instead of responding, he stared at her, raising one eyebrow in question.

"It was nothing," she said. "Just something to pass the time."

"Of course." Pleasure coursed through his body with the thought that, of all the people she might have sketched out here alone, she chose him.

In that brief moment, he knew she was as affected by him as he was by her. And he'd never felt so conflicted in all his life. Just down the path stood a woman obviously pleased that he'd chosen to court her. While directly in front of him stood a woman who appeared to have no interest in marriage to him, but fascinated him for all the wrong reasons. He handed the sketch to Jennette and turned toward Mary.

He knew in what direction he was headed.

Chapter 11

She was a complete and utter idiot, Jennette thought as she followed behind Mary and Matthew. How foolish could she be? How could she have dropped those papers in front of him? The only consolation was the fact that he'd only seen the two sketches of his face. She still held the other two next to her chest. Once she reached the house, she would burn them before anyone noticed them.

What was she thinking, drawing him as she imagined he would appear without clothes? Anyone might have come upon her and seen the pictures. But after her conversation with Avis this morning, she'd been unable to think of anything else, save him. Matthew with his cold gray eyes that warmed like coal embers when he kissed her.

Having only felt his shoulders and chest, she really had no idea exactly what he might look like without clothes. But she'd done her best to capture her image of him based on statues she'd seen at the British Museum. However, never having seen one of the more interesting parts of his body, she'd given him the obligatory fig leaf.

She shook her head, angry with herself for letting her imagination take over, and frustrated with him as he walked quietly in front of her with Mary Marston. Why had he baited her when they were all but in front of Mary? Though Mary seemed beyond hearing distance, she still might have overheard something scandalous.

His comments about inviting her to stay in his room still sent a shiver down her back. Had he asked last night, Jennette wondered how she would have replied. In her slightly intoxicated state, she might have agreed.

If only he'd asked. . . .

He glanced back at her with a devilish wink. Oh God, now he knew. He could see into her wicked soul and knew the truth of her desire for him. She had to put this to an end. Her mother had raised her in the correct manner and no proper woman took a lover.

Except Avis, her traitorous mind told her.

Avis' situation had not been the same. She wanted to find out what happened between a man and a woman to help her writing. Jennette knew what happened. Her mother had given her very specific talks about the marriage bed.

The marriage bed.

Making love was strictly for marriage.

And she couldn't marry Matthew. She'd secured her future five years ago when her foot slipped on the wet grass, and she let him take the scandalous blame.

She would always remain a spinster.

So if that was the case, what was stopping her from taking a lover?

No, she wasn't that sort of woman.

Thankfully, they had finally reached the house. Now she could burn those images. If only she could erase them from her mind so easily.

"Lady Jennette," a voice called out from the salon.

Jennette stopped and walked to the threshold to see Baron Huntley standing by the fireplace. "Huntley?"

"I haven't seen you in a while," he said, moving toward her.

"We spoke, however briefly, at Lady Elizabeth's literary salon just last week."

He looked down and blushed. "Of course."

"I didn't realize you knew the Astons." Jennette remained rooted to the spot but sensed Matthew standing behind her.

"Blackburn," Huntley acknowledged with a nod. "Huntley."

She heard Matthew's cold response. What was between them?

"I have some occasional business with Lord Aston," Huntley finally replied to her comment.

"How nice," Jennette said but had no idea what else to add. She'd known Huntley since her bow, but he had never expressed any interest in her. The man was a rake through and through.

Huntley combed his fingers through his sandy brown hair. "I suppose I should change before the luncheon. Perhaps we can talk later?"

What in the world would Huntley want to discuss with her? "Of course, that would be lovely."

Jennette turned only to face Matthew's angry face. He moved out of her way but she still caught the scent of his frustration—a tangible thing that carried the redolence of sandalwood and pine. And made her heart pound in her chest.

As she walked down the hallway, she sensed his presence behind her. Turning toward him, she demanded, "Why are you following me?"

A smile curved his lips upward. "I am going to my room."

"As am I."

"Are you now?" His voice turned husky and haunting.

"Not *your* room. *My* room."

"Now that is a shame," he said with a grin.

"Stop it! You don't want me."

He stepped closer to her. "You know I want you."

"You cannot want me. You even told John that I wasn't the right woman for him."

"He told you that?"

She cringed at the sound of disbelief in his voice. "Yes. He thought it was very kind that you worried about him. I didn't realize until the morning of the accident just why you said that to him."

His cold gaze darted between her eyes and her lips.

A part of her wanted to tell him the truth. She had planned to break her engagement but the words wouldn't come forth. The idea of breaking John's heart always seemed to stop her.

He walked to a door and waited. "Coming in?" he drawled in a deep voice that made her quiver.

She could say yes and have her questions answered. She would find out exactly what he looked

like without clothes, what he felt like, what he
tasted—

"No," she replied. "I am going to my room . . .
mine and my mother's."

His smiled deepened. "Coward," he whispered.

"I am not a coward. I just don't believe I should
come between you and Miss Marston," she said
quickly, then backed up a step. Turning away from
him, she walked down the hall.

"Coward."

His whispered word swept over her. She was a
weak coward, but in this case, she was being practi-
cal. He deserved a far better woman than her.

Matthew watched as everyone entered the dining
room. Lady Elizabeth entered with Jennette. While
Miss Marston entered next, he couldn't keep his
gaze off Jennette. Her high-waisted, pale-blue silk
gown framed her perfectly rounded breasts.

Why couldn't he keep his mouth shut around
her? Asking her to his room was completely unac-
ceptable, no matter how much he desired it. The
image of her drawing his picture as she sat alone in
the garden wouldn't leave his mind. The idea that
she felt attracted to him warmed his heart and
other more wicked parts of his body.

"Lord Blackburn, look, we are seated next to
each other."

God, he wanted that excited voice to be Jennette's, not Miss Marston's. But he understood his
duty. Marriage. And, he reasoned, Miss Marston
was the better choice.

She would bring no baggage with her, as Jennette

did. Mary's reputation was clean, no dead fiancés coming between them. Jennette's remark about how badly the gossips would talk about them was correct.

Mary was the better choice.

Now he just had to convince his damned desire of that. He held out the seat for Miss Marston as her sweet orange petal perfume swept up his nose. Attempting to control his sneeze, he took the seat next to her.

He glanced over at the woman next to him wondering just how he would feel about her in a year, ten years, forty years. Hopefully, he would grow to love her. No matter what he'd said to Vanessa, he wasn't the type of man to cheat on his wife. Even if his wife was nothing more than a duty.

"My parents will be joining us tomorrow afternoon," she commented before taking a sip of her wine.

"I would be honored to meet them."

Miss Marston gave him a secret smile. "I think you will get along famously with them."

He prayed that was so because at this point she was his only hope. *Other than Jennette,* he thought. No, she was out of the question. Spearing a piece of lamb, he decided to concentrate solely on Mary Marston.

His future bride.

The woman who would rescue him from his current plight.

The woman he would spend the rest of his life with no matter how much he desired another.

"You will ride with me tomorrow, will you not?" she whispered, leaning closer to him.

"Of course."

That brought images of another form of riding that had nothing to do with horses. He glanced down at Jennette and wondered what she would be like in bed. As much as he knew about her, she would be full of passion, an enthusiastic lover who would take everything he could give her.

Mary cleared her throat. Matthew looked over at her and instantly knew what she would be like in bed. Dull. A woman who did her duty because that was what was expected of her. She would give him the children he wanted and then she would request he leave her alone.

He really should kiss her just to determine if he could find a spark of attraction.

His wandering gaze landed on Jennette again. She appeared in an animated conversation with Baron Huntley. The hairs on his neck stood on end. Huntley was a known gambler and rake. He'd been after Vanessa as a mistress for years. When she'd chosen Matthew as a protector, Huntley had been furious. Worse even, rumor had it the man had five bastards from different women.

Matthew turned his attention to the people around him who had entered into a conversation regarding the unusual weather of the year. Joining in, he gave his opinion and his hopes that next year would be better. Perhaps then his tenants would have a good crop and pay their outstanding rents.

The men entered the large salon after their brandies and cigars. All the women had been gossiping or complaining about womanly issues until

the men entered. Then they all put on their smiles,
fanning themselves in the cool room. Jennette had
welcomed the reprieve from the men. Baron Huntley had monopolized the conversation at the
dinner table, giving her a headache.

As the men wandered the room searching for a
whist or chess partner, she wondered how she
could escape unnoticed. With her mother in the
room, Jennette knew that wasn't a possibility.
Nicholas caught her gaze and she nodded to him.
Perhaps a game of chess with him would help pass
the time.

"Interesting dinner companion," he said as he
sat down.

"The man is a bore."

"Have a care, Jen." Nicholas set up his black
pawns. "The man is a gambler."

Jennette raised her eyebrows at him. "I know
that. He is of no interest to me."

Nicholas laughed. "I didn't think he was. I'm
quite certain where your interest lies."

"Blackburn is also a gambler. I want no part of
that either. In fact, all I want is a quiet game of
chess. No discussions."

Nicholas turned his lips downward as his eyebrows did the same. "I've never heard nor seen
Blackburn gamble any amount of money."

Jennette pursed her lips. "And yet, his dearest
friend appears to be Somerton."

"Which means nothing."

"Tell me about Emma." Jennette hoped his fa-
therly pride would bring the conversation to a safer
topic.

Nicholas regaled her with all the troubles of

bringing up a ten-year-old girl. As much as she tried to listen, she couldn't help but glance over at Matthew while he played piquet with Mary. Ignoring the painful envy clawing at her heart, Jennette watched the interplay of the couple. Mary looked happy as she played but Matthew appeared bored.

Maybe they weren't as perfect a couple as Jennette had thought. She did want to see him happy and if Mary wasn't the right woman, she needed to know. Somehow, she would have to meet with Matthew in private and discuss it.

"The game is over here, Jennette," Nicholas said with a chuckle. "It is your move."

Jennette looked down at the board and realized Nicholas had her queen trapped and could put her into check in two moves. Quickly, she moved her pawn in front of her king, sacrificing her queen.

"Your attention is not on the game tonight," he said, picking up her queen. "Normally, you would give me a much tougher game. Something on your mind you want to talk about?"

"Nothing." She focused on the chessboard but knew it was a lost cause.

Nicholas took his turn and quietly said, "Checkmate."

"Well played." She moved her chair back. "Good night, Nicholas."

Jennette wanted to escape the people and the noise of the salon. She slipped from the room and wandered down the hall until she found Lord Aston's study. A small fire still warmed the study and the silence was too inviting to ignore. She poured a small glass of brandy, determined to drink only one glass, then go to bed.

Curling up into a leather chair by the fireplace, she stared at the dancing flames. A small sigh escaped her lips. In two weeks, her ship would depart for Florence. She loved her family and didn't want to desert them but leaving appeared the only way to keep her secret safe and yet, her reason for departing had changed.

No longer did she believe disappearing would give Matthew a better chance at a happy life. His only hope hinged on her finding him the perfect woman—something she could never be. And the idea of staying here and watching him fall in love was unimaginable.

"Drinking again?"

Jennette closed her eyes and sighed. "Did you follow me here, Matthew?"

"Yes." The sound of his footsteps indicated he'd moved closer to her chair. "Do you think brandy is the answer to the problem?" he whispered.

"What do you care? Drinking helps me forget. Besides, you should be with Mary." Jennette blinked. He strolled to the brandy, poured himself a snifter, then took the seat across from her.

"Mary had a headache and went to bed." He gave her a sensual grin. "I didn't think I should follow her."

"No, that would be completely inappropriate. As is being in here with me."

"And yet, you are not rushing to leave." He brought the snifter up to his perfectly shaped lips and took a sip.

Jennette knew she should run before her desire raced out of control. But her body refused to move. Lethargy had set in with just a few sips of brandy.

If she stayed, she could watch him, stare at him, imagine being with him.

God, no she couldn't!

"How are you and Mary getting along?" she asked.

"Well enough."

"But . . . ?"

He shook his head quickly. "I have to admit I am worried that she might not be up to the task of being mistress of my estates. She appeared to worry when I mentioned the number of servants."

Jennette stared down into her brandy remembering the rumors she'd heard about the conditions of his estates. "I didn't believe you had so many servants that she would need to worry over."

"I don't at this point in time. However, once I marry I shall need to hire some."

She pursed her lips for a moment. "And Mary has most likely never had a need to hire a servant."

"Exactly. They only have the house in town. How many servants could that support?"

"Not many and probably her mother and father handled everything."

Matthew nodded. A piece of chestnut hair fell upon his forehead until he pushed it back. She had never cared for hair as long as his but there was something about it on him. The reckless look suited him. Her fingers tingled with a desire to rake through those strands.

"Are you well?" he asked gently. "You are looking very strangely at me."

"I am sorry. I was lost in thought," she replied.

"About?"

About? She had to think of something quick. "Do you think Mary will suit you as a wife?"

"That's what you were thinking of?" he asked with obvious disbelief in his voice.

"Y—Yes."

"Indeed. I don't believe I have much choice in who will suit me. As long as she is pleasant enough, she will have to do."

Jennette closed her eyes as guilt struck her like a stone to her head. "I never wanted this for you, Matthew."

"I know, Jennette."

If she didn't get the subject changed quickly, she would be in tears. And she had shed enough tears for a lifetime. "Tell me how you will get your estate profitable again."

Matthew's head tilted back against the leather as he looked up at the coffered ceiling. "Well, just getting the weather to cooperate would be a big help. This damned cold is not making my tenants' lives any easier."

"But you can't control the weather so what other choices do you have?"

"Honestly, once my father's debts are paid the estates will become profitable very quickly."

Jennette's mouth gaped. "I thought the problems stemmed from the estates being mismanaged and your father's debts just exacerbated the issues."

He leaned forward. "Oh, the estates were definitely mismanaged. Money that should have gone back into maintenance and educating the tenants on new agricultural processes went to the gaming hells."

"I'm sorry, Matthew," she whispered. "I would truly like to help you."

"By introducing me to Mary, you have helped me."

And pierced her own heart. The more time she spent with him, the more she liked him as a person. She understood why he and John had been such good friends. They'd had much in common.

"If there is anything else I can do."

A long pause split the room. She was certain he was thinking money.

"I would truly like to assist you, Matthew."

"We have discussed this before. I won't take your money, Jennette." He placed the glass on the table next to him and stood. "Before I forget, have a care with Huntley."

"I have already been warned about Huntley."

"Good. I'm glad your brother had the sense—"

"Nicholas told me, not Banning."

"Oh," he muttered. "Good night, then."

Watching the fabric of his tight breeches stretch across his derrière, she realized she should correct his misassumption. But for some odd reason, she liked the idea that he seemed slightly jealous of her friendship with Nicholas.

Chapter 12

Anthony Somerton scrutinized the crowded room. Jennette stood against the wall with Lady Elizabeth and Avis Copley—or rather Lady Selby as she was now. Damn that Sophie. *Just speak of Blackburn kindly*, she'd said. And if possible, get them alone together.

How the bloody hell was he supposed to get Jennette away from her friends to spend time with Blackburn?

He couldn't walk up and ask her to ride with him. As much as he and Selby seemed to have a friendly understanding now, Anthony knew Selby would never want him speaking with his sister.

When had he become a bloody matchmaker? So he had helped Avis and Banning in some small manner. That didn't make him a marriage broker.

"Morning, Somerton." A large hand patted him on the back.

Anthony turned to see the man who was causing him all this grief standing beside him. "Morning, Blackburn."

"Pleasant day for a ride, don't you think?"

Not bloody likely. "I suppose so. With whom will you be riding?" *Please say Jennette and get me out of this mess*, he thought.

"Mary Marston," Blackburn replied.

Damn. "You seem to be spending an increasing amount of time with her. Is marriage in the works?"

Blackburn smiled tightly. "It is a possibility. Although, I have yet to meet her parents."

"They didn't attend?"

"She told me they will arrive later today."

A slow smile tilted Anthony's lips upward. Now he knew he didn't have to worry about attempting to ride with Jennette. Miss Marston's parents would certainly reject a man who had killed his own best friend.

He would make certain of that.

And if that should happen to fail, he could seduce little Mary and make her fall in love with him. It would be an easy and enjoyable task.

Matthew reined his horse to a slow trot. Mary wasn't a skilled rider, having lived in town all of her life. She knew how to look good while riding but barely could move beyond a canter.

"Thank you for slowing down, my lord," she said with a warm smile.

"You are welcome."

Hearing the gallop of a few horses, he moved slightly off the path to give the faster riders room to get around them. "Move off," he said to Mary.

She positioned her horse off the dirt path just as four riders came into view. Jennette, Lady Elizabeth, Lord Selby, and Lord Ancroft raced past them. Each of them nodded and Jennette smiled at his predicament.

"Where was Lady Selby?" he wondered aloud.

"Oh, she doesn't ride well," Mary replied. "I heard she'd taken a fall when she was young and she didn't feel she could keep up with us."

Matthew was quite sure Lady Selby could have kept up with Mary. The sound of another horse galloping up the hill made Matthew cringe. As the rider reached the crest of the knoll, he slowed his mount.

"Somerton, nice to see you again," Matthew said. He glanced over at Mary. Her eyes widened and positively sparkled as she stared at Somerton with her mouth slightly agape. *Wonderful,* the woman he was supposed to propose to appeared completely captivated by Somerton.

"Good afternoon, Blackburn." Somerton looked over at Mary and his lips twitched. "I don't believe we have met."

"Miss Marston, may I introduce Lord Somerton."

"G—g—good to meet you, my lord," she stammered.

Somerton reached across his horse for her hand. "An absolute pleasure, Miss Marston."

"T—thank you, my lord."

Dear God, the girl twittered.

"May I ride with you both?" Somerton requested, staring at Mary like a wolf about to devour a rabbit.

"Oh yes!" Mary said in an overly excited voice.

"Wonderful," Somerton said.

Wonderful indeed, Matthew thought.

"Lord Somerton, would you help me with my stirrup. I don't believe it is adjusted correctly."

"It would be my greatest pleasure," Somerton replied, raising an eyebrow at Mary.

Mary blushed a blotchy red across her cheeks. "Really?"

"Why yes, Miss Marston."

Matthew clenched his jaw out of frustration. He'd finally discovered a woman who might settle for him and his reputation only to find she was far more attracted to Somerton.

Somerton jumped down, handed his reins to Matthew, and proceeded to adjust Mary's stirrup. Somerton checked the length by reaching up to her calf and extending her leg. Mary's eyes widened and her mouth gaped. Matthew clutched the reins of his own horse, trying to gain control of his anger.

After Somerton finished the modification, they rode down the path toward the old Tudor dower house.

"Oh my," Mary whispered. "How could the Astons let that place fall to such ruin?"

"It really isn't all that dreadful," he replied.

Matthew examined the house and wondered at her comment. While a little overgrown with brushes, the structure looked sound, the roof appeared to be holding together. In fact, the little house seemed to be in better shape than his estate in Lancashire.

She would hate his estate. Cobwebs adorned most of the rooms, the roof leaked, and the furniture was all over a hundred years old and covered in dust. How would she survive the first couple of years of marriage?

The only way would be to stay in the London house and visit the estates as needed for short periods of time. Then, as the money increased, she could refurbish the house. He really wasn't asking for that much, was he?

All he wanted was a woman who could be a helpmate. A woman who would want to assist him in fixing this mess. Someone to build a future with, have children with, someone to love. He obviously wanted too much.

The image of sitting in the study with Jennette flashed through his mind. Would she have the fortitude for the task in front of him? She had been raised as a proper young lady of the *ton*. She would likely be even more put out by the condition of his estates.

"Shall we continue?" Somerton asked. "Perhaps we could catch up with the Selbys."

Matthew shook his head. "Mary isn't a very skilled rider."

"Lord Blackburn," Mary said with shock. "You shouldn't speak of me in such a manner."

"I wouldn't wish for you to get hurt," he replied calmly.

Her face softened as she smiled shyly at Somerton. "I could try a gallop if that is what Lord Somerton would like."

Somerton smiled at her. "I should hate myself if something happened to you because of me."

Her lips pouted slightly. "Of course."

Matthew gently nudged his gelding. "Come along."

The other two followed behind as anger surged within him. He'd hoped to get a few moments alone with Mary and attempt to kiss her. Now, with Somerton in tow, the opportunity appeared lost.

And for some reason, Matthew was sure Somerton had decided to ride with them on purpose.

Jennette waited patiently while her maid finished pinning her hair into a lovely coiffure. "I believe I'll wear the pearls tonight, Molly. Could you lace a strand or two into my hair?"

"Of course, miss. You look beautiful when we do. The contrast between your black hair and the white pearls is stunning."

Her mother watched from her position on the bed. "Jennette, do you think your bodice is a bit too revealing?"

Jennette glanced into the mirror and frowned. Her stays had brought her small breasts together for a slight line of cleavage. Not something she normally had.

"No, I think it's perfect."

Her mother shook her head and smiled. "Are you trying to entice someone?"

"Of course not!"

"Hmm," Mother said softly.

"Mother," Jennette warned. "I am not interested in any man. I leave for Florence in two weeks."

"So you keep insisting."

She leveled an ominous look at her mother. Jennette was in no mood to argue with her tonight. Watching Matthew ride with Mary had taken away her pleasant mood today. She had the urge to leave the party completely and return home, perhaps even to Talbot Abbey. There she could lock herself in the old nursery and paint until she had eliminated all her frustrations.

"All done, miss," Molly stated, then moved away from her to pick up the gowns Jennette had discarded earlier.

"Thank you, Molly."

Her mother shook her head as she watched Molly picking up three rejected gowns. "Where did you get this propensity for indecision? Your father was never like that and neither am I."

Jennette almost laughed. Her mother was almost as bad as Jennette when it came to making a decision on fashion. "You know I'm only like this when it comes to what I should wear."

"Of course," her mother replied.

"I believe we should make our way downstairs before they start dinner without us."

Jennette picked up her reticule and walked to the door. She and her mother strolled down the hallway to the marble steps. As they walked down the stairs, the butler opened the front door and a couple entered. Jennette had only met Mrs. Marston once, but with her sturdy frame and flaming red hair, she was difficult to forget.

"Dinner is at eight," the butler told the couple.

"That barely gives us enough time to freshen up," Mrs. Marston complained.

"I am sorry, ma'am. Lady Aston insists that dinner always be held at eight."

Jennette and her mother smiled as they reached the bottom riser.

"Lady Selby and Lady Jennette!" Mrs. Marston exclaimed. "How lovely to see you."

"And you, Mrs. Marston," her mother said. "You had best hurry or you shall miss dinner."

"Oh yes!"

The couple hurried to follow the footman to their room. Jennette and her mother continued on to the large salon where everyone congregated before dinner. A footman passed by with glasses of sherry for the guests. Her mother reached for two glasses then handed one to Jennette.

"Only three more excruciating days," her mother whispered.

Jennette couldn't agree more. Three more days and then they would return to London until it was time for her to leave. Hopefully by then Matthew would announce his betrothal to Mary, thus allowing Jennette to leave in peace. No more guilt about what she'd done to him.

Only a lifetime to relive what she had done to John. But once in Florence, she could make a new life for herself. Return to painting and take in the wonderful museums. Perhaps if she found the right man, she might take a lover and maybe, if she closed her eyes, she could pretend it was Matthew making love to her.

She blinked to keep the tears at bay. This attraction to him was absurd. Glancing over, she noticed Matthew lean in closer to hear something Mary said to him. His lips tilted upward as if whatever she'd said held some humor.

"Another sherry?"

Jennette turned with a smirk toward Somerton. He lifted an eyebrow at her in question.

"Thank you, my lord," she replied and then took the offered sherry.

"What has you with that far-off gaze in your eyes?"

She watched as his attention swung to Matthew and Mary and then back to her. Somerton had a bad habit of seeing far too much. "Absolutely nothing," she replied.

"You are a terrible liar." He sipped his sherry. "Besides, I wouldn't be too distressed."

"I am not," she lied again. Well, she didn't *want* to feel any misery at their interest in each other.

"It won't end well for them," he added in a whispered tone.

"What? It must," she insisted. "They must marry."

"Trust me, Blackburn won't marry that chit." He drained his sherry then deserted her.

Jennette looked around but Somerton had slipped into the crowd by the doorway. What exactly did he mean by his prophecy? She'd known him long enough to understand he had connections and knew secrets most didn't. Could he possibly have come into some information regarding Mary and Matthew? It made no sense. Somerton dealt with spies and criminals, not two people who might wish to marry.

Before Jennette could reason anything sensible on the topic, Lady Aston announced the time had come to move to the dining room. Jennette scanned the room looking for someone to escort her, hoping she'd find Somerton again.

"Looking for me?"

Hearing a warmly familiar voice, she turned to Nicholas. "Are you late for everything?" she asked with a laugh.

"It appears I am, lately." He held out his arm. "Shall we?"

Happy to have a man near her who didn't expect anything but a smile from her, she answered, "We shall."

He smiled down at her in a knowing way. "He's not a bad man, Jennette."

"Who?" She followed his gaze to Matthew.

"I believe you know exactly to whom I am referring."

"Why do you care what I think of him?"

"Because I know you need some advice and Banning isn't about to tell you what you need to hear. Your brother believes every bad thing he has heard about the man. I happen to know differently."

Jennette's hand shook as they walked toward the dining room. Instinctively, her gaze went to Matthew, who shot her an irritated look. "What exactly do you know?"

"I know he's been misjudged by the majority of the members of the *ton*. You have even verified what happened was an accident. And the other incident was nothing more than a young man's folly."

"What do you mean?" She raked her memory for some other issue Matthew might have had years ago. Nothing came to mind. So whatever happened must have been minor.

"It was a long time ago and truly nothing."

"Is that all you know about him?" she whispered softly.

"It's enough for me."

"But not my brother?"

Nicholas laughed. "Do you believe that would make Banning believe Blackburn is a good man? We both know your brother would find fault with any man you chose."

Jennette nodded. Her brother was as hard-headed as she was, if not worse.

"I have no plans to marry the man if that is your

intention when you tout his good points," she commented flatly.

"Of course not. You shall be leaving for Florence in just a short time."

"Yes, I will."

"Are you trying to convince me or yourself?" he whispered in her ear.

Damn him for knowing her so well. "Neither."

"Of course," he said, sounding completely unconvinced.

Mr. and Mrs. Marston entered the salon just as she and Nicholas reached the threshold. Mrs. Marston's eyes widened as she walked in the room. Her gasp made Jennette halt her stride. Dread filled her as she glanced back to see the Marstons staring at Matthew.

"Dear God, it's true," Mrs. Marston whispered.

"Get your bloody hands off my daughter," Mr. Marston shouted.

Chapter 13

Matthew stood rooted to the spot. Mary squeezed his arm, whether in fear or comfort, he didn't know. He should have known everything was proceeding too well with her.

"Did you not hear me?" the man shouted again.

Mary slowly slid her arm out of his and took a step away. Her pallid face confirmed his initial thought—Mr. and Mrs. Marston had arrived.

"I meant no dishonor, sir," Matthew replied.

"No dishonor?" Mrs. Marston said. "Did you actually think I would let a man like you near my daughter?"

Matthew quickly looked around the room and noticed nearly half the party was still in the salon, watching the sordid scene unfold.

"A man like me?" he asked in a quiet tone.

"A murdering blackguard!" she yelled.

Anger forced his hands into fists. He looked past the Marstons to see Jennette still clinging to the arm of the marquess. Her eyes were huge and full of sympathy. And the last thing he wanted from her was pity.

"Mary, get away from him," Mrs. Marston said. "This man will never touch you again."

"But Mother, he is not—"

"Do not disobey me," Mrs. Marston interrupted.

"Yes, Mother." Mary looked back at him and sent him a watery smile.

"As for you," Mrs. Marston took a step forward. "How dare you show your face at a party for decent people? No one who knows what you did will ever let you back in Society. And my daughter won't be a pawn to help you regain your position."

"And you shall never get a farthing out of me," Mr. Marston added.

Matthew inhaled deeply. One thing he'd learned after five years was to walk away. "As you wish," he said with a nod.

"Murderer," Mrs. Marston whispered loud enough for half the room to hear.

Several loud gasps circulated the room. Matthew walked toward the door where Jennette stood with her mouth agape.

"Don't think everyone in the room doesn't see the look you're giving *her*," Mrs. Marston's acid voice sounded again. "To this day I will never understand how her reputation remained intact. In my opinion you ruined her and you will not do that to my daughter."

Matthew blew out a loud breath and counted to ten.

"And you," Mrs. Marston turned her attention to Jennette. "How could your mother allow you in the same room as this murderer? He killed your betrothed and almost ruined your name in the process. You're no better than he is to allow this outrage!"

Matthew turned to Mrs. Marston with an icy fixed stare. "Malign my name all you wish," he took a menacing step toward her, "but don't ever spread your venom toward Lady Jennette."

Mrs. Marston's lips tilted upward in a cynical smile. "So the gossips were right about you loving her."

God, he hated that rumor. Especially when it was the absolute truth. No matter how he tried to deny it, he'd loved Jennette even then.

He narrowed his eyes and blasted Mrs. Marston with another glare until her mouth dropped and she took a step backward into her husband's chest. After sufficiently silencing her, he turned and strode from the room, his heart pounding against his chest in futile anger. He was finished with this party and all others.

Ignoring the open stares and whispers, he walked down the hall. The burning, hostile looks only served to increase his anger and frustration. He should have known this mad idea of hers would never work. No one would ever forget what he'd done.

Only he hadn't done anything.

Guilt etched through his mind. He'd spoken to her of his attraction that very morning. He had even kissed her for those brief few seconds. Why couldn't he have kept his mouth shut?

It didn't matter. She'd grabbed the sword out of his hand after he'd warned her not to. She had wanted to prove to him that she could do it.

The time had come to be finished with this self-castigating. He was through with the guilt. All he'd done was tell her how he felt that morning. Now he would marry her and never think of that day again.

It was her fault.

And she would be the one to pay for her actions. He was finished with her foolishness. Although she still had two weeks left to find him a wife, he knew she would never be able to succeed especially once this debacle traveled through the gossips. It was time to compromise her publicly and finish this farce.

The hell with the consequences. Her brother wouldn't call him out. Selby would insist on a quick marriage to silence the gossips. And that was exactly what she was about to get.

After slamming the door to his room, he pulled out his valise. He had two weeks to get her compromised and the idea of staying in this damned house for one more instant held no appeal. Jennette would be back in town in a few days when the party ended. Then he would do what had to be done.

He yanked off his cravat and then his jacket before setting to work on his vest. Tossing the offending clothes on the bed, he then pulled his shirt over his head. He yearned to throw something far more substantial than a mere piece of linen. Unable to do anything else, he rolled his shirt into a ball and flung it across the room.

"I'm so sorry."

In his impotent rage, he hadn't even heard the door open. His head tilted backward as he stared at the ceiling. The hushed tones of her voice floated past him, caressing him, enticing him. But the last thing he wanted was to discuss anything with her.

There would be plenty of time for talking after she became his wife.

"Leave me be," he replied in a low voice.

"Matthew, please . . . I'm sorry," she cried out from her position by the door.

"Get the bloody hell out of my room, Jennette. You're only sorry because you witnessed firsthand what my life's been like for the past five years."

"I cannot do this any longer," she whispered. "This is all my f—fault."

"Yes, it is." The moment the words were out, he regretted them.

"I have to fix this."

He flexed his fists. "Nothing can ever mend this mess."

"I know," she cried. "It's all my fault."

Hearing the anguish in her voice, his heart softened. He knew if John hadn't begged him to protect her, this scandal would have been over quickly. The *ton* would have understood what happened that day to be nothing more than an accident, but no one could understand *two* accidental deaths caused by him.

"No, it's not your fault."

"It is. I should never have let John do this to you. He had no right to make you his pawn."

He knew without looking that she was crying. A part of him wanted to take her into his arms and tell her everything would be all right. But he couldn't because nothing would ever be all right again. His life was an utter disaster.

"I have to tell them," she sobbed. "I have to let everyone know that I killed John."

He spun around to face her and his heart ached.

She covered her face with her hands as she slowly slid down the length of the door until she was crouched on her haunches.

"I have to tell them," she mumbled into her hands.

"No, you will not," he stated firmly before striding to her. He lifted her up and cupped her face with his hands. "I promised I would protect your name. You will never tell a soul what happened that morning."

"But—"

"Never." He stared into her watery, sapphire eyes until he wanted to drown in their depths. The pain he saw there broke his heart. He couldn't let her feel such anguish over his name. He'd lived with this lie for five years. He could live with it forever as long as it didn't touch her.

"It was wrong to let everyone believe such a horrid untruth," she protested.

"You will not tell anyone."

Before she could argue with him again, he lowered his lips to hers. Gently, he kissed her full lips, before moving to her salty cheeks. He wanted to comfort her, ease her pain and guilt. Kissing her tears away, he felt her shudder.

He was only kissing her to comfort her, he told himself. Make her feel better for the pain she'd caused him. Yet, the more her tongue touched his, the more he could care less about comforting her.

He wanted to feel her quiver under him in ecstasy as she reached her climax. He wanted to touch her small breasts, feel them, and suckle them until she gasped. Moving his lips back to hers, he pulled her against his bare chest. Her body molded to his as if made just for him.

Jennette moved her tongue against his as her need for comfort changed into so much more—desire. Yearning to feel his hard muscles on top of her, she skimmed her hands up his bare arms. His muscles tensed as she reached his shoulders and finally draped her arms around his bare neck. Arching her back, she sought comfort and passion from the one man she'd never expected to want her.

She shouldn't want this from him. But she did. He was the only man who could absolve her guilt, lessen the pain she constantly fought.

She wanted to feel his muscles under her fingertips. She wanted to taste him. Trailing her lips across his cheek, she needed so much more than just kisses.

Taking control back, he blazed his hot lips down to her neck.

"Jennette," he murmured against her neck. "This is madness."

"Yes," she whispered as her head leaned against the door. "Good madness."

"Bloody beautiful madness."

His hands moved to her hair and the pins that held it up dropped to the floor in a symphony of pinging tones. She couldn't take her gaze off his eyes. Usually a light gray, his eyes turned a darker shade as passion ruled his emotions.

They stared at each other for a long moment. He was giving her a chance to leave, she thought. Again, being the honorable man. But her feet wouldn't move. Her mouth would not let her speak the words to make him stop because she didn't want to stop.

Just once, her mind pleaded, *and then you'll know what it's like.*

His lips returned to hers, this time hardened with desire, not soft with comfort. She eagerly accepted his rougher kisses. As her tongue reached for his, molten heat spread from her mouth to her belly. The strangest sensations radiated from her stomach, lower to her womb. Unconsciously, her hips moved closer to him, closer to his heat.

When his hand skimmed down her back, he pressed her nearer and she felt the hardness of his erection. His fingers worked on the few tiny buttons on her gown.

"I want to see you wearing nothing," he whispered as he slid her gown down. "Nothing but your beautiful hair covering parts of your body."

Jennette bit down on her lip as she watched him drink in her body. Far from naked, she still wore her stays, petticoats, shift, draws, shoes, and stockings. But seeing the look in his eyes, she felt as if she didn't have a stitch of clothing on her body.

"Turn around, Jennette."

A little nervous tremor raced down her spine but she did as he requested. She felt his fingers work to unlace her stays. He kissed her shoulder while he loosened and finally removed them.

He pushed her hair away and his lips spread warmth across her back. A little shudder shook her body when he untied her petticoats and let them drop to the floor on top of her gown. He was right when he said this was madness. Facing the door, she closed her eyes as he brought her shift and her drawers over her hips.

Oh God, she stood there wearing nothing but her embroidered stocking and dancing shoes. She peeked back to see his lips tilt upward in a feral smile. He skimmed his fingers over the roundness of her bottom. Crouching down, he then removed her garters and her stockings fell to her ankles.

He picked up her foot, removed her shoe, and slowly traced his finger down from her thigh to her foot, removing the stockings as he went. His lips replaced his finger, warm, wet kisses trailed up her leg. He nipped the back of her calf as he moved upward.

"You have the most beautiful long legs," he whispered against the back of her knee. His hands slid from her thighs down to her ankles. "I want to feel them wrapped around my hips."

"Yes," she moaned softly. The urge to wrap herself around him was too great to ignore. She'd wanted this for so long. Tonight, she would have him all to herself.

"Soon," he replied, moving the last shred of clothing on her body. He repeated the motion of removing her other stocking and kissing her leg. Only this time, he didn't stop at her thigh.

She groaned as his lips blazed a fiery heat up her buttocks. As his lips kissed her behind, his hands cupped her breasts. Her head rolled back as he rubbed his thumb over her taut nipple sending a rush of moist heat to her core.

Slowly, he brought his hands down her belly and lower until his fingers brushed through her private hair. No man had ever touched her there. But it felt so right when he did. Spreading her folds apart, she shivered as his fingers crossed over her sensitive nub.

"You're so ready for me," he said as he slipped a finger deep inside her.

Waves of pleasure pulsed from her womb, spreading through her body. The sensations increased as he glided his finger in and out of her, replicating the actions she knew would happen in a few moments. Thankfully, her mother had not been shy in telling her everything a man did to his wife. And even though Matthew would never be her husband, she had tonight with him. And that would have to be enough.

"I want you now."

"Yes," she whispered. "Now, please."

He stood and turned her around to face him. Lowering his lips to her, he whispered, "Mine."

If only that could be true.

She felt him fumble with his breeches and wondered when he would take her to his bed. The idea of him covering her with his hard body caused a shiver to race through her. Instead, he pinned her to the door and lifted her legs.

"Wrap your legs around my waist, Jennette." His voice sounded raspy as if he were as overwhelmed with desire as she was.

She did what he'd requested and felt his erection at the entrance to her womanhood. He couldn't mean to . . . he lifted her slightly up and brought her down on top of him.

"Ahh," she cried out as he pushed through her maidenhead. The pain of his rough entry forced tears down her cheeks.

Matthew went still as the realization of what

happened hit him. She wasn't supposed to be a virgin. John had told him—Oh God, John had lied.

"I'm sorry," he mumbled against her shoulder. "I'm so sorry, I didn't know."

Gently he carried her to the bed and placed her down. Tears tracked down her cheeks. Tears he'd caused. He pushed her hair off her face and stared at the beautiful woman he'd hurt.

"I'm sorry," he said, feeling utterly helpless and insensitive.

"Why did you believe I wasn't a virgin?" she whispered.

Seeing the pain in her eyes, he had no choice but to tell her the truth. "John had implied . . ."

She pressed her lips together as more tears fell down her face. "He really said that about me?"

He gently placed his forehead on hers. "I'm sorry, Jennette. If I had known the truth . . ."

She raked her hands through his hair and gave him a watery smile. "It's all right. It's done now."

"No, it's not. I was a boorish brute and—"

She cut off his words with a passionate kiss. Pulling away slowly, she smiled at him, causing his heart to pound.

"I was told the first time could be painful."

"It didn't have to be that way. I didn't know. I was insensitive and—"

"I'm feeling a little better. I think I'm getting used to you in there."

"Oh?" His cock pulsed in anticipation.

"Maybe a few more kisses and we can try this again?" She skimmed her fingers down his chest in a flirty manner.

"As many as you want," he said, lowering his head

to hers again. Her soft lips opened for him and they found each other.

Steeled with control, he kissed down her chin, her neck, and chest until he found the little nub of her breast. Bringing it into his mouth, he heard her moan.

"Yes, more like that," she whispered.

With those encouraging words, he moved to her other nipple. Suckling deeply, he felt her quiver under him. Moist heat surrounded his shaft and he couldn't help but move slightly.

"Oh," she exclaimed.

Damn. "Did that hurt?"

"No, please do that again."

"With pleasure," he whispered.

Slowly, he withdrew from her and then gently reentered her wetness. He watched her face for any sign of discomfort but only saw her eyes widen as he reached the apex of her. Confident that the worst was over, he repeated the motion faster and felt her close around him. He had to remain in control. He had to make this pleasurable for her.

She shifted her hips, bringing her legs higher on his waist, sending him in deeper. This time they both moaned as the sensation drew them together in timeless ecstasy.

"Matthew," she whispered.

The sound of her voice urged him on. Wanting nothing more than to lose himself in her body, he increased his motions. He brought his fingers down on her clitoris, desperate for her to find her release.

Jennette moaned again as he touched her most sensitive spot. Sensations rolled like waves through her body as he stroked her. Climbing higher, she felt the pleasure radiating outward, upward until she clutched his shoulders and closed her eyes. Thousands of tiny stars lit up and she reached her release.

He increased his speed, stroking her harder as he reached for her hips and plunged in deeper. He groaned her name over and over as he spilled his seed into her. As he collapsed on top of her, they both struggled to regain control of themselves.

Jennette caressed his hair, as he nipped at her shoulder with his teeth. Her body felt sore and languid and ever so wonderful.

He lifted himself up slightly and smiled down at her. Her heart raced with the tilt of his lips. Gladness struck her as she thought about him being her first lover. The one man she'd wanted for years.

"I should leave," she said, caressing his cheek with her hand.

He grabbed her wrist and brought it to his lips. "Not yet."

"People will wonder where I am," she protested.

"Let them wonder. No one down there gives a bloody damn about either one of us unless they can gossip about it."

She tilted her head and stared at him. "I know, but my mother is one of them and she does care."

He closed his eyes. "Just a few minutes more."

She couldn't resist the pleading look on his face. And truthfully, she had no desire to leave just yet. She wanted to savor every moment, every second she had with him. She would need these memories to keep her warm once she left the country.

They moved back against the pillows and covered

their nakedness with the coverlet. He pulled her close so her head rested on his shoulder. Unable to keep her eyes open, she drifted off to sleep in the arms of the man who knew her deepest secrets. Or at least most of them . . .

Jennette watched Matthew as he showed his skill with the rapier. John parried and returned each thrust with less expertise until it became apparent to her that Matthew was holding back. Finally, John gave in and looked over at her.

"Do you want to have a try at it, Jennette?"

Matthew glared at his friend. "That is not a good idea, John. The grass is wet."

"I'll be perfectly all right," she retorted. "I've been practicing with Banning since I was ten." She held out her hand for the rapier.

"There is no plug on it," Matthew warned again. "The tip is very sharp."

Jennette shook her head. She'd show him what she was capable of, at least with a sword. "I can handle a sword."

She grabbed the sword from the handsome man. His long, thick fingers held on to hers for a moment. A spark of awareness shot up her arm. His chestnut hair was shorter today as if his valet had just cut it. But she shouldn't be noticing him.

"Come along, then." John took his position.

She stood across from him and tried to concentrate on him, her betrothed. But she knew her feelings for John had changed over the past two months. She didn't feel the attraction for John that he felt for her.

Her gaze slid to Matthew, who sat on the bench frowning at them both. He shook his head as he watched them. Jennette's hand shook as she drew the rapier in front of her. As she stepped forward, she slid a glance to Matthew to see if he was watching.

But as she pressed forward, determined to gain his attention, her foot slipped on the grass and she fell toward John. . . .

Chapter 14

Jennette woke with a start. Looking over at Matthew, her heart raced. It was true. John's death was no accident. She *had* killed him. Her attention had been on Matthew, not on the wet grass, not on the sword in her hand . . . not on her betrothed.

Her gaze had been on Matthew.

Her mind on the words he'd said to her that day. Admitting he desired her. Telling her that he must leave because it hurt to watch them together. And that kiss. While she had pushed him away in shock, she'd known in that instant that John had never made her feel like Matthew had.

She glanced over at him and pressed her lips tightly together. She'd slept with him. She let him make love to her. This shouldn't have happened. Never should she have let him do this to her.

What would John think of her? He'd loved her and she never returned his feeling as strongly as she should have.

What if she had killed him on purpose?

While she'd intended to break her engagement

to John later that day, she had tried before but had lost her courage every time. Maybe unknowingly, she had found the easiest solution to her problem.

She covered her mouth with her shaking hands as she stared at the sleeping man. What had she done tonight! She'd given in to her wildest fantasies only to realize the truth. She was a terrible person. If not for her, John would be alive.

And Matthew wouldn't be in the dreadful position in which he currently found himself.

Everything that had happened was due to her attraction to the wrong man. Why couldn't she have loved John enough? He'd been a good man. Why couldn't she keep her hands off Matthew? She'd ruined the lives of two good men. And why? Lust, desire, and yearning for something she should have left alone.

She was a horrible person.

Knowing she couldn't stay in this room a moment longer, she carefully disentangled herself from the bedcovers. Her clothes lay in a heap by the door where he'd kissed her naked body only two hours ago. Quietly, she slipped on her undergarments until she picked up her stays and realized she'd never be able to get them on alone. It didn't matter. She would run to her room.

Where her mother would be waiting for her, wondering why Jennette held her stays in her hand. Oh dear God, this couldn't get any worse, could it? There had to be someone who could help her out of this mess. Her gaze landed on Matthew.

No. He was part of the reason she was in this horrible position. Even if none of this was his fault, he would try to convince her that she was wrong about everything. But she wasn't. She had to find someone to assist her.

Avis and Elizabeth were here. Jennette closed her eyes in thought. Avis couldn't help her because Banning had barely left her side the entire party. There appeared no other choice but Elizabeth.

Jennette slid into her gown, struggled with the buttons, then crouched down to pick up her stays. She stilled her movements as Matthew stirred on the bed. He rolled over and continued to sleep.

After waiting a minute to make certain he had truly returned to sleep, she slipped out the door. She glanced in both directions and thanked God no one was about, and then raced to Elizabeth's room.

Only the dancing flames of the fireplace lit the room and spread its warmth, but it mattered not. Elizabeth hadn't returned yet. Now Jennette was stuck here waiting for a friend who had a bad habit of staying up late.

She lay on the bed, staring at the coffered ceiling and wondering how she could have created such a mess of her life. Her actions both that day and tonight would have horrified John. Tears burned her cheeks.

If she hadn't been attracted to Matthew, none of this would have happened. John would still be alive. Matthew would still have his place in Society. And she . . . ?

She would be free of this damned guilt that ate at her every day of her life.

"Jennette?"

Jennette blinked her eyes open and briefly wondered where she lay. Until Elizabeth stepped closer and the memories flooded back. "Elizabeth, I need your help."

Her friend eyed the bed and nodded. "I believe you do. What happened to you tonight?"

She should keep her secrets, but she'd been holding them in for so long she just blurted out, "I slept with a man tonight."

Elizabeth's mouth dropped. "You did what?"

Jennette cringed at the condemning sound of her voice. "I slept with—"

"Who?" Elizabeth moved to stand directly in front of the bed.

"Blackburn," Jennette whispered, staring at the coverlet.

"What would possess you to do such a thing? And with him?"

Obviously, Elizabeth had never fallen victim to lust. "I'm not certain. I went to his room to—"

"You went to his room! His room!" Elizabeth's voice rose with each sentence.

"Shh, you shall wake everyone." Jennette sat up on the bed and then patted a spot for Elizabeth. "I needed to apologize to him."

Elizabeth sat on the bed and stared at her. "Then why didn't you wait until morning?"

Staring at her hands, she replied, "I couldn't. You were in the room. You heard how horrible Mr. and Mrs. Marston were to him. I knew he would try to leave the party."

"That's no excuse. You know better than to go to any man's room."

"Elizabeth, you sound like my mother, not my friend."

Elizabeth sighed. "I'm sorry. It's just that my

mother always warned me about what happens when a lady does such a thing." She leaned in closer. "But what was it like?"

"Different," Jennette replied with a frown. "He didn't know I was a virgin until it was too late."

"He thought you had done that with another man? What type of lady does he think you are?" Elizabeth bristled.

"John and I were engaged for over two months. Perhaps he assumed we had been intimate." She couldn't tell Elizabeth what Matthew had said about John. Jennette wondered what would have possessed John to tell Matthew such a dreadful lie about her.

"But how did it feel?" Elizabeth pressed again.

Jennette bit her lip. "Once I became used to him being in there . . . it was really the most wondrous sensation I've ever felt."

"So when are you two announcing your engagement?"

"Our what?" Jennette exclaimed. She couldn't marry Matthew. Wedding him would ruin them both.

"Why do you look so surprised, Jennette? You laid with him, now you marry him. That is the way these things work."

"Not for me." Jennette rose from the bed and paced the room. "I have no plans to marry him."

Elizabeth reclined on the bed with a slight smile. "Of course, just as Avis never intended on marrying your brother."

"And she didn't until she realized she could overcome her fear of marriage. I have no fear of marriage but wedding Matthew would be a colossal mistake for both of us."

"Why?"

Jennette looked away. "The gossips would just love to tell everyone how they knew Matthew had killed John so we could be together."

"But that was five years ago, Jennette."

"It makes no difference. Besides, he's a gambler."

"Indeed? I have heard none of that. Certainly his father and brother gambled, but not Blackburn," Elizabeth said, shaking her head.

"It makes no difference. I cannot marry the man," Jennette insisted.

"If you say so," Elizabeth said in a singsong tone.

Frustration seeped into Jennette. "You believe everything your mother told you. If you make love with a man you must marry him."

"That is how it's done, Jennette."

"Not for everyone . . . not for me." She pointed a finger at Elizabeth. "Someday you shall find a man attractive but perhaps not marriageable, and you'll wonder. And you will contemplate what he looks like without his clothes. And before you know what happens, you will be in his bed and you won't care about the consequences."

Elizabeth laughed. "I hardly think that will ever happen. I am five and twenty—"

"As am I." She grabbed the bedpost. "And one day, you will start to wonder just what you've missed."

"I will not!"

Jennette shook her head. "Please just help me lace my stays. My mother is going to have my head for staying up this late with you."

* * *

Jennette slowly opened the door to her room, praying her mother was asleep.

"If you think you can sneak in, you are sadly mistaken, my dear."

Damn. She opened the door and walked inside feeling the guilt of her actions again.

"Where have you been?" her mother demanded. She crossed her arms over her chest and looked every bit the angry, worried mother.

"I was with Elizabeth, in her room talking."

"And exactly where were you when she was in the salon playing whist with Avis?"

"Waiting for her in her room." Jennette pulled at the few pins holding up her hair. Thankfully, she'd snatched some of Elizabeth's pins.

"Did you go to him?"

Jennette turned and stared at her mother. "What?"

"I know what happened in the salon. Did you go to him?"

"Why would I do such a thing?"

Her mother shook her head. "Jennette, I know how softhearted you are. I also know you feel guilty because of the way Society treats him."

"It isn't right," Jennette said, sinking to the bed. "It was an accident."

"But not the first for him."

"What do you mean?" she asked.

"Lord Blackburn ran with a fast set after Eton. One rainy night, he made a wager with a friend that his horse could best his friend's. It was dark and wet and Lord Culpert wasn't the best rider and took a dreadful fall. He died two months later from his injuries."

Jennette looked away so her mother would not notice the tears welling in her eyes. *A wager.* He'd bet on a race and the other man died. "I had no idea."

"And you know the *ton.* There is no such thing as *two* accidents."

She stifled the urge to run to him and beg for his forgiveness again. After what they did tonight, she didn't believe she could ever face him. It felt as if they had both betrayed John with their actions. That was bad enough, but she'd already been disloyal to John by agreeing to marry him when she was attracted to his best friend.

"Mother, thank you for explaining what happened. But I wasn't with him tonight." She kept her eyes locked on the fireplace, afraid her intuitive mother would discover her lie.

"As I have told you before, he is a good man. But after the Marstons' outburst, marrying him might ruin you both."

"I know that, Mother." And she couldn't do anything to hurt him again. She had done far too much already.

Matthew rolled over leisurely as he awoke. He couldn't remember the last time he felt this sated. It almost felt as if he had been dreaming. Reaching over he patted the empty space next to him.

Had it been a dream?

Had he imagined everything that happened last night? It couldn't have been his imagination because she'd been here, standing at the door. The anguish of her guilt stamped upon her face.

What had started as an attempt to comfort her

ended with her sensual, long legs wrapped tightly around him as he rutted with her like an animal. God, she'd been a virgin and he'd taken her as if she was a common strumpet.

She must hate him for what he'd done.

Guilt slid its tentacles around his heart and mind, constricting tightly. It was John's fault. John had led him to believe that it wouldn't be her first time. Matthew covered his face with his hands and groaned.

John must have suspected Matthew's feelings for Jennette. What better way to keep him away from her? Matthew should have known better than to believe his friend about Jennette's virtue. Never had he heard a word about her being anything but an honorable lady.

She hadn't even awakened him when she left in the middle of the night. If someone had seen her wandering the halls with her hair down and her dress disheveled, her reputation would be ruined.

Unless she'd been seen leaving his room, then he would save her with marriage. That might be for the best after all. If only that would absolve his guilt for his mistreatment of her last night. Or relieve his conscience for bedding the woman John had professed to love.

"This is a damnable mess," he muttered.

Sitting up slowly, he looked at his valise and wondered if he should just quit the party and return to London. But doing so would keep him away from her. He should just compromise her publicly and be done with it. Selby would force a marriage and that would be the end.

Except it would only be the beginning of a lifetime

of more remorse. Matthew swore softly. He was damned sick of all the guilt. He shouldn't have told her how he felt five years ago. He shouldn't have threatened to blackmail her into marriage when he knew he'd never be able to go through with it. He shouldn't have kissed her in the billiard room at Lady Elizabeth's house.

And he never should have seduced her last night.

But he had. His honor demanded that he marry her now regardless of the guilt, no matter her objections. He would stay and find someone to walk in on them as they kissed. It was a simple solution to a dreadful situation. Then he would spend the next forty years trying to gain her forgiveness.

And Matthew knew just the man to help him with his problem—Somerton. Somerton could convince someone with influence to accompany him to a room where Matthew and Jennette were kissing. The outrage would be enough for Selby to accept him as a brother-in-law without causing enough of a scandal for a duel.

With a plan in place, he quickly performed his morning ablutions, dressed, and readied himself for the gossips in the breakfast room. As he walked toward the door, hairpins crunched under his feet. Each pin he stepped on brought the guilt of his mistreatment of her back in full force. He'd be damned lucky if she ever spoke to him again, much less entered a room alone with him.

Pushing away the shame, he walked to the morning room determined not to let their petty talk bother him any longer. Several people looked up at him as he entered. Everyone glanced away from him and most appeared embarrassed.

"Glad to see you didn't run off," Somerton said from behind him.

Matthew turned his head and smirked. "Now, why would I do that?"

"Good man."

"I need to speak with you in private."

Somerton eyed the table. "Follow me."

Matthew followed Somerton into the music room. After closing the door, he walked toward the pianoforte. Skimming his fingers up the keys, he rethought his plan. Perhaps this wasn't the best idea. Maybe there was a better way to find a woman to marry him. But he didn't want another woman. Last night proved the inevitable—he only wanted Jennette.

"Well?" Somerton said, impatience threading through his voice.

"I need your assistance in a private matter."

"Who doesn't?" Somerton muttered with a curse. "Let me guess, since Mr. and Mrs. Marston didn't exactly give their blessings, you have decided to compromise the chit. There are far better women than Mary Marston."

"Yes and no," Matthew stalled.

Somerton shook his head. "What do you mean?"

"I do want to compromise a woman . . . but not Miss Marston."

Somerton's lips slowly turned upward. He took a seat by the small fireplace and crossed his arms over his chest. "Then who?"

"Jennette."

Her name hung in the overly quiet room. Matthew glanced over at Somerton, who appeared to be struggling to keep from laughing.

"I am quite serious, Somerton."

"I believe you." He covered his mouth and coughed. "Do you honestly think Selby will allow it?"

"I'm beyond caring. He won't want his sister's reputation ruined."

Somerton nodded, still looking as if he were trying to contain laughter. "Very well, what will you have me do?"

"Tonight, I will take her to the greenhouse. You bring the dowager Lady Selby or Lady Aston and find us kissing."

"What time?"

"Eleven. By then dinner will be finished and the gaming in full swing. No one will notice us slip away."

"All right. I will bring one of the ladies in just after eleven." Somerton rose and smirked. "Don't be late."

"Of course not."

Somerton departed from the conservatory, leaving behind a silence that overwhelmed the room. Matthew glanced around the room then sat in the chair by the fireplace. He leaned back and closed his eyes. Now that he had Somerton's assistance, the hardest part of his plan would take the forefront.

Somehow, he had to get Jennette to agree to meet him in the greenhouse tonight. She might be embarrassed by what they had done and thus not comfortable talking to him yet. Perhaps he should write her a note—tell her he wished to apologize for his actions last night.

Although, the only thing he needed to apologize for was taking her so roughly. Had he known of her innocence, it wouldn't have stopped him, but he could have made the experience so much easier on her.

He opened his eyes and rose from the chintz chair. He had to do this. She was his only hope at saving his life.

Chapter 15

"What are you doing lying about in bed as if you are an invalid?"

Jennette sighed, looking over at Avis, who stood in the doorway with her hands over her chest in a most intimidating manner. "I have a headache."

"No, you do not," Avis replied, then shut the door and walked toward the bed. "The only thing wrong with you is embarrassment."

Jennette covered her face with her hands. Elizabeth must have told Avis about what happened. How was she to face everyone after what she'd done last night?

"Well," Avis continued. "I will not allow it. That woman was a shrew."

Woman? What woman?

"Furthermore, she had no right to include you when she was reprimanding Blackburn. I have to admit, I was shocked that you stood there and let her malign your name."

Jennette felt the bed sink where Avis sat down. Perhaps her friend didn't know everything that had happened. "I was so stunned by her venom, I didn't know what to say," she replied from behind her hands.

Slowly, Jennette let her hands drop from her face. "What am I to do, Avis?"

"To do? You will get out of this bed and dress. Then we shall saunter down the stairs for dinner as if nothing out of the ordinary occurred last night."

"I can't face them," she whispered. *Or him*, she added to herself.

"Of course you can. Besides, I heard a few moments ago that they were leaving before their precious daughter became infected by the vice of this party."

Jennette laughed. "Now I know you are jesting with me."

"Actually, I am not. Mrs. Marston is dreadfully concerned about the influences here." Avis rolled her eyes.

Jennette shook her head. "The same influences Mary will have to face every time she attends a party of the *ton*."

"Exactly."

Jennette looked away from her friend. Even though the Marstons were leaving, it didn't change the fact that she couldn't face the people downstairs. Or at least one of them.

"Now, tell me the real reason you cannot seem to leave this bed," Avis said.

Jennette turned her head toward her friend. "What do you mean?"

Avis shook her head. "We have known each other forever, Jennette. What the Marstons said to you last night would never have kept you from breakfast or anything else."

"I was embarrassed!"

"Of course you were." Avis sent her a disbelieving look. "But when has that stopped you?"

"You don't believe me?"

"No," Avis replied casually. "Something else is making you remain in your room."

Jennette sighed. "You know, don't you?"

"I do now."

"Did he leave the party?"

Avis shook her head. "No. I believe most people were quite surprised by that fact. He entered the morning room as if nothing had happened last night. Do you realize that your being at the same party as he has elevated his position? Most people assume that if you can be in the same room as Blackburn, he cannot be as terrible as the rumors say. In fact, I heard several people commend him for staying."

"How can I face him, Avis?" Jennette felt heat cross her cheeks as she thought about what he'd done. "He saw me naked. He kissed my body."

"Which is what making love is all about," Avis replied in a soft tone.

"How did you get over your embarrassment with Banning?"

Avis chuckled. "I woke up with him in my bed. We were all alone in the cottage so I really had no choice but to face him."

"But weren't you embarrassed?"

"A little," she answered and then stretched out at the end of the bed. "But I overcame it rather quickly."

"Was he?" Jennette asked.

"Embarrassed?"

Jennette nodded.

"I don't think so." Avis frowned in thought. "I don't think men get embarrassed about being seen without clothes. Perhaps it's because of all the layers we women wear. We're used to having so much clothing on our bodies."

"Perhaps."

"Jennette, men enjoy seeing us without our clothing. Didn't you find it pleasant to look at him?"

"Avis, I cannot believe the questions you're asking me today," Jennette said, then grabbed a pillow and tossed it at her friend.

"And you're not answering them," Avis muttered from behind the pillow. After removing the object from her face, she said, "So answer my question."

Jennette glanced away from the prying stare of her best friend. "I did enjoy it. What I saw of him . . ."

"Hmm, it sounds as if you didn't get to see everything you wanted."

"Avis!"

Her friend chuckled from the end of the bed. "All right, I promise to stop asking such embarrassing questions."

Avis stood and pulled on Jennette's hand. "Now get out of this bed. I'll ring for Molly to help you get dressed but you are going to walk down those stairs with me for dinner."

Jennette rose slowly and then hugged her new sister-in-law. "Thank you, Avis."

As Molly helped her dress, Avis waited patiently on the bed. Jennette turned toward her with a rose-colored gown in her hands. "What do you think about this one?"

"Perfect, now hurry. You have been up here all day and people will start to assemble for dinner in the salon in thirty minutes."

Jennette scrambled into her dress then sat while Molly put her hair up into an artful chignon. She had decided on her plan of attack for the evening. Ignoring him definitely seemed the best option. No one would blame her for cutting him. All she had to do was survive dinner, then stay for a short time once the men had rejoined the women in the salon.

Once her hair was set, she stood and turned toward Avis. "All right, I am ready."

"Good," Avis replied walking to the door. "Now, should we run into Blackburn, you will give him a polite nod. If he attempts to draw you into conversation, you will allow it but only topics that are general in nature. If he should try to get you alone, find me. Unless you would like to be alone with him again."

"Avis!"

Her friend smirked. "Well, I certainly wanted more than just one time with—"

"Avis, we had an agreement. You wouldn't discuss the intimate relationship you have with my brother."

"Very well."

Avis's plan seemed far too easy. But she had no idea how intoxicating Matthew's voice sounded to Jennette. His raspy voice sent shivers of pleasure throughout her body. Somehow, she had to resist him. All of him, from his sensual gray eyes to his molded lips, to his hard, lean chest to his—

She could not contemplate any other parts of his body.

* * *

Matthew watched as Jennette entered the salon
with Lady Selby. Their arms linked together as if
to form an impenetrable force to resist all the gos-
sipy remarks. Or to stand firm against him. That
thought gave him pause. While he assumed she
would still be resistant to marriage, he hoped a
public compromising would change her mind.

What if it didn't?

What if she still refused him?

He pushed aside the negative thoughts. Her
brother would insist on marriage, if only to save her
from more gossip. As he watched her again, she
moved toward the sofa with exquisite grace. Her
long fingers grasped a small glass of sherry and
brought it up to her full lips. Ancroft approached
them with a smile.

Matthew's heart constricted as Jennette smiled
back at the future duke. Matthew still had no idea
what was between them. They obviously hadn't
been lovers even though they looked at each other
with tenderness in their eyes. He hated the idea of
jealousy, but no other emotion would make him
feel this way.

The short missive burned a hole in his coat
pocket. There had to be a way to get it to her without everyone in the room realizing. Perhaps he
could get Somerton to deliver it for him.

Glancing around the room, he noticed Somerton missing. Damn. How was Somerton going to
bring the dowager Lady Selby to the greenhouse if
he wasn't in attendance? Based on her bearing

tonight, he didn't think she would speak to him much less take a note from him.

"Don't even think of approaching her after last night."

Matthew turned at the sound of Selby's voice coming from behind him. "Why would I speak to her?"

"I know all about your plan to have her help you find a bride. That ends now. You will stay away from her."

Matthew turned and faced Selby's glittering blue eyes. "I don't think you have any say in what I do."

Selby smirked. "When it involves my sister, I most certainly do. You have caused her enough pain."

"And yet, you do nothing about Ancroft hanging on to her like a pup."

"Because I know Ancroft is harmless."

Matthew chuckled scornfully. "Harmless? The man has a bastard. With a vengeance, he'll chase after any woman he wants. As he is a future duke, women fall shamelessly at his feet."

"And still, I know Jennette is far safer with him than with you."

"Are they secretly betrothed?" Matthew held his breath, praying for the answer he wanted to hear.

"I should tell you that she is." Selby sipped his drink.

"Then she isn't," Matthew said with relief.

"No," Selby admitted. "But I would far prefer a match with him than with you."

Of course he would. Why would any man want a penniless earl with a scandal attached to his name for his sister? Especially if he could arrange for his sister to marry a wealthy marquess who would be a duke one day.

"If you attempt to do anything further to ruin her name, I will call you out," Selby said before walking to his wife.

So much for thinking Selby might agree to the marriage should he find them in a compromising position. Matthew knew he would have to depend on the dowager Lady Selby to convince her son that Matthew would be acceptable.

Somerton entered the salon, stood at the threshold, and scanned the room with his usual arrogance. Matthew nodded to him and tilted his head so that he would understand his need to speak with him. Somerton inclined his head so slightly most people wouldn't have noticed. But Matthew did.

After observing the room like a lion on the hunt, Somerton sauntered toward him.

"Yes?" he said with impatience in his voice.

"I need you to get a missive to Lady Jennette," Matthew whispered.

"Good God, man, do I look like a footman?"

"There is no one else I can trust."

Somerton shook his head. "Very well, hand it over."

Matthew casually removed the small note and gave it to Somerton. "Don't let anyone else see it."

Somerton grinned. "And I thought you trusted me."

"Only in the smallest measure."

"As it should be."

Somerton cupped the missive in his palm and walked away. Matthew continued to watch him as the footman announced dinner. Somerton neared Jennette and then appeared to trip, catching himself on her. Matthew supposed that Somerton had handed the note to her while attempting to right himself.

Jennette assisted Somerton to his feet as a small paper floated down between her breasts. How had the man done that? She leaned in closer as if he needed more help.

"For me?"

He gave her a quick, knowing nod. "I apologize, Lady Jennette," he said for the benefit of the room.

"It is of no consequence, my lord."

He sent her a quick wink as people surrounded them. "Thank you for saving me from a most ungracious fall."

Jennette attempted to keep her lips from twitching in humor but doubted she succeeded. For all his scandalous reputation, there was something oddly endearing about Somerton. Walking out of the room, she headed for the ladies' retiring room instead of the dining room.

Once there, she walked behind a screen as if to use the chamber pot. She pulled out the small note and unfolded it. Shaking her head as she read it, she could not believe he would ask her to meet him. She would never be so dim-witted again.

She had satisfied her curiosity regarding Matthew and their lust. But she couldn't let that happen again. There had to be someone who would marry him. As much as seeing him with another woman would break her heart, it had to be done.

Walking back to the dining room, she entered from the side door. She ambled past the table, looking for her seat and with whom she would be eating. Her eyes widened as she found her place and Matthew across from her.

He smiled slowly at her. Her gaze slid to Lady Aston, who looked away, but not before Jennette noticed the malicious grin on her face.

Jennette glanced over at her mother, who sent her a sympathic smile. Baron Huntley, seated to her right, welcomed her.

"Good evening, Lady Jennette."

Jennette slowly took her seat, attempting to ignore the blazing heat of Matthew's stare. "Good evening, Huntley."

"I'd heard you were feeling unwell earlier. I hope you are better now."

"I am much recovered, thank you."

Matthew raised an eyebrow at her. "Good evening, Lady Jennette."

"Blackburn," she replied curtly. But nothing could stop the heat from flaming across her face.

After the footman placed a plate of food in front of her, she pressed her hand to her stomach. She'd only eaten a piece of toast and a cup of tea all day. Now the rumbling in her stomach incited her to eat heartily, but, not wanting to look like a glutton, she slowly picked up her fork and cut a piece of beef.

As she ate, she attempted to ignore the glaring stare of the man across from her. Several times Matthew had tried to draw her into conversation, but she turned her attention to Huntley.

"Lady Jennette, I must tell you how impressed I am with your watercolors," Huntley said before taking a bite of potatoes.

"Thank you, Huntley. Where did you see one of my watercolors?"

"Lady Elizabeth's literary salon. She told me the watercolor above the sofa was your work."

Jennette nodded. "Indeed."

"Lovely." He took a sip of his wine and turned slightly toward her before leaning in and whispering, "Almost as lovely as you."

Jennette smiled tightly. "Thank you."

Luckily, Huntley returned to his dinner and spoke to the lady on his right. She glanced over at Matthew, who tilted his head as one eyebrow rose in question. Why was it so hard to ignore the man? She had the oddest desire to ask him about his morning. Had he gone hunting with the men? Or stayed behind and practiced swords with Lord Aston?

"Did you have an enjoyable morning, Lord Blackburn?" She wanted to slap her hand over her mouth.

"Very much so. I went on the hunt with several of the other men."

"Indeed."

"And you?" he asked softly. "Did you enjoy your morning alone?"

Hearing the sensual undertones of his voice made her wish she could give him a proper retort. Instead, all that came out of her mouth was, "Yes, thank you."

Dinner progressed more slowly than Jennette would have preferred. Course after course left her uncomfortably full and she wanted nothing more than to leave the awkward glances of everyone behind her. Finally, Lady Aston stood and commanded all the ladies to follow her to the great salon at the front of the house.

Avis caught up to her as she walked down the long hallway to the salon. "How did that go?"

"Dreadful. Between Huntley's thinly veiled flirtations and Blackburn's burning gaze, I am feeling quite exhausted tonight."

"Oh my, Huntley?"

"Yes. He complimented me on the watercolor landscape above the sofa at Elizabeth's home." Jennette looked over as Avis frowned.

"But that's an oil landscape."

Jennette smiled tightly. "Exactly."

Avis covered her mouth with her hand, suppressing a grin. "Did you correct his assumption?"

"Of course not. You know as well as I that women don't paint in oils. That's far too masculine a pursuit," Jennette said scornfully.

"Just as women don't write books that might go against the mores of the day," Avis replied.

Jennette patted Avis's hand. "Your book will be published. And one of my oils will end up in a museum."

"Lady Jennette, might I have a word?"

Jennette moved to Lady Aston's seat. "Of course."

After Jennette sat on the sofa next to her, Lady Aston began, "My husband's mother is getting on in years and Aston believes she should live with us. Personally, I won't have that woman in my house. So I have decided to refurbish the dowager house on the property."

"That sounds like a fine idea." Jennette had no idea why Lady Aston was telling her this tale.

"I know you decorated your sister-in-law's home. I would very much appreciate if you would take a look at the dowager's house and make some recommendations."

"I would be happy to." A little thrill of excitement rushed through her. If she couldn't paint, she loved to decorate rooms. "I will go out there first thing in the morning to have a look."

Lady Aston gave her a condescending smile. "I don't know how to thank you."

Jennette brushed aside the nagging sensation that something wasn't right about her request. Instead, she excused herself to go to the ladies' retiring room. After taking care of her business, she started to head back to the main salon. But as she passed a large window, her gaze landed on the greenhouse. A small light flickered from behind the glass.

She should not go to him.

And yet, even as she had that thought, she walked away from the salon and toward the exterior door.

Matthew paced the long gravel path of the greenhouse, passing the fall vegetables and the flowers forced to bloom out of season. All he had to do was wait for her to arrive, talk to her, and kiss her, until her mother and Somerton walked in on them.

Simple enough.

So why did his heart constrict every time he thought about compromising her?

She'd paid a heavy price for her actions five years ago. She had watched her fiancé die before her eyes. An action she'd caused. Her suffering ate at him.

And now he was going to cause her more pain.

He stopped and stared at a small red tulip almost ready to bloom. The color reminded him of John's blood. John would despise him for even thinking about compromising her. Matthew had promised to protect her name. Ruining her would be breaking his pledge to John.

John was dead, he reminded himself.

Nonetheless, guilt washed over him. How could he do this to her? He touched the silky petal of the flower and thought about the texture of her raven hair. He yanked the bud off its stem and threw it across the room.

Why couldn't he be the scoundrel? Why couldn't he hurt her?

"Matthew?" her whispered voice sounded from the door.

He turned and stared at her, immediately comprehending the reason he could never see her hurt. And more importantly, why he could never be the one to wound her. The wind had whipped strands of her black hair out of its upswept style and caused them to fall upon her delicate face. Her blue eyes sparkled in the dim light of the greenhouse.

He loved her.

He could not do this to her. He wanted her willingly, not because she'd been forced out of duty to keep her name secure.

"Get out of here."

"You asked me to come here," she replied, slowly walking into the room. "What did you wish to speak with me about?"

"Get out, now!" Couldn't she sense the urgency in his voice? He had to make her leave.

"Matthew . . ."

"Jennette, I believe someone is coming. If you don't get out now you know what will happen."

She licked her lips and nodded. "I see. Good night, then."

"Don't take the main path back to the house."

She turned and walked to the door. After cracking the door open, she paused, and said, "Thank you for not compromising me, Matthew."

He watched her depart and prayed no one would see her leave the greenhouse. Hearing voices, he picked up the candle and walked to the door. He headed straight for the couple walking up the path.

"Somerton," he said with a nod. "And the ladies Selby, nice evening, isn't it?"

The dowager Lady Selby eyed him and the greenhouse. "Yes, I believe the weather has become so much more pleasant."

"Indeed it has."

"I've heard there are some interesting plants in the greenhouse," the younger Lady Selby commented. "Would you care to join us?"

"Actually, I am just returning from the greenhouse." He looked up at Somerton. "There is nothing much to see."

Chapter 16

As the sun broke through the clouds the next morning, Matthew strode out of his room furious at himself for thinking Jennette would ever come willingly to him. She'd loved John, not him. The frustration he felt was eating at him. There was only one way to rid himself of the aggravation—a good long ride.

After walking to the stables, he waited while a lad saddled a gelding for him. He admired the horse, wishing he could afford such quality horseflesh again. At the rate this plan with Jennette was going, he might never be able to buy another horse.

He climbed into the saddle and headed down the path toward the valley. The gray November sky and cool wind chilled him but did nothing to ease his ineffective anger. With irritation nipping at his heels, he spurred the horse to a run. The brown and gray scenery flashed past.

As he crested a small knoll, the ivy-covered dowager house came into view. He slowed his horse to a canter while he examined the home. Coming nearer, he noticed a horse tied to a post in front.

Odd, there was only one horse, so he doubted it was a liaison. He wondered if a rider might have become ill or hurt and stopped there for a rest. Knowing he had better check, he reined in next to the other horse. The mare appeared to be fine.

Walking into the house, he shouted, "Hello?"

In the small parlor, dusty white cloths covered all the furniture and cobwebs hung from the ceiling. Why would anyone willingly enter this old house? Walking back into the hall, he approached the staircase and shouted, "Is anyone up there?"

"I'm upstairs," the muffled feminine voice replied.

"Is everything all right?" he asked, striding up the stairs as fear etched its way down his back. Something had to be wrong for a lady to be in this ruin all by herself. The place was all but falling down.

"Matthew?"

Just as he reached the top riser, he saw Jennette walk out of one of the bedrooms. Fear turned to anger. "What the bloody hell are you doing here? Are you meeting someone? Ancroft perhaps? Or maybe Huntley is more your taste."

She dropped the pad she'd been holding and crossed her arms over her chest. "How dare you imply such a thing!"

He stepped closer as anger mingled with jealousy to create a dangerous combination. "Oh, I dare. Why else would a woman be in this hovel alone?"

Her eyes glittered like the icy North Sea as she took two strides toward him. Before he knew what had happened, she'd slapped his cheek. The tingling crossed his face feeling like a hundred splinters of wood.

"My maid was ill. You of all people should know I don't take lovers," she hissed.

Why did she bring out every bit of jealousy imaginable in him? Deflated, he replied, "You're right. And I must apologize for my reaction."

"Pardon me?"

Pulling her closer to him, he smiled down at her. "I said, you are right."

"Why are you here, Matthew?"

He noticed she'd said nothing about the fact that she was up against his chest. "I saw the lone mare and thought a rider might have been hurt and sought refuge here. Why are you here?"

"Not to meet a lover." Rosy color infused her cheeks. She retreated a step. "Lady Aston asked me to look at what it would take to refurbish the house."

"Why would she ask you?"

"Because I love to redecorate rooms. I refurbished both my brother's house and Avis's before she married Banning. I also assisted Sophie with her home."

Based on her fashion sense, he assumed her work would be wonderful. Even seeing her here in a morning gown of pale green with an apron covering her, she looked exquisite.

"Isn't this place too far gone?" he asked, looking around at the peeling wallpaper and warped floorboards.

"No, it definitely needs quite a bit of work. But it's not too far ruined." She pulled at his hand and led him to the bedroom. "Look at that window."

Matthew looked at the window and shrugged. "It's a window."

She rolled her eyes. "No, it's a Palladian window. Facing the south."

"And?"

"And you know nothing about light or color or anything," she said, throwing her hands in the air. "The window is a beautiful Palladian, facing the south so all the sunlight comes through the glass. It warms the room and brightens everything in it. This is a perfect bedroom for an aging widow."

Her enthusiasm infected him. He smiled at her. "It's beautiful."

She retrieved her pad from the hall and quickly sketched the room. "Oh, I just love this room. Now picture a pale green silk on the walls, floral curtains, and a lighter wood for the furniture."

Matthew did his best but still couldn't picture the room as clearly as Jennette seemed to. "But this isn't a very big room."

She turned to him with a grin. "Exactly!"

He shook his head in confusion. "Why would the dowager want to make this her bedroom when there is a larger bedroom?"

"Come with me." Jennette stomped off without a glance back to him.

Matthew followed her into another bedroom and cringed. Even with the curtains open, the room appeared dark and gloomy.

"Why would anyone want to sleep in here?" she asked. "The dowager Lady Aston should have the bright and airy room. This should be a guest room."

Looking around, he realized the room was only

slightly larger than the first bedroom she liked so much. "I believe I see your point."

Jennette sat down on the bed and her hand flew across the pad, noting everything about the room. She looked up at him with a gleam of passion in her eyes. He suddenly realized just how much she loved what she was doing here. The cobwebs hadn't sent her shuddering away. The creaky floors and evidence of rodents hadn't forced her to leave either.

He watched as she attempted to move a large trunk. "Wait. I shall help you."

Together, they moved the trunk away from the wall, exposing a small hidden door. "Why is that here?" he asked.

Jennette stared at the door and pursed her lips. "I'm not sure. As I was sketching the wall, I noticed the slight indentation."

"A secret passageway, perhaps?"

Her eyes lit with intrigue. "Maybe!"

"Shall we find out?"

"Yes!"

Matthew slid the door open and glanced inside. Pulling his head back out, he smiled up at her. "Sorry, it's just a storage area. No secret passage, no hidden treasure."

"Damn." She covered her mouth with her hand, eyes opened wide.

"Damn?" He stood and laughed at the ease with which the word rolled off her tongue. "Have you always hidden this propensity to swear?"

"Yes. Banning has admonished me so many times but that's hardly fair when every shocking word I know is because of him."

"It's hard to be a lady."

Jennette laughed. "You have no idea. Men get to say anything they want and no one cares. But ladies must be proper at all times. Not a sullied word can pass these lips."

"Except in the bedroom," he whispered. "There lovers can be themselves, say what they desire."

He watched her swallow as her eyes darkened.

"I am all done in this room," she said quickly.

Point taken, Matthew thought. He followed her as she inspected the third bedroom. Dusty crates and trunks filled this room, making it appear as though the previous owner never had moved in. Jennette slowly opened one of the trunks and gasped.

"Look at this dress," she exclaimed. She stood and turned with an ornate gown, fashionable maybe a hundred years ago, in her hand. "Isn't this the most beautiful dress you have ever seen?"

"No," he replied, shaking his head.

"Indeed? When have you seen a prettier gown?"

His lips tilted upward. "The night you wore that sapphire gown with the peacock embroidered at the bottom."

"Oh," she whispered, then glanced back down at her pad. "You don't need to stay here while I finish."

"I certainly do. Others might come upon you here . . . alone . . ."

"I shall make certain I lock the door after you leave."

"I wouldn't be a gentleman to let you stay here in this decrepit, old house that is all but falling down. You might get hurt."

Jennette moved past him, leaving the room but

her jasmine scent remained. He stalked her. She opened a door, making her way to the attic rooms.

"Oh my," she said with a sigh when she reached the top step.

"What's the matter?" he asked following behind her. The door shut as he walked up the steps.

"Lady Aston specifically stated that her mother-in-law would need three servants. But there is only one bedroom up here and the lowest level is a dirt-floor cellar."

Matthew reached the top and surveyed the room. "It's certainly big enough for three rooms. Each would be approximately the same size as the bedrooms downstairs."

"Yes, but that will increase the costs."

"I believe Lord Aston can afford it." He had to admit to be taken aback by her concern for the cost of the project.

She walked around the room and shook her head. "This is much more work."

"You can do it."

She whipped her head around to him. She smiled shyly at him and said, "Thank you."

"Let me see your pencil." He held out his hand until she dropped the lead. Walking around the room, he drew lines on the walls and floors where new walls could be built. "What do you think?"

Jennette sat on the musty mattress and eyed each marking before she picked up another piece of lead from her apron. Drawing the approximate dimensions on the paper, she shook her head.

She pointed to the marking nearest the middle window and said, "That wall must go on the other side of the window. Otherwise one servant would have two windows while another servant would have none."

He stepped back toward the bed and looked at the lines on the wall. "You're right. I hadn't noticed that. I was basing the walls purely on room size. Now this room will be bigger but at least there will be a window."

She looked around the room and shivered. The idea of being alone with him in this room had set her nerves on fire. She needed to finish her work and leave before she did something completely irrational . . . again.

He walked back to the lines he'd drawn and her gaze wandered to his buff-colored riding breeches. The soft leather stretched across his tight derrière. Her pulse increased as she stared at his backside, remembering how it felt to have her legs wrapped around his hips.

Heat seared her cheeks when he glanced back at her. He couldn't possibly know her thoughts. And yet, the seductive grin he sent her made her think otherwise.

"Jennette," he said softly.

"Matthew, please . . ."

"May I see your ideas for the room?"

Jennette blew out a breath, thankful that he seemed to understand they could not fall into bed again. He strolled across the room and she wondered if he hadn't felt the same pull of desire. Maybe she imagined the look of desire she thought she'd seen in his eyes. He sat next to her on the bed and glanced down at her drawing.

The man smelled of leather and horses, creating a strange swirl of emotions rolling through her. His thigh brushed against her and it took every ounce of control she had not to turn to him and kiss him.

His finger pointed to one wall she'd drawn. "I think that wall will need to be brought in a little. Otherwise, there won't be much room in the hallway."

"Of course," she whispered. What happened two nights ago had been an accident. Their emotions had been overwhelmed by the Marstons' slanderous comments. Besides, any man would have made love to a woman who so brazenly entered his room without even knocking.

He leaned in next to her, his shoulder encountering hers, his head all but touching hers. She wanted to be the upright lady, the woman who slapped her fan against his arm in protest to his close contact. Instead, she turned her head toward him.

Staring into his eyes, she lost any thought of being a proper lady. The back of his hand skimmed her cheek, drawing down to her neck. He wrapped his hand around the crook of her neck and brought her closer to him, to his lips, to the deep desire she wanted to know better.

His lips caressed hers until she opened for him. She wanted to feel the fire of passion flare between them again. She didn't care if that made her a strumpet. She had wanted him for so long and had never dared admit it to anyone save herself.

The sound of the downstairs door slamming shut broke them apart.

"Oh God," she whispered.

Matthew rose and raced to the steps. As if in a daze, she followed him, praying whoever might be downstairs would leave before finding them in the attic.

"No one's here," a deep masculine voice sounded from the second floor.

"But . . ." The feminine voice sounded timid.

"Come on, Annie." Footsteps fell across the floor below them.

Matthew looked at her and shrugged. Jennette looked at him and wondered what he was thinking. The rooms below had gone silent except for the occasional creaking floorboard.

Quietly, they both tiptoed to the bed and waited for something to happen. Matthew pulled her down onto his lap. She could feel his erection rising.

"Did you hear that?" Annie said.

"Probably just a mouse in the attic. No one is here."

"But what about the horses?"

The man groaned. "No one ever comes to this depressing place. There's a pond just beyond the house. Most likely someone tied the horses and walked to the pond. We checked the rooms and no one is here."

"All right."

Matthew leaned in and whispered, "Do you know an Annie?"

Jennette shook her head and replied, "Possibly a servant."

Soft moans echoed up through the floorboards. Moisture started to pool between Jennette's legs with the image of what they must be doing.

"God, your tits are huge," the man said. The sound of suckling floated up from the downstairs.

"Oh, Robert."

"The only Robert I know at the party was Lord Aston," Matthew whispered with a chuckle. He brought his hand up and rubbed her taut nipple.

Jennette slapped his arm. "Shh, they'll hear us."

"Oh, Robert!"

"Take me in your mouth, Annie."

Jennette frowned slightly, wondering exactly what Annie was putting in her mouth. She glanced back at Matthew to see his eyes widen. Whatever they were doing, it had obviously excited him.

"Damn," Matthew whispered.

"What are they doing now?"

Matthew closed his gray eyes and clenched his fists. "She was taking him in her mouth—"

"Him?"

He ground her bottom against his hard shaft. "His cock."

"In her mouth?"

The groaning and moaning from the room below grew in volume. "Yes," Robert shouted enthusiastically. "I want to do that to you."

"Yes," Matthew replied with a groan. "And now he wants to return the pleasure."

"I thought he'd already suckled her nipples."

"Not there, Jennette." He skimmed his hand up her thighs until he found her wetness.

"There . . . no."

"Oh yes."

"Have you done that before?" She couldn't believe she'd just asked him that question.

"Many times."

"Oh."

The sounds of Annie's moaning increased. "Oh Robert, yes. Please now . . ."

"On all fours, Annie. I want to take you like an animal."

Jennette squeezed her legs tighter in an attempt to ease the tingling. Hearing the bedstead creaking and knowing what they were doing was driving her mad. Matthew's finger split her folds apart. He rubbed her nub, driving her insane with longing.

"Please, stop," she whispered.

"Not until I feel you shaking with desire. Until you're so ready for me, you make as much noise as they do."

"Robert, harder, harder," Annie's voice squealed. "I'm coming."

"Now, Annie," Robert shouted and then groaned loudly. "God, you're wonderful."

"Oh, Robert, don't stop yet, I'm coming again," Annie moaned in pleasure.

Jennette shook with desire. She wanted that release but held back knowing she couldn't make a sound while they were still below. "Stop, Matthew."

"Never," he whispered in her ear before he nipped at her shoulder. "God, I want you, Jennette. I want you just like this, you on my lap, riding me."

"Yes," she moaned softly.

"Soon."

Already, she could hear the sounds of them moving downstairs.

"Don't you want to do this again?" Annie's muffled plea echoed upward.

"Not today, darling. Too many people about with that damned party of my wife's. Tomorrow."

"Leave," Matthew pleaded to the thin floorboards.

He kissed the back of her neck as he unbuttoned the front of her dress. Thankfully, she'd worn her front-lacing stays today. He made short work of them and quickly reached under her shift for her breast. Drawing his thumb across her stiff nipple sent shivering desire to her womb.

A small moan erupted from her as he squeezed her breast while his other hand still rubbed her clitoris.

"Shh," he whispered. "They should be leaving soon."

"I can't take much more of this."

"You must. I want to take you in my mouth, taste you."

"Oh God," she said softly. The image of Matthew's mouth between her folds sent even more wetness between her legs.

Finally, the front door banged shut and she realized the couple below had left. "I think they have departed."

Matthew kissed up the side of her neck. "Hmm, I think you're right."

He lifted her from his lap and laid her on the small bed. As he removed her dress and undergarments, she shivered in the cold room.

"I want to see you this time," she said brazenly.

Matthew smiled down at her. "As you wish."

He rose off the bed and proceeded to remove his riding clothes. Each layer that fell to the floor made her gasp anew. While she'd seen his chest two nights ago, she'd never viewed his entire body. Attempting to scrutinize him like the artist didn't work. When he pulled his breeches and undergarments off, her eyes widened with passion.

"Touch me, Jennette."

She rose up onto her knees and skimmed her fingertips from the base of him to the tip. Hearing his groan, she assumed she was doing this right. Remembering what he'd said about taking it in her mouth, she brought her lips to the head of his penis. She swirled her tongue around, tasting the salty flavor of him.

"God, Jennette."

Slowly, her mouth covered him. Imitating the movements of two nights ago, she slid him in and out of her mouth. He reached down and grabbed her other hand, bringing it to the sac between his legs.

"Gently," he moaned.

With a light touch, she caressed him there until she felt him tighten.

"Enough," he rasped.

He moved over her, kissing her roughly as if unable to control the passion driving him. She returned his kisses with just as much force, craving his touch, his lips, the scent of him. Nothing else mattered when he kissed her. The world around them fell away until it was only the two of them. No scandals, no accidents, and no guilt.

He moved to her nipples. Suckling one then the other until she thought she might explode from the sensation. His mouth skimmed down her stomach, until he reached the curly hair between her legs. She watched as he opened her to him. His eyes darkened with desire and then his mouth moved on her.

She closed her eyes as pleasure radiated through her body, spiraling upward out of control. "Matthew," she moaned as his tongue danced through her folds.

Higher her desire flew until she reached the top.

Quivering, she called out his name as she shook with pleasure. This was where she wanted to be forever with him.

"Come here," he said dragging her up to him. He moved to a sitting position and placed her in front of him. Slowly, he drew her down onto his shaft.

Matthew clenched his muscles as her wetness closed around him. He'd never been with a woman who excited him as she did. And after having her, he never wanted another. Once she'd fully enveloped him, he lifted her hips slowly until he heard her moan again.

He wanted to make this wonderful for her to make up for their first time. "Are you still sore?"

"Only a little," she replied in a breathy tone.

"Just like that, Jennette."

Slowly, she caught the rhythm and moved over him, sliding him deeper into an abyss of pleasure like none he'd ever experienced. Feeling her tighten against him and hearing her moans, he clasped her hips and took over. Just as she reached her climax, he released the tight grip he'd had on his control. He brought her down on him one last time as she clenched against his erection. Spilling himself into her, he groaned with the most incredible pleasure.

As they moved back to lie on the bed, the sound of the attic door locking echoed through the room.

Chapter 17

"What was that?" Jennette remained motionless on the bed, afraid to make any noise.

He blew out a breath. "I believe we've been locked in."

She sat up, pulling the old coverlet over her nudity. "We're what?"

"Give me a moment and I'll go check."

He pushed off the bed and dragged his breeches over his legs. After he reached the bottom step, she heard him turn the knob and then swear. He walked back up, shaking his head.

"Someone locked us in."

"Who would do such a thing?"

He sat back on the bed and tucked a lock of her hair behind her ear. "Hmm, Robert, Annie, Lady Aston—"

"You?" she asked bitterly.

"It wasn't me. If I couldn't compromise you last night, do you honestly believe I would today?"

She shrugged lightly. "I really don't know any more."

"I did not even know you were here until I walked inside," he replied, pacing the room.

"Why would Lady Aston do this?"

"She might have believed you were the one having an affair with her husband. Or perhaps she might have discovered we were here and thought to trap you with me, thus ruining you."

She covered her face with her hands. "Of course she did. The woman wanted to marry Banning but my mother intervened and Lady Aston ended up wedded to Aston. It's not me she's trying to punish but my mother."

Tears slid down her cheeks. The idea of being forced into either a scandal or marriage only made her angry. This was her life. Why couldn't people just leave her be?

Strong arms brought her against a hard chest. Without thought, she wrapped her arms around the man who could end up as her husband. But she couldn't let that happen. She had ruined his life once; she would never do it again.

If only things were different. She wanted to be the one to help him through the mess his father left him. Her money would allow him to get his estate in order and keep his tenants from being evicted in the cold winter. But mostly, she could build a life with him. At some point, he might even fall in love with her.

She stilled with the thought of loving him. Did she love him? An attraction to him was one thing but love was something completely different. Yet, having his arms around her felt right.

"It will be all right, Jennette," he murmured softly.

Her family couldn't afford another scandal. She'd made a promise to her father not to bring any scandal to their name and now she'd failed him twice. There had to be a way out of this mess without creating a disaster for him and her family.

"I don't think it will be," she replied, brushing a tear from her cheek.

"Yes, it will."

"No, Lady Aston will find us here together. She shall take great joy in telling my mother and then if Banning doesn't call you out, he will force us to marry. The gossips will love this. First the accident and now I'm found in your arms."

He caressed her hair. "Of all people, your brother certainly can't talk about scandal. His wife created enough shame by compromising herself in front of a large group of people."

Jennette nodded. "Which is why I hate this so much."

His hand stopped its gentle movements. "Is it?"

She moved away from him and looked him in the eye. "What do you mean?"

"Is it really the scandal that is bothering you or the idea of marrying me that you hate?"

"What?"

"You didn't wish to marry me before so I can only assume you would not want to marry me now." He walked to the windows and looked down.

"I wouldn't want to bring more dishonor upon your name, Matthew. Marrying me is only going to make things worse." For both of them. Once she married him, her money was legally his. He could do anything he wished with it, including gambling it all away.

"I suppose you are correct."

"Is there any way we can get out of here before someone comes?"

He turned and stared at her. His gray eyes burned through her, seeing into her soul.

"No," he said. "There are no trees close enough to climb and the fall could kill us. It appears you're stuck with me."

She tried to suppress the leap her heart made with his words. If there was no other way out of this mess then she would have no choice but to marry him. Her conscience might allow that to pass, but the logical part of her mind knew better. He was a gambler, just like his brother and father. Marrying him would be a dreadful mistake she might regret for the rest of her life.

"I suppose I am." She looked around the barren room. "How long do you think it will take someone to find us?"

"If it is Lady Aston, my guess is she would like us to be here for quite a while so she can gloat that we must have been doing something scandalous."

Which, of course, they had. Jennette stood, covered herself with the blanket, and walked toward Matthew. He stood by the window, still staring at her.

"I'm so sorry, Matthew." She reached up and combed his hair off his forehead. "It seems every time we are together I create a disaster for you."

His lips tilted up slightly. "Not all the time."

"When haven't I?"

He pulled her close and nipped her shoulder. "We seem to be all right when we're in bed together."

A thrill of excitement raced down her spine. "Oh?"

His lips moved up her neck to the sensitive lobe of her ear. "We definitely seem to manage just fine there."

Her head rolled back allowing him more access to her neck. "I think you're right."

"Always," he said, then picked her up and brought her to the bed.

Matthew rolled off Jennette and brought her to his chest. The silky texture of her raven hair tickled his shoulder. Hearing her labored breathing only made him smile. She was such a passionate woman. And yet, so fearful of scandal. He wanted to know everything about her.

"What do you want most out of life, Jennette?"

She skimmed her fingernails down to his stomach. "My parents adored each other. And now I see Avis and Banning so obviously in love it . . ."

"Makes you envious?" he whispered.

"Yes," she admitted softly. "I want a husband who will love me, remain faithful to me, and give me children. Lots of children."

He smiled thinking of her cradling their child. "I thought you wanted to be an artist."

"I already am an artist," she retorted softly.

"Touché."

She laughed. "Not that I wouldn't mind having my paintings on exhibit at the British Museum or any other museum. Any place other than just my friends' and family's homes."

Matthew thought back to that picture he'd noticed at Lady Elizabeth's home . . . "JMT". "Did you paint the landscape in Lady Elizabeth's hall?"

"Perhaps . . ."

"That painting was so beautiful it stopped me. I was compelled to look at it."

She glanced away with a slight smile. "Thank you, Matthew."

"It wouldn't surprise me a bit if your work did end up on display there."

Her hand stopped moving, then she glanced up at him. "All right, we talked about me. What do you want?"

Matthew sighed. "I don't want to feel like a failure. I want my lands secure and my tenants happy."

"You are not a failure. Your father caused this problem. By trying to fix it, you will be a success."

"Not without my name."

She stiffened.

Damn. Just as they were starting to learn more about each other he had to bring up their past. "I'm sorry, I should not have said that to you," he murmured against her hair.

"Yes, you should have because it's the truth." She moved away from him but put her head on her hand and looked at him. "I could never take back what happened . . . but if I could . . ."

"I know."

She licked her lips and then bit down on the lower one. "What do you think John would say if he saw us like this?"

He couldn't tell her that he believed John had already suspected their attraction. "I think he might be happy."

"Why?"

"He asked me to protect you, Jennette. I almost wonder if he knew what might happen between us."

"He could not have known," she said roughly.

Damn, he was an idiot. He knew how much she loved John. She must feel as if she betrayed John by being with him. "I'm sorry. I can only imagine how hard this must have been on you. You loved him so much."

She looked away from him as her cheeks turned rosy. He was such a fool. Did he actually believe she might love *him*? Even after five years, it was obvious that she still loved John. Was she just using him as a substitute for John?

And then there was Ancroft.

At least he could question her about him. "What does Ancroft mean to you?" he whispered.

Closing her eyes, she said, "I'm sorry. I never should have let you believe what I did. Nicholas and I are as much like brother and sister as Banning and I. Nicholas's father was not a very agreeable man so Nicholas spent holidays and most summers with us. He took great pleasure in teasing me over everything, again, much like Banning. And yet, I've always been able to talk with him in a way I can't with my brother."

Matthew had no idea what to say to her. His jealousy of Ancroft now seemed petty and immature. And yet, he was curious why she hadn't told him the truth at the beginning.

"Why didn't you tell me this when I asked you the first time?"

She chuckled. "You were so furious when you found us out on the terrace."

"You were wearing his jacket and he had his arm

around you!" They had looked like lovers, not friends.

"And you looked as if you wanted to tear him apart."

"I did," he admitted.

"Why?"

He couldn't tell her how jealous he'd felt that night. He had no right to be resentful of their relationship. Even at this point, he wondered if he had any rights where she was concerned.

"I know of Ancroft's reputation. I didn't want to see you hurt again," he finally replied.

"Oh," she said in a flat tone.

Had she wanted him to admit how he actually felt? She couldn't possibly care when she obviously still loved John.

After pushing the covers off his torso, he sat up and looked down at the clothes strewn across the floor. "We should dress before someone finds us."

Jennette nodded slowly.

As he dressed, the realization struck him that he didn't want this afternoon to end. He wanted to continue their conversations and learn even more about her. What did she fear the most from marrying him? What was it that he felt certain she was hiding from him?

He would love to talk to her in more detail about his estates and his plans for the future. What ideas would she have for refurbishing his homes? He wondered if she would have any issues with hiring servants. Most ladies learned early on the proper way to hire help.

She could refurbish his houses. They could have children who would learn how to manage the estates properly. There was a conservatory in his home in Essex that would be a perfect place for her to paint. They could be happy.

He glanced back at her as she hurriedly dressed. They would be happy . . . if she could ever love him as much as she'd loved John.

They waited in silence for another twenty-five minutes, but she dared not ask him of his thoughts. With every minute that passed, his face darkened until he looked as if he might just strangle whoever walked through the door. The sound of horses neighing forced her to her feet. She raced to the window and looked down.

"Who is it?" he asked in a harsh tone.

"I cannot be certain." She tilted her head, attempting to get a better view of the person. "I think it's a man."

"A man?" He exhaled sharply. "Your brother?"

"I don't believe it's Banning."

"Then who?"

"I already told you I don't know. I can't get a good sight of the man." She turned away from the window and crossed her arms over her chest. "What difference does it make? We're caught."

"So we are."

Jennette pressed her lips together upon hearing the rough tone of his voice. He sounded very angry at the idea of marrying her.

Footsteps fell heavy on the wood floors. Doors opened and slammed shut on the lower level.

"Where the hell are they?" a man's voice sounded from the second floor hallway.

"Somerton?" Matthew murmured. He strode for the attic door and shook it. "Somerton, we're in here."

The door shook confirming its locked state. "Give me a minute to find the key," Somerton said as his footsteps faded away.

Matthew glanced back at her, his face dark with emotions she couldn't read. Finally, Somerton's footsteps grew louder.

She stared down the steps as the door creaked open. She prayed he was alone and hadn't brought her brother with him. The door opened fully, revealing the tall form of Viscount Somerton. With his shorter-than-normal hair and arrogant smile, he looked far more like a devil than her savior.

"Well, well, what naughty mess have I caught you both in?" Somerton asked with a chuckle. Looking up at her, he said, "Good God, the Selby family does make my life interesting."

"Is anyone with you?" Matthew demanded.

"No, but you must hurry. Lady Aston is all atwitter because she is certain that something horrific must have happened to Lady Jennette. I overheard her speaking with her maid but it won't be long before she brings this to the Dowager Lady Selby or Selby himself."

"Lady Aston," she said, shaking her head. She had been right all along.

Matthew glanced up at her and nodded. "Are you ready to leave?"

"Well, that all depends," Somerton said before Jennette could even answer.

"On what?" Matthew asked.

Somerton crossed his arms over his chest and

stared at them both with prying eyes. "Do you plan to marry each other?"

"Yes."

"No," Jennette replied at the same time as Matthew.

Matthew turned toward her, anger burning in his gray eyes. "Why not?"

Staring at his handsome face, she knew she had to tell him the truth. "Because I won't marry a gambler who will squander my inheritance at the gaming hells."

Matthew's face turned pale. "You think I'm a gambler?" he whispered.

"Very well, then," Somerton said. "She stays locked in here."

"What?" Matthew and Jennette exclaimed together.

"If Lady Aston did this, then she is going to expect someone to be up here. So," Somerton said, looking up at Jennette, "you will be here . . . alone."

"Why are you helping me?" Jennette asked. Somerton took his reputation as a serious scoundrel to heart. He never seemed the hero to her.

Somerton tilted his head and smirked at her. "As I said, you Selbys make my life interesting. If you marry this poor sod that will stop."

"Very well, in the continued interest of making your life exciting, I shall stay here," Jennette said, smiling at the rogue.

Matthew walked back up to her. "Are you certain?"

"Yes. It is for the best." If Somerton's plan worked, there would be no need for a forced wedding. Certainly, this was for the best. She pressed her lips together and hoped he wouldn't notice the tears stinging her eyes.

"Come along, Blackburn. We don't have much time."

He stared at her a moment longer. Their gaze held and she felt as if he could read her soul.

"Very well," he said tightly. He walked down the steps and stopped at the threshold. "But you should know that the only thing I've ever gambled on was you . . . and I lost."

She clenched her fists so hard her fingernails bit into the palms of her hands. She had done the right thing. Now he wouldn't be disgraced because of her again. He wouldn't be forced to marry a woman who wasn't good enough for him.

She walked to the window and watched as he and Somerton jumped on their horses and raced down the path away from the house. Tears trickled down her cheeks. Her heart ached with the pain of letting him go. She knew it was the right thing to do but the ache in her heart hurt so dreadfully.

But she knew she couldn't have him. He deserved a far better person than her. Someone with no past.

She would only ever be his lover, never his wife.

Chapter 18

"I'm starting to wonder about you, Blackburn." Somerton slowed his horse as they neared the main house.

"Oh?"

"You know as well as I that you just passed up the best chance of compromising her. And yet, you did nothing when I said she must stay in that house alone." Somerton smiled in a knowing way at him.

Matthew glared over at him as they continued their slow canter toward the stables. "Being caught kissing a lady in the greenhouse is one thing. It is quite another to be discovered having seduced the lady in a deserted dowager house."

Somerton appeared to consider his words. "I suppose you are correct. A kiss Selby might excuse. Not what you actually did back there."

"You are making an assumption there."

Somerton smirked. "Of course it was just an assumption. I'm quite certain you two could keep your hands off each other," he added sarcastically.

"There was absolutely no kissing or touching, right?"

There was no point in replying when everything he said would be a lie. Every time they kissed, it was amazing. And led to far more incredible things.

"It's all for the best, Blackburn."

"Why is that?" Matthew jumped down and grabbed the reins.

"Have you ever thought that maybe Jennette isn't ready yet?" Somerton jumped off his horse, grabbed the reins, and started walking toward the stables.

"Ready for what?"

Somerton stopped and looked back at him. "Marriage."

Matthew laughed. "She is five and twenty. Well past the age most women marry. She'd planned to marry John five years ago."

Somerton shook his head. "She believes you are like your father and brother. Besides that mess, is she in love with *you*?"

"Good God, man. Why is that important?" And yet, as soon as the words left his mouth he regretted them. He remembered her statement about wanting a husband who loved her and would be faithful to her.

"It is important," Somerton whispered harshly. "Very important to her."

Matthew frowned as he glanced over at the faraway look in Somerton's eyes. "Never knew you were such a romantic, Somerton."

His blue eyes darkened. "I am not. But Jennette is and you should appreciate that."

Was Somerton in love with her too? "I will remember your words."

Somerton shook his head as he led his horse to the stable boy. "Why don't you court her? Let her come to know you better. She will see that you're not a gambler and wastrel."

"I don't have time for writing her love notes and sending her flowers. I have to be married before the year is out."

"What are your plans once we return to town?"

"I don't have an idea." Somehow, Matthew had to break through the barriers that held her bound.

Matthew handed the reins to the stable boy and turned to walk in the house. They had already decided he must return with Somerton and claim they'd been riding for most of the afternoon. Somerton grabbed his elbow and led him toward the path away from the house.

"Have you ever considered just asking her if she would marry you?"

"Why are you so concerned about my relationship with Jennette?"

"I can only assume that means no," Somerton replied with a shake of his head.

Matthew clenched his jaw until his teeth ached. "You are the one who just said she needed more time."

"She *might* need more time. If you did seduce her, which by the way I would be surprised if you hadn't, you should propose to her." Somerton's normal smirking smile was gone, replaced with a dark scowl.

"When did you become the upright member of the *ton*, espousing the values of the day? Last I'd heard, you were the one with the reputation of a rake. How many ladies have you seduced and then left without a by-your-leave?"

"I content myself with widows and whores who don't want or care about marriage."

Matthew stared at Somerton, noticing the slight blush that crossed his cheeks.

"Ask her to marry you," Somerton demanded.

"And if she refuses my offer?"

"Then you better hope she is with child so she has no choice."

Matthew frowned. He'd been foolish not to take any precautions with her. She could easily be with child—his child. And the thought sent a rush of warmth to his heart. Until he remembered her tendency toward stubbornness.

"I'm not entirely certain that would change her mind regarding marriage."

Somerton chuckled softly. "Selby loves his sister, but he would never allow her to ride out a scandal when there is a child involved."

"She doesn't need his consent to marry. Nor does she need his approval to ride out a scandal. She has enough money to do as she pleases."

"You're right, of course," Somerton commented. "But she cares deeply for her family's name."

Matthew stared at him. Did Somerton know more than he pretended? Matthew knew the importance of her family name but how did Somerton? Could he also have stumbled upon their secret somehow?

"Then what am I to do?" he whispered and halted his stride.

"Offer for her."

Offer for her. Yet, the idea of her refusing him brought back too many memories of rejection by his own parents. He was the second son. As long as David had remained healthy, there had been no reason to pay any attention to him. Matthew gave himself a mental shake. None of that mattered anymore.

"I shall take your words under consideration," Matthew replied.

"Do more than that—propose to her."

"Let's get inside and make sure we greet Lady Aston in our riding clothes," Matthew said, eager to change the subject. At this point, his life was spiraling out of control.

They walked around to the front of the house and the butler opened the door to allow them entrance.

"Good afternoon, my lords."

"Good afternoon, Hanover," they both said in overly loud voices.

Hearing the sound of feminine voices coming from the front salon, they walked deliberately toward the noise. Matthew tried to distinguish the voices until he made out Lady Aston's overbearing tone.

"She has been gone all day. I believe a few of us should ride out to make certain she is all right. Even worse, Lord Blackburn has gone missing, too."

The volume of chatter increased again. Matthew hurried his stride until he reached the salon.

"Did someone call my name?" he asked, standing at the threshold with Somerton by his side.

"Lord Blackburn?" Lady Aston's face blanched. "No one had seen you in several hours, we thought . . ."

"Lord Somerton and I were riding."

"Oh," she whispered. A slow blush crept across her cheeks.

"Did I hear you say something about Lady Jennette gone missing?" Somerton asked.

"Um, yes."

"Then we need to search for her," Matthew said. "She might have taken a fall." He looked over at Somerton. "Find Selby."

Lady Aston spoke up. "He and Lady Selby rode into town for a few items."

Damn. Having Selby with them would have been for the best. He glanced over at Lady Aston as his hands fisted tight. He had no doubt that she had planned the scheme and most likely locked them both in the room.

Lady Aston looked down at her hands. "Perhaps we should search the dowager house first. I asked her to look over the place and make recommendations on refurbishing it."

"Of course," Somerton replied with a twitch to his lips. "Will you be joining us?"

Lady Aston straightened in her seat. "I shall at that. I will change into my riding habit and join you at the stables."

"We will be eagerly awaiting your presence," Matthew said.

As the minutes ticked by, Jennette wondered when someone would arrive to set her free. The long afternoon rays of the sun were shortening quickly. Soon it would be dark and the thought of staying here all night made her tremble. With no fireplace to warm the room and no candles to light it, the hours until dawn would seem endless.

She should have insisted that Matthew take her with him. They could have contrived some story that people would believe. Standing, she rubbed her behind. The hard-wood chair she'd been sitting in for the past hour had made her sore. She glanced out the window and saw a group of riders heading toward the dowager house.

"Thank God!"

To make the scene even more realistic, she opened the window and yelled out, "Help! I'm locked in the attic!"

She watched as Matthew and Somerton reined in their horses and pointed to her position at the window. Lady Aston looked up and her mouth gaped.

"We're coming, Lady Jennette," Somerton shouted in return.

Listening closely, she heard the group dismount and enter the first floor. She couldn't leave anything to chance. This scene had to be believed.

"I'm up in the attic," she yelled again from the door.

"Upstairs," she heard Matthew say.

"I believe there is a key in the bedroom," Lady Aston said.

Of course, the bitch knew the exact location of the key. Finally, the lock clicked and the door rattled open. Matthew, Somerton, Lady Aston, and another woman crowded into the room. Jennette backed up the stairs, as Lady Aston glared at her.

"Who is here with you?" she demanded.

"What do you mean? There is no one here. I came up here to sketch the attic rooms and I heard someone lock the door. I banged on the door and then looked out the window but I have no idea who it might have been." Jennette walked up the steps into the attic room to retrieve her pad and lead.

Lady Aston followed her. With eyes like a hawk, she scanned the room, looked under the bed and even in the small linen-press. Thankfully, Jennette had aired out the room of the musky scent of their lovemaking and remade the bed.

"What is she doing?" Jennette asked in an innocent tone. "She is the one who asked me to come here."

"Exactly," Matthew replied. "So it begs the question, why would she assume a man would be here with you?"

Lady Aston shot him a quelling glare. "I rode by earlier and there were two horses out in front."

"Yes, my lady." Jennette hoped her cheeks appeared red as if in embarrassment. "Before the door locked on me, I was up here and another couple went to one of the bedrooms downstairs and . . . well . . . I don't believe they knew I was up here."

Lady Aston pursed her lips. "And exactly who was down there?"

"I cannot say for certain." Jennette stared at the ground, praying she portrayed the appropriate amount of innocence.

"I think you know who was here." Lady Aston stood in front of her and glared. "I believe you are hiding something."

"Lady Jennette, perhaps if you know who was here, you should tell her," Matthew said softly.

Jennette stared at Matthew and Somerton and shook her head slowly.

"Yes, tell me," Lady Aston demanded. She folded her arms over her chest waiting for an answer.

"The woman called him Robert," Jennette said with an exaggerated sigh.

Lady Aston's face paled. "Robert?"

"Yes, ma'am," she whispered.

"Did you hear the woman's name?"

Jennette nodded but hated to give out the poor servant's name. She doubted the young girl knew just how much trouble she could get into when she let Lord Aston into her bed.

"Tell me her name, Lady Jennette," Lady Aston demanded in an overly loud tone.

"Annie," she replied.

"What were they doing down there?"

"Oh, ma'am. I cannot answer for certain," Jennette said, looking away from the probing stare of Lady Aston.

"Try," Lady Aston insisted.

"It sounded as if they were . . ."

"What?"

"Having sexual congress."

"I'll kill him," Lady Aston whispered. She walked toward the window and muttered, "How did I miss them?"

"Perhaps one of them locked Lady Jennette in the room," Somerton offered.

Lady Aston's cheeks regained their color. "Of course. Probably that little strumpet, Annie. She will be off this estate by nightfall."

"Lady Aston, what if I was wrong?" Jennette said. "Their voices were muffled and—"

"Do not try to save that whore's job."

"I believe we should depart before it gets dark," Matthew said. "We have dinner to prepare for."

"Yes, I need a bath after being in this dirty house all day," Jennette commented in an attempt to be done with this mess.

"Indeed," Lady Aston replied. She appeared very distracted after the announcement of her husband's affair with a servant.

Jennette still felt dreadful for the girl, Annie. Perhaps she could find her a job. Victoria was always looking for someone to help with the orphans.

"Let's be off," Matthew said.

Lady Aston and her friend huffed off down the stairs. Jennette mouthed a thank-you to both Matthew and Somerton. If not for Somerton's plan, she would be completely and irrevocably compromised. And while a part of her loved the idea, she knew it was wrong and not to be considered again.

As much as she hated the thought, she had to renew her plan to find Matthew a wife.

Time was running out.

Jennette walked down to dinner feeling miserable. She reviewed her list of potential brides for Matthew and found them all lacking. Each of the women would love the title Countess Blackburn, but none of them had the resourcefulness to know how to help him with his estates. Assuming any of their fathers would agree to a match, which at this point was a major flaw in the plan.

She frowned as she walked through the hallway. How could a woman with no experience deal with the everyday workings of multiple estates?

She slipped into the salon unnoticed and sat in a blue leather Hepplewhite chair. Matthew sat alone in a seat across the room. Others in the room still ignored him after Mrs. Marston's outburst. Jennette longed to go to him, sit next to him, and talk to him more about his estates. But after her decision today, it made more sense to attempt to pay him no heed.

As if there were any possibility of that happening.

Even from this distance, his gaze burned her, scorched her, baring her soul for him to see. She squirmed in her seat under his constant stare. Moist heat slid through her folds as she crossed her legs.

"My, my, what a look on your face."

Jennette blinked and looked up to see Somerton smiling down at her. He dropped to the chair beside her.

"Whatever are you talking about, Somerton?"

Somerton chuckled softly. "It came to my attention today that you believe something about someone that isn't quite the truth."

"Oh? And who might that be?"

"I think you know to whom I am referring." He leaned in closer to her and whispered, "I know that was you watching us as we departed Norton's a few nights ago."

Jennette breathed in deeply. "It could not possibly have been me. I would never go near a gaming hell."

"And neither would the man with me. Blackburn isn't a gambler."

"And let me guess, neither are you?"

Jennette slid her glance to the man next to her. Somerton's lips twitched as he sought a rejoinder.

"Actually, I am. I'm quite good at it, too, which is why I should know a gambler when I see one. And Blackburn isn't one. He was assisting me that night."

"Why are you so concerned with what I think about Blackburn?" she whispered back to him.

"Because unlike me, he is a good man." Somerton rose and walked away before she could question him further.

Jennette glanced over at Matthew. Could she have been wrong about him? The fact remained that his father and brother had both been consummate gamblers. Most men had the fortitude to resist the temptations of a wager unless for sport, but Matthew's relatives couldn't seem to help themselves. Could he?

"Good evening, Lady Jennette."

Jennette glanced up to see Baron Huntley standing over her. What did he want? "Good evening, Huntley."

"Might I sit with you?" He inclined his head toward the empty seat next to her.

"Very well," she answered when she preferred that he disappear.

"I heard about your dreadful experience at the dowager house this afternoon."

Oh God, the gossip had started already.

"Rumor has it that Aston and a scullery maid were swiving right under your feet," he leaned in and whispered. "That must have been dreadful."

"Very," she replied.

"Or was it?" he questioned in a low, seductive tone. "Did your mind wonder exactly what they were doing?"

"It was quite obvious what they were doing, Huntley. And I believe this conversation is completely inappropriate," she said, slapping her fan on her palm.

"I just wanted to let you know that I'd be more than a willing teacher."

Dear Lord, of all the men in the *ton* to make such a proposal, Huntley was the last man she'd choose. "Huntley, your proposition is most unwelcome."

"That didn't stop your sister-in-law," he said with a leer.

Some people just wouldn't let Avis's debacle rest. "Well, I am not Avis."

"True, but you must be curious about what happens between a man and a woman."

"Actually, I am not. I am a spinster and prefer to stay that way." How blunt did she have to be?

Huntley looked away but not before she noticed the frustration lining his face. His sudden, fervent attention seemed odd to her. He'd never appeared interested in her in any manner. She wondered if his newfound interest meant he was having financial difficulties. Her fortune never seemed to bring out the best in men.

"Very well, then, Lady Jennette. But remember, if your curiosity ever gets the better of you, know that I'm here for you."

"I shall indeed." She glanced around, thankful that no one save Matthew took any notice of Huntley's conversation. Luckily, Matthew sat too far away to hear any of their talk.

"Huntley?" Banning took the seat Huntley had just vacated.

She fired him a furious glance. "Never."

"Good thing. So I heard that Somerton and Blackburn saved you from another escapade today." Banning leaned back in his chair until it almost tilted.

"It was nothing," she said, her gaze returning to Matthew's place across the room.

"I heard that also." Banning paused for a moment. "And yet, I can't help thinking there is far more to this adventure than anyone is saying."

"And as usual, you are attempting to make this little incident into something it's not."

Banning clenched his jaw. "When either of those scoundrels is involved, something bad is bound to happen. And when both are involved there is trouble."

Jennette laughed softly. "I thought you and Somerton had become friends."

"Trust me, Somerton has no friends. And Blackburn deserves none, especially you."

"I am not his friend." *Just his lover . . . and never anything more.*

"But it doesn't explain why you are continually gazing at him," Banning said.

"I am not," she complained, and instantly turned her head toward her brother.

"You just were until I brought it to your attention." He brought his chair upright. "Jen—"

"Please don't try to tell me what a horrible man he is, Banning."

"I wasn't about to. I wanted you to know that the only reason he would want you is for your money."

"I know," she muttered softly. Even if he wasn't a gambler, without her fortune he would never pursue her.

She closed her eyes against the shot of pain that pierced her heart.

Chapter 19

After another excruciating dinner, Jennette walked to the salon for cards with the other women. The men were enjoying their brandies and speaking of politics while the women congregated for gossip.

"Lady Jennette, I have a note for you."

Jennette turned to the maid who had her hand outstretched. She retrieved the note and thanked the maid. Opening the missive, she frowned.

It is imperative that you meet me in Aston's study at 10.

No one had signed the note, but the handwriting didn't appear to be Matthew's or anyone else she knew. The slanted, flowing handwriting looked feminine. Lady Aston, perhaps. The lady had gone quite pale when she discovered her husband's infidelity. Maybe she wanted to ask her more questions.

She walked into the salon and scanned the room. Lady Aston was indeed missing and it was almost ten now. With a shrug, she strolled down the hall to the study. Two orange trees occupied the space by the windows and filled the smaller room with a sweet scent. She pulled an orange blossom off a tree and inhaled the delicious aroma.

"You came."

Jennette whirled around at the sound of Huntley's voice. "What are you doing here?"

He rolled his eyes. "I sent you that note."

"Oh. Then what is so important that you had to speak with me now?"

"Lady Jennette, after hearing what happened to you today, I haven't been able to get the image of you off my mind." He took a step closer. "All alone in that room, hearing Aston and that maid rutting like animals. I can only imagine what it must have been like to listen to them."

The man was a complete and utter pig. "What does that have to do with me?"

He stepped even closer. She had no place to go but into the orange tree.

"Did hearing them excite you?"

Jennette glanced around trying to find a way around him. But he now stood directly in front of her. With a plant and windows behind her, there appeared to be no place to go.

"Did you get damp thinking about what they were doing? Aston filling that servant with his hard cock. Did you touch yourself? Bring your finger deep inside you? Or rub that little nub of yours? Did you come?"

"Don't be vulgar, Huntley."

He inched closer until his chest was all but against her. "I want to know how you taste. My cock wants to be deep inside you, riding you, breaking through that virginal barrier."

Her heart pounded. A bead of sweat rolled down her back. Knowing she couldn't wait any longer, she raced past him. She had caught him off guard. With only two steps left to the door, he yanked her arm back toward him.

"You are going nowhere." His hot breath smelled of old brandy and stale cigars.

"Don't do this, Huntley," she pleaded.

"I have no choice. I want something and the only way to get it is by fucking you."

"Money," she panted. "I shall pay you. Whatever you want."

His wet lips touched her neck. "I don't want your money."

If he didn't want her money, what could he possibly want from her? Most men desired her fortune.

"I'm not an innocent," she admitted, hoping that would stop him.

"Even better. No virginal tears, just pleasure for both of us."

He clasped her hands and brought them behind her back. His lips approached hers and fear terrorized her. She couldn't let him do this to her. As she opened her mouth to scream, his mouth battered her lips. His tongue chafed at hers. She struggled against his grip but that only seemed to excite him more.

Huntley ground her hips against his erection. Feeling his hardness brought on full panic. She had to get herself under control. There had to be a way out of this situation. Remembering what Banning had taught her, she brought her knee up between his legs as hard as she could.

Freedom came in an instant.

"You bitch," he screamed and fell to the floor.

The door opened and Jennette looked over to see Matthew, Somerton, and, oh God, Banning.

"What the bloody hell is going on here?" Banning said.

Somerton quickly shut the door and backed himself against it.

"Jennette," Matthew whispered.

"Matthew." She ran to him, desperate to be in the warm comfort of his strong arms.

He brought her against his hard chest. She barely heard the pounding of his heart in her ear over the loud groans of Huntley.

"Did he . . . ?"

"No," she answered into his jacket.

"Well done, Lady Jennette. Looks like you took care of the cur," Somerton commented.

Jennette glanced back to see Banning drag Huntley to his feet.

"What the hell did you do to my sister?" he shouted.

"Selby, keep your voice down or you'll have the entire party at the door," Somerton said harshly.

Her brother pushed Huntley against the wall, keeping a choking hold over him.

"I had to," Huntley whimpered.

"Did you think I would accept a man like you for my sister's husband?"

As she listened to the interrogation, Matthew caressed her hair, comforting her, making her feel safer than she ever had. But the burning question needed an answer. She turned away from Matthew's comfort and faced Huntley.

"Why did you attempt to do this, Huntley?" she demanded. "I deserve an answer."

Huntley glanced away from her until Banning pried his chin forward to look her in the eye.

Matthew had had enough of this foolishness. He strode toward Huntley, shoved Selby away, and grabbed Huntley's cravat, tightening it until his eyes bulged.

"Answer the lady's question."

"V—Vanessa," he mumbled so quietly only Matthew heard him.

"What did you say?" Matthew's world spun around him.

"Vanessa Fulbright."

Matthew released his grip on Huntley's cravat. "Get him out of here, Somerton."

Somerton only smirked. "My pleasure."

"Wait," Selby started. "He needs to give me the name of his second."

"No," Jennette said coldly. "No one is going to duel over me."

Selby turned toward his sister until they were both glaring at each other with their arms folded over their chests. If there was any humor in this situation, it would have been the comical, identical expressions of Selby and Jennette. Only there was nothing remotely humorous here.

Matthew dropped to the nearest chair as brother and sister battled it out. If anyone should call Huntley out, it was he. But he had no right to do so because he hadn't even proposed to her.

"Jen, your honor has been dealt a blow. It is my job as your brother to see that honor restored."

"Seems to me," Somerton commented from the doorway, "that she restored her own honor by unmanning him."

"Exactly," Jennette agreed.

Somerton tugged on Selby's arm. "Let this go. I really don't want to be your second twice in one year. I shall handle Huntley."

"Very well," Selby said. "Take care of him."

Somerton leveled Huntley a wild smile. "I haven't killed a man in such a long time," he drawled.

"No," Jennette said, looking horrified by his words.

"No," Selby agreed.

"And what do you say, Blackburn?" Somerton asked softly.

"He has no say in this matter," Selby answered, glaring at Matthew.

"Kill him, Somerton," Matthew replied, staring at Selby's icy blue eyes. "Just make certain it is a long, slow, and excruciatingly painful death."

"Matthew!" Jennette exclaimed. "No one is going to die over what happened here."

"Oh, very well," Somerton said with a sigh. He dragged Huntley toward the door, stopping in front of Jennette. "Anything you might want to say, you stupid fool?"

"I apologize from the bottom of my heart," Huntley mumbled to Jennette.

"Accepted," she said.

"Jennette, let's go," Selby said, walking to the door.

"No. I need to speak with Lord Blackburn about an important matter."

Selby shook his head. "Be quick."

"Alone, Ban."

"Never."

Somerton pulled Selby. "Leave them be, Selby. She's made her choice whether you like it or not."

Selby glared back at Matthew, then at Jennette. Before he could say another word, Somerton dragged him and Huntley out of the room. The door slammed behind them.

Matthew sat in the chair, staring into the dancing flames of the fire. He heard her approach but had no idea what to say to her. Everything that had happened tonight was his fault. He should have been clearer with Vanessa. Telling her he didn't love her would have hurt her, but she was strong and would have recovered. Instead, he had given her false impressions that he might come back to her when he knew that would never happen.

"Why are you so quiet?" she whispered.

"This was all my fault, Jennette."

She sat on the arm of his leather chair and played with his hair. "Why do you think that?"

"God, I want some brandy." He rose to his feet, more to get away from her than to find the brandy. He'd never felt so guilty in all his life. "Would you like some?"

"Yes, but what I really want is for you to sit down and talk to me."

"Brandy first." He poured two snifters and brought the drinks back to their seat. Then he moved to the sofa.

Instead of staying in her seat, she moved closer to him. "What are you about tonight, Matthew?"

He had known Jennette long enough to be certain she wouldn't cease her questions until he answered them. "This is all my fault, Jennette."

She frowned, two small lines indenting her forehead. Again, she reached over and gently caressed his hair. "How could this be your fault? Huntley did this, not you."

"He only did this because my former mistress either asked him or is holding something over his head." Matthew gulped his brandy down. The warming liquid did nothing to ease his frustrations.

"Why would she have done that?"

Matthew closed his eyes and leaned his head back against the soft velvet of the sofa. "She was in love with me. I knew that before I ended it with her but I thought . . ."

"Thought what?" she whispered.

"I thought if I gave her hope of my return that I wouldn't be breaking her heart."

Her soft hand moved to caress his face. "And people call you a rake and a scoundrel."

"Yes, that's me. The softhearted rake who can't break his mistress's heart."

"I think that's rather sweet."

"Not when it caused you to almost be raped." He moved his head closer to hers. "I can never forgive myself for that."

"You have nothing to absolve yourself of. This was Huntley's fault. He should have refused her." Jennette glanced away, biting down on her lower lip.

"What is wrong?" he asked softly.

"Nothing at all." She shrugged but he could tell she was avoiding the question.

"Jennette?"

"Perhaps I am not the best person to speak of forgiving oneself."

"Especially when it wasn't your fault."

She wiped a tear away. Unable to see her crying without comforting her, he pulled her against his chest.

"B—But what if it was my fault, Matthew?"

Her fault? How could she possibly think the accident that killed John was her fault? "I was there, Jennette."

"So was I."

"Your foot slipped in the wet grass," he said, holding her tighter. While he'd always known she felt guilt over John's death, never would he have imagined the depths of her remorse. She'd spent the last five years playing the part of the frivolous woman with no cares. A part he'd commanded her to play.

"Jennette, if anything, I should take more blame," he said softly.

"Why? You didn't have the sword in your hand. I—I did."

Matthew flexed his fingers and then pulled them into tight fists. "If I hadn't spoken to you that morning . . . If I hadn't ki—"

"No, it wouldn't have mattered. What happened was my fault entirely," she cried.

"Jennette—"

"*I* wasn't watching the field as you'd told me to," she said with a sob. "*I* should have kept my eyes on John and the field."

She pulled away, rose, and then started pacing. There was a wildness to her expression he'd never seen before. Her long black tresses had fallen out of her chignon and flowed down her back. She took a long draught of her brandy and refilled her glass.

"Jennette," he started softly to comfort her. "I saw you. I was there. You were watching the field and John."

"No, I wasn't. My gaze was elsewhere. I never should have thought to pick up a sword that day."

Matthew walked toward her and caught her shoulders in a loose grip. "I was there, too."

"Then *you* should have noticed where my attention landed that day." Tears streaked her cheeks.

Confused, he took a long breath and released it slowly. "I have no idea what you mean. What were you looking at?"

She stared up at him, her eyes as wet and blue as the ocean. "*You!* I was looking at you. Not John my betrothed, not the wet grass, or the field. *You!*"

Matthew watched as she raced from the room, tears still streaking down her cheeks. He was unable to process what she'd said, and his feet refused to move and follow her.

Had his words caused her wayward gaze? She had been looking at him. What did she mean by that? Had he made some movement that caught her eye? Had he coughed or cleared his throat?

Thinking back, he couldn't remember doing anything but watching them both. And feeling a stab of envy for the love they had for each other.

Or had they?

She couldn't have meant that she'd glanced back

at him because she fancied him. That thought made no sense. She and John had loved each other. The six-month betrothal that Jennette had insisted on wasn't that out of the ordinary. John had told him she needed the time to make the plans for the wedding of the Season.

He slowly sipped his brandy in thought.

Had she given John that reason as an excuse?

She might have delayed the wedding because of her insecurities about him. Perhaps she'd sensed what Matthew knew, that John had been unfaithful to her. The only reason Matthew had told her about his attraction was due to John's disregard for her. She deserved better than an unfaithful husband.

Unless she was unsure of her own feelings toward John.

She'd only been twenty at the time. While not terribly young for marriage, she might not have been as ready as she thought.

She was looking at you, his mind reminded him.

He shook his head. Jennette did not have feelings for him five years ago. The kiss he initiated broke off because she had pushed him away. He wasn't even certain she had feelings for him now, other than lustful ones. This situation seemed to be worsening. He had the perfect opportunity to propose to her tonight. Instead, she raced from the room in tears.

The door opened and banged against the wall. Selby stood in the threshold with a murderous rage in his eyes. "Is she gone?"

"Yes."

"Good. We shall have that talk now."

Right. The reason he, Selby, and Somerton were coming here in the first place. Selby wanted more information on what had happened with Jennette at the dowager's house.

"Have a seat. Have some brandy," Matthew said, pointing to the decanter in the corner.

Selby shut the door and then walked to the brandy. Holding it up, he said, "Looks like you've already had your share."

"Your sister helped." Damn, he shouldn't have said that.

Selby shook his head. "Of course she did."

"So you want to know what happened at the dowager's house," Matthew said before draining his snifter.

"No."

"Then why did you insist Somerton and I meet with you here?"

"Oh, I wanted to know that then." Selby gently placed his snifter on the table, in contrast to the anger etched upon his face. "Now, I want to know what happened in here."

"You were here, Selby."

"After I left."

"I talked to her about what happened and apologized for my part in it."

"Oh yes, Vanessa Fulbright. Your mistress, am I correct?"

Matthew folded his arms over his chest. "No. She is my former mistress. I ended things with her before I started my bride search."

"Obviously, you didn't end things well enough," Selby's voice grew louder.

"I realize that now," Matthew replied forcefully.

"And after you apologized, what happened?"

Matthew stood to his full height. And much to his pride, was at least an inch taller than Jennette's brother. "Nothing. She became upset when we started to discuss something that happened five years ago. Then she left."

"I will not allow a marriage between you two," Selby said softly.

"When at last I checked, I found your sister to be well above the age of majority. She doesn't need your consent." Unfortunately, Matthew knew she would want her brother's approval.

"I will go to court and get my grandmother's will overturned. Jennette will have nothing because I refuse to allow the man who killed my sister's betrothed to marry her."

Matthew clenched his fists. The money didn't matter to him any longer. The only thing that mattered was Jennette. Together they could solve their problems and face the gossips. Perhaps it would be for the best if Selby turned over the will. She already thought he was a gambler. By not bringing her fortune into the marriage, she would see he had no desire for the gaming hells.

And perhaps someday she might even learn to love him as much as he loved her. He strode to the door and then glared back at her brother.

"Do what you must, Selby."

Chapter 20

After arriving back in town last evening, Jennette had been on tenterhooks. Nervous energy filled her for no apparent reason. When the footman asked if she wanted the trunk left in her room for the voyage, she'd snapped at him. When the maid brought her tea and toast, and the tea was luke-warm, she had yelled at her.

She had never cared before if her tea wasn't piping hot. There had to be something to do that would ease the panicky sensation burning through her belly.

The entire carriage ride home, her thoughts were on Matthew. In her heart, she knew marrying him would only bring more scorn on him. The gossips were cruel to him before and they would assume he killed John to have her for himself.

And what would they say about her?

Perhaps they would think she had more in-volvement in the killing. People might say they planned this together to be rid of John. Society would ostracize her family. They would shun her mother, Banning, and Avis. Her family's name ruined.

"All because of me," she whispered aloud.

"What is all because of you, my dear?" her mother asked.

Jennette whirled around, stunned to see her mother standing at the threshold of her room. She'd never even heard the door open.

"Jennette, don't you think it is time to talk to me? Believe it or not, I was once your age and remember the trials of falling in love."

"I'm not in love," she exclaimed. Was she? Five years ago, she'd thought she loved John, only to have his best friend hold more appeal. Was she just a fickle woman who couldn't decide on a man?

"Of course you are," her mother said, waving her hand at her in dismissal of her objection. "I haven't seen you this preoccupied . . . ever."

"That is only because I'm leaving in a matter of days."

Her mother sat in the floral chair and shook her head. "You still have six days and no, you aren't leaving."

Jennette frowned. "What do you mean I'm not leaving? The trunk is over there," she said, pointing to the trunk in the corner.

"Why can't you just admit you love the man?"

It was too hard and far too painful. "Because it will all be for naught."

"Why? Has he found another woman to marry?" Her mother held her hands out for the warmth from the fire.

"Not that I am aware."

"Then why?" her mother pressed again. She sat back against the cushion and stared at Jennette.

Jennette walked across the room to be away from her mother's prying glances. "The gossips would never let it go."

Her mother laughed softly until Jennette turned back to her. "So you are willing to be miserable for the rest of your life because of the gossips?"

"It's not just me, Mother. Think about what those wagging tongues will say. My actions will affect your life, Banning, and Avis, too."

"Oh, so you believe by not marrying the man you obviously love you will protect poor old me. And Banning, and Avis, of course."

"Yes! Avis and Banning's courtship debacle is still running on the tongues of those miserable people. I cannot add another reason for them to talk about us."

"Jennette, sit down," her mother said in her strictest voice.

Feeling like a scolded little girl, she sat obediently in the chair next to her mother. She stared at her hands. Why did she ever pick up that sword? *To show him*, her mind reminded. To prove Matthew wrong. *To gain his attention*.

"My darling girl, I want an honest answer. Do you love him?"

Jennette tried to speak but the words stuck in her throat. She loved everything about him—the way his hair constantly fell into his face. The way his eyes crinkled when he smiled. The comfort and safety she felt in his arms when he held her. The fact that he would choose to marry a woman he didn't love just to keep his tenants in their homes.

She nodded.

"Then the only thing that matters is you and Blackburn finding happiness," her mother said softly.

"How can I be happy knowing I have made the rest of my family outcasts in the eyes of Society?"

Her mother gazed into the flames of the fireplace. "Do you think it was any different when I married your father?"

Jennette finally looked over at her mother's loving face. "What do you mean?"

"Your father was thirty-two years older than I. The gossips immediately assumed that he must have forced himself on me and that I was with child. Or the other rumor circulating involved my family using me as payment for some debt owed to the earl."

She reached over and clasped Jennette's hand. "No one even contemplated the idea that I was in love with him. There had to be a more sinister reason for marrying him."

"I'm sorry, Mother. You never told me this."

"There wasn't a need until now. If I had let the gossips guide my life, I would never have married your father. I wouldn't have known such a great love. And I wouldn't have had you and your brother."

"But . . ."

"Jennette, I have never asked this of you and I only do now because I think you have to admit it aloud." Her mother squeezed Jennette's hand tighter. "Did you feel like this with John?"

Jennette blinked quickly. She'd never told a soul how she really felt about John. With a deep breath, she whispered, "No. I thought I loved him when he proposed, so of course I agreed."

"Is that why you pressed him for a longer engagement?"

She nodded. "I needed the time to sort through my feelings for him."

Her mother laughed softly. "I would imagine having John's best friend with him most days didn't help the situation."

"No. Even then, I noticed Matthew. Oh Mother, what am I to do?"

"Even then you felt this way about him?"

"Not quite," Jennette replied flatly. "I definitely felt an attraction to him. But I didn't know him enough to be in love with him then."

Her mother smiled lovingly at her. "And now that you do know him?"

"I want to spend every minute with him. I want to help him restore his finances and his estates. I want to have children with him." Tears welled in her eyes. She'd never wanted anything more than this in her entire life.

"Does he love you in return?"

Jennette paused. She honestly didn't know the answer. He made her feel loved but he'd never spoken the actual words. Could he love her as much as she did him? If so, why hadn't he told her?

He'd told her how he felt five years ago. His words were imprinted in her mind forever.

"Jennette, I know this is wrong. You're John's betrothed but I must tell you how I feel. I am attracted to you in a way I should not be. Physically. And while I know you won't do anything to hurt John, I thought you should know why I can't be around you both any longer."

"Jennette?"

She blinked at the sound of her mother's voice. "I'm sorry?"

"I asked you if you believe Blackburn loves you in return."

"I don't know for certain."

"Don't you think you should find out before you plan out a life that might not happen?"

Jennette sighed softly. What if he didn't love her? She'd always said she wanted a marriage like her parents'—one based on mutual love for each other. She'd seen the loveless marriages of the *ton* and would prefer to remain a spinster than have that type of union. She also knew several women who had loved their husbands only to have them not return the emotion. They became extremely bitter, especially as their husbands turned to their mistresses for love.

"Jennette?"

"How would I find out if he loves me?"

Her mother smiled at her. "There is only one way. You have to admit to him how you feel. If he loves you in return he will tell you."

"And if he doesn't?"

"Then you have a rather large decision to make. Do you think he could come to love you? Or is he the type of man who would marry you for your money and then return to his mistress?"

Jennette bit down on her lower lip until she tasted the metallic flavor of blood. She toyed with a loose thread on her gown. "I don't know. He knows that I'm an heiress. And with his father and brother's gambling . . ."

"Was he pursuing you just for your money?"

"Initially, yes. But once I told him I'd find him a bride, he seemed satisfied with that option. Do you think he might be a gambler, Mother?"

"Hmm," her mother mumbled. "I think the only person who can give you a satisfactory answer is Blackburn. When did you two become close?"

Jennette felt the heat of embarrassment cross her cheeks. She couldn't tell her mother when that had actually happened. Her mother would force a wedding whether Jennette loved Matthew or not.

"When we would talk about what type of woman he wanted for a bride. He spoke of his estates and you could just see the love he had for the land and his tenants."

Her mother's dark brows tilted upward. "And you want to be the one to help him."

Jennette nodded. "More than anything."

"Then perhaps you should go speak to him. See how he feels about you and then you can make your decision as to whether you will be traveling to Florence or staying here with your family and new husband."

Jennette leaned over and kissed her mother's soft cheek. "I cannot go to his home alone."

Her mother smiled at her. "I know I would if I were in your position."

"Thank you, Mother."

"You know which decision I'm hoping for," she commented with a smile. "Go tell this young man how much you love him."

Matthew blew the dust off his father's desk in the study of his London home. Someday this would be different. But not for a long while if he married Jennette. While the idea of marrying her after she was no longer an heiress should anger him, it didn't. They would find a way to survive without her money.

After sorting through the letters he'd received from the creditors, he knew he had one more piece of nasty business to attend to before he could speak with Jennette. He glanced over at the clock on the mantel and decided noon was late enough for Vanessa to be out of bed. Pulling on his greatcoat, he planned the rest of his day. Vanessa first, then he would call on Jennette at her mother's home.

Before he proposed, he had to know if she would ever be able to love him as she had John. If she thought there was the slightest chance, he would ask for her hand.

With his day planned, he left for Vanessa's house. The air was brisk and a few snow flurries landed on his old beaver hat as he walked the eight blocks. The wind whipped around the buildings, making him wish he had taken his horse to make this trip shorter.

He walked up the steps to her house and raised the knocker. After banging loudly, he waited. Finally, Davis opened the door.

"Good afternoon, my lord," Davis said with a frown. "Is she expecting you?"

"Not that I'm aware."

"I see." He opened the door and waved him in. "Please wait in the salon and I shall see if she is at home."

"Tell her I insist she speak with me."

"Yes, sir."

Matthew waited in the salon, noting that nothing had changed in the eight weeks since he'd ended it with her. He wondered if she had secured another protector.

"Matthew," Vanessa exclaimed as she strolled into the room. "What an unexpected surprise!"

"Indeed. Can I assume this means you haven't spoken to Huntley in the past three days?" he asked gruffly. Every time he thought about what almost happened to Jennette anger filled him.

A small frown marred her face. "I—I don't know what you are speaking of. Huntley is not my protector."

"I never said he was, but we both know that is his desire," Matthew retorted.

"Well, we knew that when I chose you," she answered. Davis brought in a tea tray and placed it on the table in front of the sofa. "Tea, my lord?"

"No. I only came for answers, Vanessa."

"I've missed you dreadfully." She walked up to him and kissed him softly. "Have you missed me?"

"No."

Her face lost its color. "Oh."

She returned to the sofa and poured herself a cup of tea. "Why are you here, then?"

"I think you know why I am here, so just tell me why you put Huntley up to it." Matthew leaned against the pianoforte and folded his arms over his chest. His patience had worn thin.

"I really do not know what you are talking about. What exactly did Huntley do and what does it have to do with me?" she asked in an innocent tone before sipping her tea.

"He told me you asked him to force himself on Lady Jennette."

She laughed in a malicious tone and placed her

teacup on the table. "I never told him to *force* himself on her."

"Then what did you ask of him?" His voice grew louder.

"He told me you and Lady Jennette were becoming close. We both know she is not the woman for you, Matthew." She leaned back with a satisfied look on her face.

"What did you ask him to do, Vanessa?"

She shrugged. "I only suggested that if he were to seduce Lady Jennette, I might take him as my protector."

"Indeed?"

"Yes. Lady Jennette would only make your life worse than it already is," she answered.

Matthew clenched his fists. "And how exactly would she make my life so horrible?"

"Well, think of the dreadful gossip if you decided to marry her. You both would be outcasts among Society. You might even have to go into seclusion at one of your deteriorating estates."

Vanessa rolled her eyes and continued her diatribe against Jennette. "Lady Jennette would despise you for making her into such a disgrace. The ensuing scandal would ruin her family's name, too."

"So you took it upon yourself to ruin Lady Jennette's life by having Huntley almost rape her."

"Almost?" she mumbled in a hushed tone.

"Yes, almost. He didn't succeed. Her brother and I stopped him before anything of consequence happened."

"I see." She pretended to straighten her skirts.

"Still, Matthew, she wouldn't want to be made a fool of by marrying you."

"I believe that decision should be up to her, not you." Matthew could not believe the woman seemed to have no remorse for her actions against Jennette. How could he have misjudged Vanessa so significantly?

Vanessa swallowed visibly and sat up straight in her seat. "Do you love her?" she whispered.

"Yes."

"But you weren't supposed to fall in love with her. Or anyone," she sobbed.

"Vanessa, you were my mistress. My lover but not my love. I'm sorry."

"You never intended on returning to me, did you?" she asked, then wiped away a tear.

"I am sorry for deceiving you. I had hoped to spare your feelings," he said softly.

"Spare my feelings?"

"Yes. I knew you loved me but I didn't have the same feelings for you. I had hoped you would find another protector before I married," he admitted.

"I see." She pulled at the folds of her skirt, stretching the muslin then crinkling it into clumps in her fists. "I think you had best leave, Matthew."

"Of course. As long as we are both clear that I will not be coming back to you."

"I understand perfectly," she replied harshly.

Matthew yanked on his greatcoat. "I certainly hope you do."

"Oh, trust me, Matthew. I understand."

The ominous tone of her voice made him turn and stare at her once more before he left the house.

* * *

Vanessa stared at the door after Matthew left. If he thought for one minute this was over, he was wrong. How dare he say he didn't love her! She'd given him her heart and her body.

The sound of heavy footsteps turned her head toward the staircase.

"Did I not tell you he was in love with the chit?" Huntley said, straightening his cravat as he walked.

"I told you to seduce the girl, not force yourself on her," Vanessa yelled, standing to face him. She cringed every time she saw the purplish bruises on his face. Someone had beaten him nearly senseless.

"She wouldn't be seduced, so I thought the only way to get what you wanted was by force."

So that explained the bruises. Selby must have caught him and beaten him, as deserved. Huntley was a complete and utter idiot. If not for his finances, she would have dissuaded him years ago. But he might prove useful for a few more weeks. Vanessa stood and walked over to him. She pressed her lush body against him and felt him start to harden again.

"Can you get me into Ancroft's fancy-dress party?" she asked in a husky tone.

"I wasn't invited. Ancroft is good friends with Selby."

She drew her fingernails up the heavy cloth of his trousers and over his hard cock. "Please?"

"One condition," he moaned as her palm rubbed against the head of his penis.

"Anything you want," she purred.

"I want you here, right now."

"But the servants," she protested. The man was insatiable. They had done this only a few hours ago.

"Let them watch."

She swallowed down the rush of excitement at possibly being watched by the servants. Removing each button from its hole, she asked, "Can you get me into the party?"

"Anything you want," he answered as she took him into her mouth.

Chapter 21

After knocking several times, Jennette slowly turned the doorknob of Matthew's town home. She glanced back toward the street to make certain no one noticed her and then slipped inside. The darkness of the place sent a shiver of fear down her back. Did he actually live in this gloomy house?

"Hello? Lord Blackburn, are you here?"

Where were the servants? She knew he must have let some go but certainly some had remained out of loyalty to his family. Walking toward the salon, she almost tripped over a loose marble tile. She glanced up to see huge cobwebs in every corner and a thick layer of dust on the tables. After she opened the heavy draperies, the condition of the house became clearer.

It was an utter disaster.

"Oh my, the man needs me desperately," she said aloud.

She had to see if the rest of the house was in such abhorrent deterioration. As she walked down the marble hallway, she could tell this house had once been a great home. But now, pictures were gone, leaving only their imprint with darker wallpaper in their place.

One room was completely devoid of furniture as if everything had been sold. And it probably had been sold, she thought. She walked further into the house. The kitchen at least looked as if someone came in and fed the man. The coals in the fire were still glowing.

She walked back to the front steps and upstairs. She felt a twinge of guilt for trespassing. At least she now knew exactly what she was getting herself into with him. Thankfully, she loved to refurbish a home and once they had paid his father's debts, she could start on this home first. She turned the knob on the first bedroom at the top of the stairs and released a long-held breath.

The bedcovers were a rumpled mess, there were clothes strewn across the floor, but instead of disgust, she only felt pity. The man had no valet, no footman, no butler, and possibly only a woman who came into cook for him. Her heart went out to him with the sacrifices he made to prevent his tenants from being put out of their houses.

"Who's here?"

He's home. Her heart raced with anticipation. "I'm upstairs," she replied, then proceeded to fold his trousers and place them in the walnut clothing-press. She could hear his footsteps coming closer so she hurried to finish picking up his room.

"Jennette?" He walked through the door with a look of shock on his face. "What are you doing here?"

"I came to see you," she said, then realized they were standing in his bedroom.

"You shouldn't be here," he replied, looking around the room. His cheeks reddened in discomfiture. "Why did you clean my room?"

She never wanted him to feel embarrassed by her discovering the condition of his home. "I assumed your valet was off today."

"You know I have no valet. I'd planned to clean later in the day."

"Matthew, I wanted to talk to you."

He stepped closer to her. "And I you."

"Why did you want to speak with me?"

He pulled her closer to him. "You ran out on me at the Astons' party. You were upset and I had no way of comforting you."

Jennette stared at the brass button on his jacket. "I was upset."

"Then you should have stayed so we could talk," he whispered softly, then kissed her jaw. "It's only been a few days and yet, I've missed you dreadfully."

"Have you?" she asked as her lips tilted upward.

"Mmm," he said, moving his lips to her ear. "We really need to talk."

"Yes, talk," she replied as the heat of his lips against her ear sent moist heat to her womb. They really should talk before they do this again. . . .

He shifted his lips to hers and she was lost. She had no desire for conversation, only for him. Brushing his hair back with her hands, she returned his kiss. His tongue swept across hers, deepening the passion she felt for the man she loved.

As his lips trailed down her neck, she knew they should stop and talk first. But she needed him. Now. If he didn't return her feelings, this would be their last time together. This might be the last time she could be this intimate with Matthew.

And she could never do this with another man. He was the only one she wanted to comfort her, to be with her. If she couldn't have Matthew, she wanted no other.

After loosening her gown, he slid it off her body slowly, leisurely, as if they had all the time in the world. And they did. Her mother would understand her need to be with him. The rest of her clothing dropped to the floor in a pile until she stood completely naked in front of him. Unlike the first time, she felt no embarrassment.

"I want to undress you," she said with a seductive smile. "I want to touch every part of you."

His eyes darkened to slate. "As you wish, my lady."

He held out his arms for her to remove his jacket. She skimmed her fingers up his chest to his shoulders, watching his reaction. As she slipped the jacket off him, Matthew kissed the nape of her neck sending shivers down her back. She wanted him now but she needed this slow.

She unraveled his cravat and then slid it over her breasts, teasing him. She loved to watch the emotions play across his face. Lifting his white, linen shirt slowly over his chest, she revealed hard muscle and warm skin. Finally, he grabbed it out of her hands and ripped it over his head.

"Getting impatient?" she whispered in a husky voice.

"Yes."

"I'm sorry, because I have far too much patience today." She reached for his trousers and then looked down at his boots. "Those have to go."

His smile turned positively sinister. "Then take them off."

"Sit down."

Her body burned from his passionate gaze as he sat on the end of the bed. She stood in front of him and pulled until the first boot popped off his foot. After repeating the motion with the second boot, she put her hands on her hips.

"Now stand," she ordered.

"Very well."

She closed the distance between them, letting her breasts rub against his bare chest until he moaned. She moved her fingers down his chest until she reached the buttons on his trousers. One by one, she released the buttons until she could slide his trousers down his legs.

Once she had him completely nude, she brushed her breasts against his chest and wrapped her arms around his neck.

"Jennette," he mumbled against her shoulders. "I want you now."

Arching against him, she whispered, "Now, Matthew."

Jennette relinquished control to him. She needed him to love her with his strong body, to prove there was even a small chance he might love her.

Leisurely, he lowered her to the bed. The dim afternoon light caught the silvery flecks in his eyes as he brought his sensual lips down on hers. Tenderness and passion mixed until desire overtook them both. He moved his lips down her neck to her breasts and suckled deeply until she squirmed and bucked under him.

"Matthew," she whispered. The words wouldn't come out of her mouth. Fear of rejection kept her admitting her love.

His lips traveled down her belly, even further until he reached the spot he knew she loved. Her body cried out for his when his tongue rasped against her nub. Feeling the sensations building, she fought against them. She wanted him inside her, filling her, making them one.

"Now, Matthew," she demanded in a hoarse whisper. She could feel his lips smiling against her thigh.

"Anything you say, my lady." He rose up, brought her legs with him, and entered her quickly, deeply.

Jennette shut her eyes, feeling the sensations of being with the man she loved.

"Open your eyes, Jennette," he said.

She blinked to find his face close to hers. Matthew grabbed her arms and brought them over her head, linking hands with her. His body lay atop hers as he slid farther into her and then back out. Pleasure built and she stared into his eyes, watching his expressions.

There was love in his eyes, she was certain. She should tell him. But the pleasure changed to pressure and she had no control. Lifting her legs higher on his hips, he sank in deeper, sending her quickly over the edge.

"Matthew," she cried but the words she needed to say refused her.

"Oh Jennette," he thrust once more before stilling his muscles and spilling his seed into her.

She watched as his face contorted in pleasure, and she smiled, knowing she had done that to him.

* * *

Matthew awoke slowly. He rolled to his side and watched Jennette sleep. They had a very bad habit of not being able to keep their hands off each other. While this would be a good thing in a wife, she still hadn't agreed to marry him. Most likely because he hadn't asked her yet.

He hadn't wanted to become so carried away with her before they talked. But their lovemaking always amazed him. This afternoon had been different, far more tender and sensual than any other time.

She blinked her eyes open and smiled at him. "I thought we were supposed to talk," she said softly.

"Hmm, I think we became preoccupied with other things."

"I think you're right. We seem to always have that problem." She rolled to her side and caressed his face. "Matthew, why didn't you tell me how bad your situation was?"

"I thought I had."

"I just never imagined you living like this." She looked around. "I could have at least helped you by hiring a few servants—"

"No," he interrupted. "I told you before I would not take your money." Resting against the pillows, he pulled her closer.

"Matthew," she stared then paused, looking away from him.

"Yes," he drawled.

"Are you a gambler?"

He chuckled softly. "No, Jennette. I have wagered

a few times but I never had the urge to waste my money on a game of chance."

"What about the wager with Lord Culpert?"

Matthew closed his eyes as his jaw clenched tightly. "It was a silly bet to see who was the better horseman. No money was ever going to exchange hands with that bet. His groom determined later that the horse had a cracked hoof."

"Oh," she whispered.

"I'm not like my brother or father. Even if I had a fortune, there are far better things to do with money than waste it on a wager."

With her silence, he assumed she was satisfied with his answer. Not that it mattered terribly since her brother planned to turn over the will. They would create their own fortune. Once he discovered what she still felt guilty over.

"Tell me what you think happened the day of John's death."

She stiffened until he started to rub the long length of her back.

"You can tell me, Jennette," he murmured.

"I hate even thinking about it much less speaking of it."

"Tell me, Jennette," he insisted.

"I've tried my best not to remember that day, hoping if I could put it out of my mind somehow it might not have really happened." She pushed her hair behind her ear and looked up at him.

"The night we first made love, I dreamed about it again. Only this time, everything seemed clearer to me. I remembered holding the heavy sword in my hand. And when I should have been looking at

John and paying attention to my feet, I couldn't help but look back at you."

He pressed a kiss to her forehead. "Oh darling, it was just a dream."

"No, Matthew."

"I watched you closely that day because the grass was so slick. I'd told John not to let you take the sword but you both insisted. So I kept my eyes on you. You didn't look back at me."

She shook her head vehemently. "I did, Matthew. You might not have noticed but I did."

"I would have noticed." He caressed her long tresses. The question burned his mind, forcing him to ask so he could learn the answer. "Nonetheless, why would you have been looking back at me?"

"I couldn't help myself," she admitted in a whispered voice.

"Were you attracted to me then?" he asked, praying for the answer he wanted to hear.

She nodded against his chest. "Yes."

Now he started to understand her guilt. How dreadful to be attracted to a man who wasn't her betrothed and then to accidentally kill the man she loved. And to have the man she was attracted to tell her of his desire right before she picked up that damned sword. No wonder guilt consumed her.

"The worst part," she whispered, "is I think John knew."

The only way they had a chance of being together was if she knew the truth. The entire truth. As much as he hated to tell her, he had no choice.

"He knew. At least, he knew I was attracted to you."

Her tears rolled onto his chest. If he could take

away all her pain he would, but he knew she had to come to terms with this mess. Perhaps talking to him would help her.

"Do you think he'd noticed my attraction to you?"

"I can't be certain." He caressed her hair. "He never mentioned it to me."

"What if he did know?" she murmured into his chest. "I cannot live with that."

"Perhaps that is why he asked me to protect you," he whispered aloud.

"I tried so hard not to let my attraction show," she said, wiping a tear from her cheek.

"Maybe he sensed your attraction, although I never did."

"You didn't?" she said with a sniffle.

"No. For all I could see you both were very much in love." Her desire for him never meant she loved him. If only she could love him as she did John, he thought again.

"Jennette, if the situation were reversed and John had killed you, would you have wanted him to feel such guilt over an accident?"

"Of course not."

"There's something else you should know." He dreaded telling her but wondered if this might be the only way she could forgive herself.

"What?"

"John wasn't faithful to you during your engagement," he whispered. "When I confronted him about it, he disregarded my comments."

She stilled. "Do you mean he kept his mistress?"

Matthew shook his head, feeling worse about what he had to tell her next. "John couldn't afford a mistress. He'd taken up with a couple of widows who didn't need money."

Slowly she raised herself up off his chest and stared at him. "What do you mean John couldn't *afford* a mistress?"

How could she not have known? "John's father had cut off his allowance because of his wild behavior. He had no income."

"So he thought to marry me knowing my father would give him a large dowry and my family would never let us starve." She blinked. "And of course knowing I would inherit a huge fortune when I was twenty-five." She paused and stared down at him. "Why didn't you tell me then?"

"I wanted to," he said, looking away from her. "I tried to tell you that morning but John interrupted us."

"Oh."

"Would it have made a difference?"

"Yes and no," she whispered so softly he barely heard her.

"What?"

"I'm not certain I would have believed you after your admission that morning."

Matthew shook his head and sighed. "Of course you wouldn't have. I'd just blurted out my feelings for you. I was hurt and angry that you were so in love with John . . . and not me."

"I wasn't in love with him," she mumbled.

"You what?" His heart pounded in his chest with the hope that she could love him.

Sobs wracked her body. "I knew then that I didn't love him. I—I was going to break the engagement.

I'd tried a few times before but I had decided to break it off with John *that day*."

"Oh, Jennette," he said, holding her tightly. "You have never told anyone this, have you?"

"How could I? I killed him. For all I know, I did it on purpose."

He pushed her away from him and stared down at her. "Never say that again. You did not kill John on purpose."

"How can you be sure? I'm not even certain. Everything that happened that day is a blur." She combed her hair back with shaking hands. Tears still fell like a summer storm from her beautiful blue eyes.

He grabbed her shoulders and gave her a gentle shake. "I saw what happened. Your foot slipped. That was all. John couldn't react in time because the grass was slippery."

Matthew hoped he was making some semblance of sense to her.

She stared at the bedcovers as if unable to move. "Do you think he could have forgiven me?"

"If he had survived, I have no doubt that he would have absolved you of all guilt."

She nodded.

"Come here," he said, bringing her back into his arms. "He was my best friend, Jennette. It would tear him apart to know how you've lived with this guilt."

"It doesn't seem quite right that the man whose life I ruined is the one trying to help me with my life," she commented, wiping a tear away.

"Who better?"

For the first time in days, he heard her laugh.

The sound warmed his heart and made it ache at the same time. He wanted to hear her laughter for the rest of his life.

"Jennette," he paused for courage, "I—"

"Blackburn, where the devil are you?"

"Dammit!" Matthew exclaimed. "Wait downstairs, Somerton."

Jennette's lips twitched. "He does seem to have the worst timing, doesn't he?"

"Unbelievably poor timing." With the moment to confess his love gone, he yanked his trousers up his legs and then found his linen shirt. "Damned poor."

"And what should I do?"

"Stay here. I shall get him out of the house." Matthew tugged on his jacket and walked to the door. Looking back, his heart ached again. She looked like a waif with her hair covering her breasts and tears still on her face. He wanted to go back and comfort her, not talk to Somerton.

Matthew cursed once more before opening the door and heading down the stairs. He searched the salon only to find the room empty.

"Where the devil are you?" Matthew complained.

"I'm in some filthy, dusty room with no light and a desk."

Matthew walked down the hallway to the study. He hadn't bothered to open the heavy velvet curtains this morning, so he did so now.

"Thank God. This place is a disaster," Somerton commented.

"Why are you here?"

"I actually have something for you." He handed

Matthew a heavy invitation. "Seems we're both moving up in the world of Society."

Matthew stared at the invitation to a fancy-dress ball at the Marquess of Ancroft's home tomorrow night. "Why?"

"I believe he heard how we saved Lady Jennette from a most unfortunate event."

"Of course." If Selby hadn't told him, Jennette most likely had.

"Will you be attending?"

Since Ancroft was such a good friend of the Selbys, it might be a perfect time to announce an engagement. If he could only get Somerton out of the house, giving him a chance to propose to Jennette in peace.

"I believe I shall," he replied.

Somerton poured a glass of port and leisurely sat in the cracked-leather chair. He looked as if he did not intend to leave anytime soon. "So, have you screwed up your nerve to ask her yet?"

"I haven't seen her since the party," Matthew lied.

"Well, I'm quite certain she will be attending Ancroft's ball so talk to her then."

Matthew glanced around the room and wondered what he had to offer her. Not his name, not a fortune, not even a decent home in which to live. He did have a title making her a countess but that was about all.

"Have you decided how you will tell her brother?" Somerton asked.

"No. The man threatened to go to court to have her grandmother's will turned over if she married me."

Somerton drained his glass and slammed it on the table. "Damn him. I will talk to him."

"No."

Somerton thrummed his fingers on the arm of the chair. "I know him better than you. I can convince him that you love her, not her money."

"I do not need your help with this," Matthew said, feeling a twinge of anger.

Somerton shrugged. "Of course you don't." He rose and tilted his head. "I shall take my leave now."

Thank God. "Good afternoon, Somerton."

Matthew walked Somerton down the hall to the door. As soon as the heavy wood door shut behind him, Matthew raced upstairs to Jennette. He entered the room and frowned.

"Jennette?"

No sound came in return. Her clothes were gone, the sweet smell of her had departed, too. As he sat on the end of the bed, he noticed a note on the pillow.

It was getting late and my mother would have started to worry about me. Thank you for talking to me. Your words were a great comfort. I didn't have a chance to tell you that I have found you a bride. She does not believe your name is a problem and is old enough not to need the consent of her parents. She will be dressed as Aphrodite at Nicholas's fancy dress ball. Please attend so I may introduce you both.

Yours,
Jennette

She found him a bride? He ripped the note to shreds and tossed them in the dying coals of the fireplace. Bloody hell. After all they had been through, she still wanted him to marry another woman.

Well, that wasn't about to happen. He would go to her mother's house and insist she marry him. Didn't she realize they had not done anything to protect against a child? She could be carrying his baby in her womb at this moment.

Matthew combed his hair and strode down the cracked marble stairs, careful to miss the steps in the worst condition. After pulling on his greatcoat and hat, he walked to her house on Bruton Street. In his anger, the biting wind had no effect on him.

He banged on the front door and waited for the butler or footman. The door opened slowly.

"May I help you, sir?"

Matthew handed the older man his card and waited.

"Yes, my lord?"

"I am here to see Lady Jennette."

The man's fluffy white eyebrows drew into a frown. "I am sorry, my lord. Lady Jennette is out."

"Where is she?" he demanded.

"It is not my position to ask," the butler replied.

"Where is she?"

"Is there a problem, Grantham?" Lady Selby asked from behind the door.

"Lady Selby, I must speak with your daughter."

"Open the door, Grantham," Lady Selby insisted.

The door opened fully to reveal Lady Selby standing with her hands on her hips staring at him. "Lord Blackburn, my daughter is not at home. She did tell me if you called upon her to tell you that she will not speak to you until tomorrow night's ball."

Matthew stood there staring at the older woman. Jennette wouldn't even speak to him? Perhaps she really had found him a bride and this was her way of being done with him. After all, he was nothing but a fortune hunter like John.

Chapter 22

"This has to be the most uncomfortable costume I have ever worn," Jennette complained to her maid.

"Yes, ma'am. It's the shell," Molly replied, trying one last string to keep her shell attached to her gown.

Aphrodite rising from the sea. Perhaps not her best idea for a masked ball.

"How am I to sit in this?" she said with a laugh.

Molly chuckled with her. "Very carefully or the sheer will rip."

"No, I shall stand all night. Hmm, dancing may be out of the question, too."

Molly tied the mask with white feathers sticking out of the side. "Can you even see?"

"Barely. This costume is mad."

"But it is beautiful, ma'am."

Even with all the issues with her dress, excitement rippled through her. Tonight, she would tell Matthew she loved him and she was the perfect woman to be his bride. She would do her best to right his reputation. Several of her friends were influential amongst the *ton*. Hopefully, she could count on them for support. It didn't matter what the others thought or believed because her family supported her and they always would.

"That's the last of the ties holding the shell in place, ma'am," Molly said.

Jennette turned to the mirror and immediately knew the reason she'd chosen this costume. Aphrodite rising from her clam shell was the most beautiful thing she'd ever worn. The pale, pink sheer fabric of the shell against the white flowing Grecian gown created an elegant effect.

"Have a wonderful night, ma'am."

"Thank you, Molly." She planned to have the most magnificent night of her life. When she returned to her room tonight, it would be as the future Countess Blackburn. Tomorrow she would start her wedding plans. A simple wedding at Selby House. Avis would love to be the hostess for her wedding breakfast.

As she walked down the steps, she smiled at her mother waiting below.

"You look positively radiant," her mother stated. "Any special reason?"

"Do you think Banning will accept him?"

"Yes. Once he sees how much you love Blackburn, he will understand. Plus, Avis will make certain he gives his approval."

Jennette nodded. "Shall we?"

Her mother's eyes welled with tears. "My little girl," she mumbled softly.

Jennette squeezed her mother's hand as they walked into the carriage. "How am I to sit in here?"

she asked with a laugh. She finally managed to sit and wondered why they even bothered to drive when Nicholas's home was only two blocks away.

When they arrived, she scrambled out of the carriage eager to enter the house and find Matthew. Walking into the ballroom, she scanned the room and realized the flaw in her design. It was a masked ball and she had no idea what he planned to wear.

After discounting all the men with hair either too light or too dark, she found him. He wore the same highway costume he'd worn to her birthday ball when he found her in the garden. His lips slowly tilted upward as she walked toward him. The mask he wore hid most of his face but she had no need to see his visage. She knew the structure of his face, the small lines that formed when he smiled at her, and the way his brows creased when he frowned. And after they married, she had every intention of painting him nude.

"Aphrodite, I assume?" he asked when she reached his position by the door.

"A highwayman. Hmm, I believe I might have seen this costume at another time."

"Are we to wait for Jennette to introduce us, then?" he said with a chuckle.

"I don't think that will be necessary," Jennette replied.

Her heart swelled with love. This was the man she'd wanted and needed all her life. She couldn't wait to start their life together. After seeing his town home, she wondered if his estates needed as much work. She certainly hoped so. She hated to have nothing to do with her time. His estates would keep her busy for years.

"There is a waltz starting, shall we?" He held out his arm for her.

"Yes." At least she would be close to him. She desperately wanted to sneak away with him to a quiet room where she could kiss his lips, feel his tongue rough and velvety against hers. The thought of losing herself in his arms brought warmth to her cheeks and elsewhere.

The music started and they floated across the room. His hand burned through the layers of her clothes. She yearned for his kisses, his touch.

"Hmm," he said. "I thought Aphrodite was without clothing as she arose from the sea."

Her lips twitched. "I thought the *ton* might find that just a bit too scandalous."

"Jennette, we need to talk in private," he whispered so no other dancers would hear him.

"Yes."

"Does Ancroft have a room in which we could meet?"

"Perhaps his study. It's down the hallway on the left. Third door."

"Meet there in an hour," he said softly. "It's imperative that I speak with you."

"An hour?" She tried to keep the disappointment out of her voice. She wanted to speak with him now.

"If we're caught slipping away immediately after dancing—"

"Of course," she said, but didn't really understand. If the purpose of their meeting was to agree to marriage, what did it matter if someone saw them?

She wanted so much more than a conversation with him, but there was an odd tone to his voice tonight. Almost as if there was something wrong. Perhaps he wanted to propose to her properly and felt a little nervous. She could understand with the amount of butterflies in her stomach tonight.

As the dance ended, he walked her over to her mother and bowed formally over her hand. Jennette's nerves prickled watching him stroll away from her.

Something *was* wrong.

The urge to chase after him became tangible. Her mother's hand clasped onto her arm. "Is something amiss?"

"I am not certain, Mother. He acted strangely with me."

"Nerves, my dear. Nothing more. Men like to pretend they are the stronger gender but in truth, we are." Her mother's gaze went to the dance floor. "Do you think any of these men could handle childbirth?"

Her mother always had the ability to make her laugh. "No, I suppose not." Jennette glanced around and noticed both Avis and Elizabeth across the room. "I need to speak with Avis."

"Very well, my dear. Just don't be long when you meet Blackburn. We would not wish to cause more talk."

Her mother's intuition amazed her. "Yes, Mother."

Jennette sauntered through the crush until she made her way to her friends. A footman with glasses of lemonade and wine stopped in front of the group. Jennette immediately picked up a glass of white wine and slowly sipped it.

"Well?" Avis asked as soon as the footman departed.

Jennette shrugged. "We danced. That was all."

"He didn't pledge his love in the middle of the dance floor?" Elizabeth said.

"Of course not," Jennette replied in a hesitant tone. "I am to meet him in the study soon."

"But . . . ?" Avis said, then sipped her lemonade.

"I wish I knew. Oh, I wish Sophie had attended. She could let me know if I'm worrying for naught." Jennette grabbed a glass of wine from a passing footman.

"Why?" Elizabeth asked.

"I just have the strangest feeling something is wrong. He didn't act or speak with me as he normally would. What if I am wrong about his feelings for me? What if he only bedded me because I was convenient? What if this was just the best way for him to get me to marry him, so he could have my money?"

Avis smiled condescendingly at her. "Jennette, you worry overmuch. Besides, Banning told him that he would turn over your grandmother's will if he attempted to marry you."

"Banning said what?"

"Shh," Elizabeth warned. "People are looking."

"Banning was bluffing. He wanted to test Blackburn's love for you," Avis said.

Jennette held her stomach as it began to roil. "Oh God, I think I am going to be sick."

"No, you will not," Avis said sternly. "There is nothing to worry yourself over. Blackburn loves you."

"But he's never told me that," Jennette whispered. "He has never spoken those words to me."

Jennette drank her wine down quickly and

wished for more. Not that the wine seemed to help either her stomach or her nerves.

"He needs my money, Avis. Without it, he cannot help his tenants. He can't pay his father's gambling debts. He shall have no ability to refurbish his homes."

"Jennette, if he loves you, none of that will matter," Elizabeth said softly.

"Elizabeth, don't be so romantic. He has to marry a woman with money," Jennette answered coldly. She suddenly felt as if her world were splitting apart into pieces too small to ever put back together again. She leaned against the wall, afraid she might faint.

He would never offer for her now.

She had to find him and tell him the truth about her money.

Matthew watched Jennette from across the room. Never in his thirty years had he felt this nervous about anything. Somehow, he had to convince Jennette that marrying him wouldn't be a mistake. Even though he had nothing to offer her but his love, it would be enough. God, that sounded so sanguine. While in truth, he had nothing.

She appeared more beautiful than he'd ever seen her. The white silk of her dress shimmered like pearls in candlelight against her skin. He shouldn't feel so tense. She told him his potential bride would appear as Aphrodite.

She'd worn that dress as a message to him. Encouraging him to propose and she would agree.

And yet, he couldn't eradicate the feeling that

something was going to happen tonight. Something dreadful. This heavy mood just would not lift.

"Are you ever going to get up your nerve and ask her?"

"Good evening, Somerton," Matthew replied with barely a look sidewise to him. "Are you ever going to keep your nose out of my business?"

"Not with this."

"And why not?"

Somerton smirked and raised an eyebrow at him. "Let's just say I have a vested interest in seeing you two married."

"Oh?"

Somerton shrugged nonchalantly. "I think you two belong together."

"Am I supposed to believe that? Everyone knows you don't care about anything." Matthew glanced down at his watch—twenty more minutes of this inane conversation.

"Perhaps you found my fatal flaw," Somerton said with a grin.

"A hopeless romantic?"

"If you need to think that to propose to her, then believe it."

"And yet, I don't see you working to improve your reputation in order to find an appropriate bride," Matthew said.

"I have no need for a wife," Somerton answered a bit harshly. "I don't need money. I have too many cousins so an heir isn't a priority, no matter what my father says. And if I need a woman, there are plenty who would love to warm this rake's bed."

Matthew looked up and noticed Selby walking directly toward them. This could not be good.

"Selby," Matthew said with a nod. "To what do I owe this pleasure?"

"For the past two days, I have had two people whom I care deeply about do nothing but regale me with all your finer points, Blackburn. I still don't believe them but thought a quick talk with you might allay some of my concerns." Selby nodded to a quiet corner of the room.

"Oh, this should be excellent," Somerton remarked.

"Stay out of this," Matthew and Selby said at the same time.

"Very well," Somerton said, then skulked off.

Matthew walked to the corner and behind the large palm. "What do you want, Selby?"

"One simple answer," he said, folding his arms over his chest. "Do you love my sister?"

"Yes," Matthew answered simply. "I have absolutely nothing to offer her but my love."

"And if I take her money away?"

Matthew shook his head. "I would still love her and still ask her to marry me."

Selby smiled, revealing deep dimples just like his sister's. "I believe my sources were right."

"Sources?"

"My wife and Ancroft."

Ancroft defended him to Selby. The idea tilted his lips upward. "Good people."

Selby smiled fully. "Yes, they are. And they both care very deeply for Jennette and none of us would like to see her hurt."

"I will never hurt your sister."

"I'm starting to believe you," Selby said, then stepped out in front of the large palm.

Matthew sighed and shook his head, glad the interrogation from Selby was completed. He glanced around the room to find Jennette still in deep conversation with Lady Elizabeth and Lady Selby. Jennette leaned against the wall as if her knees were about to give out.

Something was wrong with her. He stalked across the room to talk to her. The quintet ended their musical set, creating a crush of people moving off the dance floor. Caught in the crowd, he had no choice but to slow his pace.

A woman dressed in a scarlet gown walked to the stage. She hammered a knife against her wine glass to garner the attention of the party.

"What the devil?"

Matthew stopped and turned to see Ancroft grimace. "Not an expected announcement?" Matthew asked.

"No," Ancroft answered. "And I have no idea who she is."

They both waited for the room to quiet and the woman to make her announcement. The woman held up her glass and smiled.

"I am afraid most of you don't know me, but I decided it was time for the truth to come out," she said.

"This cannot be good," Ancroft commented.

Matthew tensed. The woman's voice, though distorted by the crowd and room size, sounded familiar. The sense of unease that had haunted him most of the evening returned with a vicious bite.

"For too long now, a man among you has been scorned and his reputation has been left in tatters. But what most of you don't know is that Lord Blackburn is and always has been the innocent party in the death of John Ridgeway."

Whispers circled the party and gazes moved from him to Jennette.

"Oh God," Matthew whispered.

Ancroft stared at him. "What the devil is she talking about?"

Vanessa cleared her throat and said, "Lord Blackburn was not the person who killed John Ridgeway. The woman who killed him duped Blackburn into protecting her name. Lady Jennette Selby did the deed. She is the one who should be scorned."

Matthew and Ancroft raced to the stage to stop her.

"Lady Jennette killed Mr. Ridgeway because she was in love with Lord Blackburn," Vanessa announced just before Matthew reached her.

Chapter 23

"Oh my God!" Jennette exclaimed as the curious gazes of the *ton* landed on her. Shock wrapped its fingers around her, holding her motionless. She wanted to move, leave the room, but her feet remained in their position.

"Get her out of here," Avis said to Elizabeth. "Take her to your house."

"Of course."

Jennette felt as if she were in a dream. Elizabeth led her out the side door and the numbing cold hit her in the face. Not even the wind and driving rain could awaken Jennette from her stupor.

Everyone knew the truth.

She would never be able to show her face in Society again. Her name was ruined, as well as her family's.

"Who was that woman?" she finally asked, once safely ensconced in Elizabeth's carriage.

Elizabeth looked at her gown. "I heard a man say the name Vanessa as we passed by him. I don't know a Vanessa, do you?"

"No," she mumbled, unable to tell Elizabeth the truth. Matthew, the man who insisted she tell no one, had told his mistress. The woman he paid to have sexual congress with for the past year or two.

"Jennette," Elizabeth started slowly, "is it . . . true?"

There was no point in lying to her friend about it any longer. The truth had been freed from its cage.

"Yes," she whispered.

"Why didn't you tell me?"

"John asked Matthew to protect my name. I couldn't tell anyone." She looked out the window, gazing at the passing homes. "I never even told my family."

Elizabeth reached over and grasped her hand. "I understand."

But Jennette didn't understand. Matthew had impressed upon her the importance of keeping what happened secret. He'd told her no one could know or they risked the possibility of another inquest.

Another inquest.

She lied during the first investigation by agreeing that Matthew had killed John. If another inquest was called for, she might hang for lying to them. No one would believe her now.

Why?

Why would that woman have made her announcement now?

Jennette clutched her stomach as the nausea returned. She could only think of one reason for Vanessa's actions. Matthew had asked her. He'd been acting peculiar all evening. He didn't know how to tell Jennette that he couldn't marry her. If he believed Banning's remarks about her grandmother's will, he would not marry her. Vanessa's announcement cleared his name. Now he had the freedom to marry any woman in the *ton*.

Any woman, save her.

Now she was officially ruined.

And even worse, no one would believe that John's death was accidental. Vanessa had made certain when she told everyone that Jennette loved Matthew.

Sadness and remorse slowly turned to a burning rage. Matthew had ruined her. The man she thought she loved and would spend the rest of her life with destroyed her. The idea of living without money appeared more important than creating a life together with love. Even if Banning had found a way to take away her money, she and Matthew could have survived. She could have sold her paintings or taken up portraits to make money.

Only none of that mattered now.

Her life here was over. Staying would only create more issues for her family. They deserved better than a life of gossips talking about them behind their backs. Or people questioning them as to whether or not she was a murderer. As the carriage slowed to a stop in Hanover Square, she knew what she had to do.

Matthew and Ancroft pounced on the stage just as Vanessa finished her vitriol-filled proclamation. They dragged her off the platform and down the hall to the study. Vanessa only laughed as they shoved her into the room. She slowly untied her red mask like the seductress she'd always been.

"You are free now, Matthew," she said, almost

sounding giddy. She moved closer as if she thought to put her arms around him.

Matthew took a step backward. He'd never been more repulsed by a woman in all his life.

"No, all you have done is ruin my life and Jennette's," Matthew said angrily.

"Why?" Ancroft asked in a strangely soft voice.

The door opened and Selby glared at them all. "Who the bloody hell is she?"

"Vanessa Fulbright, my lord," Vanessa replied with a flirtatious smile and curtsy.

"I should have known." Selby grimaced. "Is it true, Blackburn?"

Matthew knew he couldn't ruin Jennette. She had lived with her guilt long enough. This was one way he could protect her . . . again.

"No. The *lady* here is nothing but a disgruntled mistress, my lord. When she discovered I loved your sister she decided to use the gossip to her advantage."

Vanessa's blue eyes turned icy cold. "You liar! You told me what happened two years ago."

"I was foxed, Vanessa. I was trying to make myself appear better in your eyes, nothing more. I'm shocked you actually believed that story," he said in a casual voice that belied his true feelings.

"If you have ruined my sister, I will kill you," Selby said in a low, feral tone.

"You have nothing to fear, Selby," Matthew replied, staring at Vanessa. "No one will believe a whore."

"Nor will anyone else want to be her protector," Ancroft added with a smug grin. "After all, mistresses are supposed to keep secrets. Obviously, you can't be trusted."

Matthew watched Vanessa's mouth gape when she realized the mistake she'd made. Her face paled under the artificial color on her cheeks.

"Go home, Vanessa." Matthew opened the door for her. "While you still have one."

As soon as the door shut behind her, Matthew turned toward Selby and said, "Where is Jennette?"

"Avis told her to go home with Lady Elizabeth."

"How was she?" he asked with dread. He couldn't imagine what she must be going through. The urge to go to her overwhelmed him.

"I was across the room. Avis had her gone before I even reached their position in the room."

"I have to go to her," Matthew muttered. "I have to talk to her."

"Give her tonight to talk to my mother and her friends, Blackburn," Selby requested.

"I cannot do that, Selby."

"She needs to talk to them," Ancroft added. "I know her. And now that Vanessa is gone, you can admit the truth."

Matthew dropped to a chair and raked his fingers through his hair.

"Did she kill him, Blackburn?" Selby sat across from him, leaning forward in his seat. Worry for his sister etched deep lines into his face.

Matthew nodded once. "It was completely accidental. She took my sword but then her foot slipped on the damp grass. John couldn't react in time. The sword went through his lung."

Selby closed his eyes. "Why didn't she tell us?"

"John begged me to protect her name. When I

told her there would be an investigation, she almost fainted. I impressed upon her the importance of not telling anyone, even her family. The consequences were too high. I knew there would be an inquest and if anyone had spoken the truth there would be doubt in the investigator's mind."

"Then why did you tell your mistress?" Selby bit out.

Matthew shrugged, glancing away from Jennette's brother.

"He wanted to look better in her eyes," Ancroft replied. "I'm sure we both can understand that."

Matthew nodded again. "And let's not forget the power of brandy to loosen a man's tongue," he said bitterly.

"No one will believe Vanessa," Ancroft said with confidence. "In fact, I need to return to the party and make certain all the biggest gossips know that Vanessa is nothing more than a drunken, disgruntled former mistress."

Ancroft quietly shut the door behind him, leaving Matthew alone again with Jennette's protective brother.

"I owe you an apology," Selby said, sincerity lining his voice. "I had no idea what you did to protect my sister."

"You weren't supposed to know. No one was."

"Why did you do it? Did you love her then as the rumors implied?"

Matthew shifted in his seat. "I didn't love her then. There was an attraction but that was all."

Selby laughed softly. "And yet you say you didn't love her?"

"I did not." God, he wanted this finished. He

needed to talk to Jennette, not her infuriating brother.

"Then why? Why lose your name over an accident that you didn't cause."

"Because no matter my feelings for Jennette at the time, John was my best friend. I could not let him die worrying about what would happen to her," Matthew replied as anger laced his voice.

"Damn, Blackburn. Are you deliberately trying to get me to like you?" Selby asked, then stood as if to leave.

"I don't give a rat's arse if you like me, Selby. I only care about how Jennette feels about me."

Selby threw his head back and laughed. "Good man, Blackburn."

"I need to see her. She won't understand why Vanessa knows what happened."

Selby shook his head. "Give her time. Avis will tell her why Vanessa knows."

"She needs to hear it from me," Matthew insisted, rising to his full height.

"And she will. Tomorrow. She is going to have to come to terms with what happened. If you try to see her too soon, she will only send you away." Selby paused by the door. "My sister has a tendency to be a little stubborn."

"A little?"

"Don't worry," Selby opened the door and smiled back at him, "you shall come to love that about her, too."

As the door shut behind him, Matthew whispered to the empty room, "I already have."

* * *

"I really must go home," Jennette insisted to Elizabeth for the fourth time in the past fifteen minutes.

"Your brother and Avis will come to get you soon." Elizabeth looked anxiously out the window.

Jennette clenched and unclenched her fists. There had to be a way to get home before her mother or brother. Once they arrived, there would not be a chance to leave. They would attempt to talk her out of going away. Everything will work out, they would say in condescending voices.

But she knew better.

Matthew betrayed her. And she had lied to the investigators five years ago. That was perjury. Even if they decided John's death accidental, she could still be in trouble for lying to them.

"Elizabeth, do you have anything I could change into?"

Elizabeth turned and smiled weakly. "Of course, I should have realized how uncomfortable you would be in that costume. I shall find something. You're so tall nothing will fit you in the length."

"Thank you. Anything is better than this outfit."

"Yes. I'll fetch you something." Elizabeth walked out the door.

Jennette slowly stood and strolled to the threshold of the salon as if to follow Elizabeth up the steps. Once she saw Elizabeth reach the top stair, Jennette raced out the front door. She had to hurry. The white gown was like a beacon in the dark night.

She stopped at the top of the square and wondered the best way to get home. Continuing down George Street seemed the fastest. Thankfully, she still had her mask. Quickly, she tied the mask on and prayed no one would notice the woman dressed as Aphrodite, complete with shell, hurrying down George Street at eleven in the evening.

She couldn't contain a giggle. It was the first time she'd even smiled since that bitch made her announcement. But thinking about Vanessa brought tears to her eyes. She'd been so certain Matthew loved her. Obviously, money mattered more than her love.

And nothing mattered now except leaving.

Her resolve strengthened with each step she took toward home. Wiping away her last tear, she lifted her head high and ignored the stares from the few people out tonight. She rubbed her arms as she walked, wishing the cold would numb her emotions, too. If she could just make it home before some unscrupulous person discovered her, out alone and dressed as if she had plenty of money.

When she turned down Bruton Street, she half-expected a crowd of people with a noose in front of her house. Nothing looked different. The light of candles burning only in the foyer indicated that no one had arrived here yet. She grabbed the wrought-iron railing and walked up the steps.

The door opened before her slippered foot reached the top step. "Good evening, miss," Grantham said as she walked through the doorway.

"Lady Jennette," Grantham paused with a frown.

"Yes, Grantham?"

"Is everything well?"

She finally reached home. Her sanctuary from the outside world. Tears flowed down her cheeks. This would be the last time she ever entered this house.

"No, Grantham. Nothing is well."

"Would you like some tea brought up?"

"No, thank you. Tea cannot fix this problem." Jennette walked up the stairs to her room. Molly followed behind her.

"Just help me dress and then leave me," Jennette said to her maid.

"Yes, ma'am." Molly must have sensed her mood because for once the maid said nothing as she assisted her out of the costume.

"I need my black wool dress," Jennette said once she stood in her stays and petticoats.

Molly turned and frowned. "At this hour?"

"Yes."

"Very well." Molly pulled out the black gown and helped her into it. "Is there anything else I can do for you tonight?"

"No." Jennette waited until the maid's hand touched the doorknob. "Thank you, Molly. For all your patience with me over the years."

Molly stood there for a moment, her eyes narrowed with confusion. "Ma'am, you have never been an issue," she said slowly.

Once Molly left the room, Jennette raced to the linen-press. She pulled out several of her sturdiest dresses and tossed them into a portmanteau. Moving to her desk, she opened the secret drawer that held her traveling money. She had been putting half her allowance in here in case she ever needed it. This would be enough to get her settled in Florence. She could arrange with the bankers for her inheritance later.

But when she picked up her ticket, her shoulders sagged. Her ship didn't leave for five days. Even if she could stay at an inn for that time, her brother would find her. Her family would convince her to remain here. Jennette could not do that.

After what Matthew did to her tonight, she could never show her face in Society again. She had ruined her family's name by hiding the truth about John's death. Her options had run out, it was time to leave.

As she packed her money away, she thought about what to do. There had to be ships leaving sooner. Maybe even with the morning tide. Unfortunately, most of the ships leaving London were trade ships, not passenger vessels. She prayed there would be at least one ship that would allow her passage. The trip to Portsmouth where she could find a passenger ship would take too much additional time.

While she'd always thought Florence would be the perfect place to live, too many of her friends knew her destination. Perhaps it would be better to try a different country, farther away from England. She returned to the linen-press and picked out a black hat with a veil. She hadn't worn this hat since her father died.

Glancing in the mirror, she knew she looked the part she would need to play. The grieving widow moving to be closer to her . . . her . . . cousins, she decided. With tears still welling in her eyes and her heart in pieces, she felt every bit the part.

Never had she imagined a pain like the one she felt tonight. She'd been so sure of his love.

She looked over at the small clock on her night-stand and pressed her lips together. If she didn't leave now, her family would find her. Now, she just had to sneak out the back door.

Knowing Grantham would not leave his post by the front door until her mother returned, she would have to opt for the servants' staircase. She peered out the door of her room and noticed no one in the hall. On tiptoes, she raced to the small rear staircase. Stopping at the top step, she listened for voices from below. Most of the servants should have retired for the night by now.

Her luck held as she walked down the creaky steps. Entering the study, she released her breath when she found no one around. An eerie silence filled the entire house tonight.

A commotion at the front door indicated her mother, if not Avis and Banning, had returned home. Her feet refused to move forward. Instead, with one hand on the doorknob, she listened.

"Yes, ma'am. She returned home an hour ago," Grantham said.

"Thank goodness," her mother said. "I will go to her now."

"Ring if you need anything, my lady."

"Thank you, Grantham. We shall be all right, you may retire for the night."

Jennette desperately wished she could give her mother a hug before she left. She wanted to see her mother one last time. But she could not. For all she knew, the investigators would be knocking at the door any minute. Because of her actions, she would never see her family or friends again.

She opened the door, looked back, and whispered, "Goodbye, Mother."

Chapter 24

After pacing his dusty study all night, Matthew could not wait another moment to see her. He'd spent the night chastising himself for telling Vanessa what had really happened five years ago. He should have known better. A mistress wasn't always discreet no matter how much money lavished on her.

Especially a mistress who thought she was in love.

He'd had no idea what love truly felt like until Jennette. Now he almost understood why Vanessa acted as she had. He would do anything to get Jennette back into his life.

He hadn't seen her since last night and it felt as if it had been months. He missed her smile, her sparkling eyes dancing with humor, the sound of her laugh.

But before he could see her, he had to make himself look decent. He raced up the stairs to ready himself. After quickly shaving and changing into decent clothes, he splashed more water on his face. Hearing the front door open, he assumed it was

Somerton. He was the only one who ever called on him . . . except the one visit from Jennette.

"Who's there?" he shouted down the stairs, hoping it was Jennette and not Somerton.

"Selby. Is Jennette here?"

Matthew raced down and almost skidded into Selby. "What do you mean? Isn't she at Lady Elizabeth's?"

"Dammit!" Selby yelled, throwing his hat across the hall. "You were my last hope. I thought she might have come to you for an explanation."

"I haven't seen her since last night. *You* told me to stay away until morning." He never should have listened to Selby. Speaking with her last night would have calmed her.

"She left Lady Elizabeth's around eleven and returned home. Then, a short while later, she departed out the door in the back of the house." Selby cursed again.

Matthew grasped the banister for support. How could she have left? *Fear and embarrassment, you idiot,* his mind reminded him.

"Where else might she have gone?"

"I haven't been able to check with Miss Seaton or Miss Reynard. She might have gone to one of them last night."

Matthew stared at Selby's pale face. "But you don't think so, do you?"

"Let's check with her friends before we go to the wharf."

"The wharf!" Matthew's voice rose. "Why in God's name would she have gone there?"

"We're wasting time, Blackburn. We need to speak

with her friends." Selby picked up his hat and then swung the door open. He strode for his carriage.

"Selby!"

"In the carriage, Blackburn."

Matthew followed as anger and frustration bit at his heels. An overwhelming ache radiated from his heart. He had to find her. The idea of life without her made his entire body slow to a stop. He would find her. It didn't matter where she went, he would travel to the ends of the world to find her.

She had to forgive him.

The carriage stopped in front of Miss Seaton's home for orphaned children. He charged up the stairs before Selby reached the first step. After he banged on the door, a small woman with blond hair and spectacles slowly opened it.

"May I help you?" She glanced around him and said, "Lord Selby, this is a surprise."

"Miss Seaton, please excuse our intrusion. Have you seen my sister?"

"Jennette? Not since two days ago." Her blue eyes rounded behind metal spectacles. "What happened to her?"

"She is missing. If she stops by, please send word to Avis and my mother," Selby said.

"And keep her occupied here until one of us comes for her," Matthew added.

Miss Seaton frowned but nodded just the same. "Good day."

Matthew turned around and went back to the carriage. "Where does Miss Reynard live?"

"Only three blocks away."

"Why would she have gone to the wharf, Selby?"

Selby grimaced. "She had planned to leave for Florence in four days."

Matthew stared silently out the window. His heart felt as if someone had ripped it out of his chest. She had planned to leave and not marry him. Not once in all their conversations had she mentioned her intentions to leave. He raised his fists to the side of his head. None of this made sense.

She'd written that note to him telling him she'd found him a bride. She had dressed as Aphrodite. Why would she have gone to all that trouble if she intended to leave anyway?

"Her ship doesn't leave for four days, so she could be at any of the inns by the docks," Selby said, interrupting Matthew's internal debate.

"None of which is terribly savory," Matthew replied. "Why would she leave here instead of Portsmouth?"

Selby raised a black brow at him, reminding Matthew of Jennette. "Time is of the essence. She knows I will be searching for her, and quite possible you, too."

"Selby . . ."

"What?"

"She might have exchanged her ticket for passage on a trade ship that leaves earlier." *Or had already left.*

Selby frowned and shook his head. "I know."

As the carriage stopped in front of Miss Reynard's house, Matthew's foreboding grew. The possibilities of what might have happened ran rampant in his head. She could be hurt. Someone might have kidnapped her.

Or, she might have just left you for good, his mind reasoned.

Dread slowed his pace. Selby knocked on the door and an ancient butler showed them both into the small antechamber. Selby talked to the man but Matthew didn't even listen. His mind continued its crazed debate about why she left and where she could be right now.

"Lord Selby and Lord Blackburn, welcome."

Matthew looked to see an exotic woman with dark hair and almond eyes the color of slate looking at them. He'd heard of Miss Reynard and how she had become the toast of the *ton* with her ability to make matches and tell fortunes.

"I need your help, Miss Reynard," Selby said.

"Of course you do. But I think Lord Blackburn requires my assistance even more than you, Lord Selby." Miss Reynard smiled softly at Matthew and then clasped her bare hands with his. "She is safe."

"Where is she?" he asked insistently.

"She feels she must leave."

"Then she was here!" Matthew said.

"No, my lord. She has not been here in days." She squeezed his hands in comfort. "But I do know my dear friend. She must have decided she had no choice but to leave."

"Where?"

Miss Reynard shook her head and frowned. "I do not know for certain. In fact, I don't think she knows where she is going. I sense she is safe but in terrible pain."

Pain. "Physical pain? Did someone hurt her?" he whispered.

"You will have to discover that for yourself."

"Come along, Blackburn. Miss Reynard cannot help us," Selby said, dragging him away from the medium.

Anger surged within him like a raging flood. When the door shut behind them, he said, "She knows more than she is telling."

To Matthew's amazement, Selby laughed.

"Miss Reynard is never forthcoming with her information. But if Jennette were in any real danger, she would have let me know."

"How can you be so confident?" Matthew asked.

"Without Miss Reynard's assistance, my lovely wife would have made a huge mistake. When Miss Reynard discovered what Avis planned, she came to me. I trust her." Selby clambered into the carriage.

"Now what?"

"The wharf. We shall check the inns and all ships sailing either today or in the next few days."

"That could take days!"

Selby closed his eyes. "We *will* find her."

If only Matthew had such confidence. The long trip to the wharf only reminded him that every second exhausted could mean losing her forever. As much as he wanted to, he didn't have the funds to chase her all over the globe.

They had to find her before it was too late.

Before he lost the only woman he ever loved.

Jennette picked up her new ticket and then returned to the inn she'd retired to last night. Thankfully, the inn appeared to be decent enough. Still, she had shoved a nightstand in front of the locked door last evening in case any drunken sailors had taken notice of her.

As she entered the gathering hall, several men turned and stared at her. She released a breath blowing the lacy veil out in front of her. Even though she was wearing her widow's dress, one man slowly approached her.

"Afternoon, ma'am," he said with a small grin. "Do you need any assistance?"

"No, thank you. I know exactly what I am doing."

He raised an eyebrow. "I'll bet you do," he said in a low voice. "I'll bet you know exactly what yer doin'."

"Excuse me. I need to get my things and leave."

The man licked his lips as he surveyed her from breast to toe. "What ship are you sailin'?"

Dear God, no. What if this man was a sailor on the ship? "I never said I was sailing anywhere. Perhaps I just arrived and happen to be waiting for my coach."

"Awfully long wait, if yer askin' me."

Jennette drew herself up to her full height and looked him directly in his bloodshot eyes. "I don't believe I was asking you anything."

The other men in the room chuckled as this sailor's cheeks became as red as his eyes. Before he could say another word, she walked around him and up to her room. Once the door locked behind her, she let out a long-held breath. She lifted the black veil covering her face. This entire situation was mad.

How could she take such a long voyage without incurring another sailor's attention? She had no protector, not even a maid with her. Hugging herself, she glanced around the pitiful room. With only a small bureau, bed, and nightstand, the room was still twice the size of the cabin she'd secured.

How could she do this?

How could she leave *him*?

She shook her head and tensed her muscles. This was all his fault. His mistress announced to the world what she'd done and the only way Vanessa could have discovered the truth was if he'd told her.

She should hate him.

Or at least try.

Instead, all her soft heart could imagine was Matthew lying beside her in bed. His heart beating softly in her ear. His strong arms comforting her.

"No! I will not let him do this to me any longer," she shouted in the empty room.

Digging her watch out of her gown pocket, she realized that the ship departed in four hours. The man who sold her the ticket had told her that she could board now. The time had come to start her life anew.

A new life . . . a new identity. No one would be able to find her now.

She lowered her veil again, then picked up her valise and with a quick look in the mirror, she started her new life.

Matthew rushed into the next shipping office. They had been searching half the day with no luck at all. Selby had decided to try a different agency. As Matthew raced into the room, the man behind the counter cringed.

"I need your help," Matthew said when he reached

the counter. "Did a woman come in here today seeking passage on one of your ships?"

The man scrutinized him. "Why do you want to know?"

"She's my wife. We had a terrible argument but I now realize that I was wrong. I must apologize and get her back."

The man laughed. "We've all been in that situation."

"Can you help me?"

"Yes. A woman dressed as a widow came in here this morning and wanted to exchange a ticket to Livorno to anything that would sail this morning. A Mrs. Talbot."

Matthew clenched his fists. He'd missed her. She had already sailed and now he had no way of reaching her. He just had to get through this—then he could return to his dilapidated home and drink himself to oblivion. But for Selby's sake, he had to find out where she went.

"What city did she depart for?" he whispered harshly.

"New York."

"Thank you." He turned to leave but stopped as the man spoke up again.

"Sir, she hasn't left yet."

Matthew spun around. "What?"

"We had no ships leaving this morning. The soonest will leave with the evening tide at five."

"Can I get her?"

The man nodded with a smile. "Just be off the ship by half past four. Tell the sailor on guard that Charlie gave you permission."

Matthew reached over the counter and shook

the man's hand. "Thank you, Charlie. I will never forget this."

"Get your wife, my lord."

With lightning strides, he reached the ship and raced up the gangplank. He only had an hour to convince her that she couldn't leave. The sailor on guard pointed him to her cabin.

Once he reached her cabin, he stood outside the door for a few moments. Finally, he knocked on the door.

"Mrs. Talbot, it's the captain. Might I have a word with you?"

Chapter 25

Jennette smiled hearing the captain's low voice outside her door. The first mate had told her the captain would introduce himself once he had the time. She'd expected their meeting would occur after they had set sail.

"Just a minute, Captain."

She glanced in the mirror and sighed. The bedraggled sight reflected back looked in no condition to meet anyone. She pushed the stray hairs back into her chignon and knew there was nothing she could do about the dark circles under her eyes. If nothing else, she looked the grieving widow.

She started to open the door only to have it pushed out of her grip. Stumbling backwards, she gasped when she noticed him.

Matthew slammed the door behind him and glared at her. "Do you have any idea what you have put me and your entire family through today?"

Anger surged in her. How dare he come in her room? How dare he find her?

"Get out. I have already written a note to my family so they will know where I am."

His gray eyes turned to hard slate. "And me? I suppose you were going to send me a note too?"

"No," she said, glaring back at him. "You don't deserve a note or anything else from me."

"Oh?" He took a menacing step closer to her.

She parried with a step sidewise. "After all, you were the one who finally realized the only way to regain your name was to have your mistress tell everyone the truth. You don't need me any longer. You have your name and now some innocent miss will love to be the next Countess Blackburn."

His hand snaked out and clutched her arm. As he pulled her close to him, she tried to ignore his wholly masculine scent. She couldn't let herself fall victim to his intoxicating charms.

"You are quite wrong about everything," he whispered. "I don't have my name back. And I don't want an innocent miss in my bed or my life."

Jennette pulled back and frowned at him. "How could you not have your name back? She told everyone the truth."

His lips tilted upward. "Do you honestly think anyone would believe a disgruntled mistress?"

It didn't matter. He had arranged with Vanessa to make that announcement. She pulled out of his grip to get away from her mesmerizing attraction to him. She had to keep her senses alert. Being near him did terrible things to her mind.

"Well, I guess you should have thought about that before you had her make her announcement to half the *ton*," Jennette spat.

Matthew stilled. "You think I put her up to that announcement?"

For a quick moment, she almost believed the innocent look on his face. "Yes, why else would she have done it?"

"Because she didn't want me to marry you," he said with a sigh. "She was in love with me."

She crossed her arms over the black wool covering her chest. "Why would a mistress care who her protector married?"

"Because she knew I would never come back to her if I married you," he said gently.

"How could she know that for certain? Many married men take mistresses," she retorted before walking the short distance of the room. There was not enough room to pace in here! With his overwhelming presence, the small cabin seemed to shrink.

"Because she knew I loved you. And I, unlike many men in the *ton*, wouldn't take a mistress when I loved my wife."

Jennette stopped mid-step. He loved her. Her heart leaped in her chest and then slowed. It mattered not if he loved her. Nothing changed just because he'd said those lovely, heart-wrenchingly beautiful words.

"Then how did she learn about what happened to John if you didn't tell her?"

Matthew glanced down to the floor of the cabin and sighed. "I did tell her," he admitted in a whispered tone.

"Why?" Jennette's voice rose.

"I was drunk and bitter. It happened two years

ago." He looked into her blue eyes and held her gaze. "I'm sorry. I had no idea she would ever speak of it. Mistresses are supposed to keep secrets."

The look in his eye was so genuine Jennette almost ran to him then. But she couldn't. There was still too much that he hadn't explained. And nothing he'd said changed her situation. She might still hang for John's death. The only thing to do was make him leave and put the pieces of her heart back together again . . . alone.

"Thank you for telling me what really happened." She walked to the door and opened it. "Good-bye, Matthew."

His eyes widened and slowly he smiled. "Do you really think I'm leaving?"

"I believe you had better before I call for assistance."

"Call all you want." He took the two steps to the door and slammed it shut. "They all believe I am your husband. So who do you think is going to interfere with a married couple? According to the law, I can forcibly remove you from this ship and no one could stop me."

"Why would they think we are married?"

"Because I told them we had argued and you thought to leave. We both know that as my wife I can drag you back to my house, even against your will." He placed his hands on his hips and gave her a devious smile.

"I cannot believe you did that!"

"I did. And if you don't pack your bags right now, I will put you over my shoulder and carry you off this boat."

"You wouldn't . . ." Her voice trailed off because, staring into his eyes, she knew he would dare to do such an outrageous thing. And the idea that he would melted her heart. He wouldn't force her to return if he didn't love her.

"I cannot go back, Matthew." She turned away from him.

He stepped behind her and gently placed his large hands on her shoulders. Leaning toward her ear, he whispered, "I will be there with you, Jennette. For all times."

"I killed John. I ruined your name. I scandalized my family's name." A tear slowly tracked down her cheek. She wanted desperately to believe everything would be all right. But she knew better.

"My name doesn't matter as long as you are with me."

"Matthew, please stop. We both know your name means everything to you."

"Not if you aren't with me." He turned her around and looked down at her. "Jennette, I have nothing to offer you except my love."

"Please, don't do this," she pleaded. She hated the thought of turning him down. If she could just prevent him from proposing to her and then get him to leave.

"Jennette, please marry me. Be my wife and we shall face the gossips together. We'll show them that waspish talk doesn't matter when you're in love."

Her heart raced. She couldn't do this. She could not! "No!"

"What?"

"I cannot marry you. I can't go back to town. I have to leave before they discover the truth."

"Who and what truth?"

"The investigators, you fool. Now that Vanessa told everyone that I killed him, there will be another inquest. I lied to them five years ago." She covered her mouth with her hands and mumbled, "Oh God, you lied to them, too."

Matthew grabbed her shoulders and brought her closer to him. There was no way he was going to let her go now. He knew she loved him. But somehow, he had to find a way to get her to admit it and trust him enough to face the gossips.

"Jennette, no one will believe Vanessa. She isn't a lady. She's just a bitter mistress who lost her protector."

"I saw the looks on the faces of the people at the party. They were horrified."

"By her actions, not yours," he said softly, trying to calm the wild look in her eyes.

"I can't go back there, Matthew." She flung herself into his arms, wrapping her arms around his neck. "Come with me. We can build a new life together in America."

He slowly disentangled himself from her clinging body. Cupping her face, he said, "We cannot do that. I am the earl. I have responsibilities to my tenants, to my estates, to you. I cannot leave and you know that."

"I do know that," she mumbled. "Then I shall have to go alone."

With his thumbs, he wiped away her tears. "Jennette, I promise you, everything will be all right. No one will believe her. Your family and friends will support you. Your brother has been out of his mind since he learned you were missing. You can't leave them."

He paused before whispering, "You can't leave me."

She closed her eyes as tears continued to fall. "I don't want to leave you . . . or my family. But how can I stay?"

"You have to trust me," he said softly. "I'm not going to let you leave, Jennette." He leaned in and kissed her cheek. "I shall be by your side the entire time. I won't let anything happen to you."

"You are far too good for me," she whispered. "I don't deserve such an honorable man."

He laughed softly. "Hardly honorable. Just a man in love."

She blinked her blue eyes and stared at him. "I love you, Matthew."

"I know, Jennette," he said with a smile. "I think I've known since that first night we made love. You never would have given yourself to a man you didn't love."

"I do love you, Matthew," she whispered.

"And do you love me enough to disregard the gossips?"

She bit down on her lip and nodded slowly.

"I will never let anything happen to you, Jennette. I will protect you with my name, my title, and more importantly, my love."

She wrapped her arms around him. "I love you, Matthew. And I want more than anything to be your wife."

"Then so you shall. But if we don't leave now, I'm going to make love to you here."

Jennette kissed his mouth tenderly. "And that wouldn't be good?"

Matthew laughed. "Oh, it would be good but we would spend our honeymoon traveling to New York."

She leaped backward. "The ship! It's leaving soon."

"Not with us on it."

Epilogue

Anthony watched the faces of the people at the wedding breakfast held at Selby's home. Lady Jennette Blackburn clung to the arm of her new husband as they greeted the guests at their wedding party. Finally, he had finished this mission.

"Thank you for coming, Somerton," Lady Blackburn said with a gracious smile.

"You are very welcome. How could I not attend and make certain this scoundrel actually went through with his vows?" Anthony smirked at Blackburn.

Blackburn smiled at his new bride. "There was no chance I would back out, Somerton."

"So I see." He was genuinely happy for them. But, seeing the one woman he came to this breakfast for, he excused himself.

After reaching Sophie, he said to her, "We need to talk."

"Not *now*, Somerton."

"Now," he said roughly. He clasped her elbow and led them to a quiet corner.

She rolled her eyes at him. "This is their day. Come to my house tomorrow."

"No. We will discuss this now."

"There is nothing to discuss," she replied in a hushed tone.

Anthony leaned in closer to her and whispered harshly, "I have helped you twice now. First Selby and Avis, now Jennette and Blackburn. You owe me."

Sophie tilted her head back and laughed softly. "I owe you nothing, Anthony. How many times have I assisted you when you needed to find someone for that position you *don't* have with the Home Office?"

"All I want is her name."

"Not yet," she answered coyly. "I have one more friend who needs our help."

"I am not a damned matchmaker," he retorted as the strangling anger circled him.

"Of course, you aren't. I am." She patted his arm with her fan. "You are just my assistant."

"I want her name."

"No."

"I want to strangle you," he whispered.

"I know. But you won't because you want that woman's name and you know that there is no one else who can help you find her." Sophie smiled in such a sweet manner that everyone watching would think they were friends.

"But not until I help you . . . *again.*"

"Exactly. Now turn around because Selby is about to toast the happy couple. And they are only happy because we helped them, whether they know it or not."

"I really want to kill you," Anthony said.

"I know. Now do be quiet."

Selby cleared his throat and lifted his glass of champagne into the air. "I truly never expected this day to come. My little sister has finally found a man to love her. I wish them both all the love in the world. May they be as happy fifty years from now as they are right now."

As Jennette watched the guests slowly leave the wedding breakfast, her heart could barely contain all the love she felt. Their first public appearance since they left the ship a week ago had gone quite well. Only a few people had declined the invitation and for all she knew they had other plans that couldn't be broken. She wished Nicholas were there, but his daughter had been struck ill and he had to be with her.

To her amazement, Matthew had been correct so far. No one believed Vanessa. They all still assumed Matthew had killed John. And Matthew never let anyone think otherwise. Slowly, people were beginning to believe the story that they had fallen in love while she helped him find a bride.

While a part of her wished she could clear that assumption and his name, she knew he would never allow it. He needed to protect her. And she now realized he needed that to forgive himself for letting her take his sword that day.

They said their farewells to her mother, Avis, and Banning. Jennette walked with her new husband toward the carriage she'd bought him as a wedding gift. The Blackburn crest emblazoned the black door. A footman opened the door for them.

"I love you," he said to her once they had settled in the coach.

"And I love you. I have a little surprise for you," she said as love filled her heart to the brim.

"Oh?"

"I'm a week late."

Matthew stared down at her. "Is that unusual?"

"Very. I'm quite timely."

"Do you think?"

She smiled at him. "I certainly am hoping."

Pleasure lit his face. "I am, too."

"I love you," she said for the tenth time that day. "I never thought I could be this happy . . . until you."

"And do you believe I didn't marry you for your money?"

She reached up and stroked his cheek with her hand. "I never believed you wanted me only for my money. Except perhaps that first night at my birthday ball."

Matthew reached over and pulled her onto his lap. "That was the only time."

"I know." She kissed him fully and felt the spark of desire skipping up her arms. "You know, we could take the long way home."

"My thoughts exactly."

About the Author

CHRISTIE KELLEY was born and raised in upstate New York. As a child, she always had a vivid imagination and the bad dreams that go along with it, or perhaps the dreams were caused by her five brothers and three sisters. After seventeen years working for financial institutions in software development, she took a leap of faith and started her first book. Seven years later, *Every Night I'm Yours* was bought by Zebra Books.

She now lives in Maryland with her husband and two sons. Come visit her on the web at *www.christiekelley.com*.

Put a Little Romance in Your Life With
Georgina Gentry

Cheyenne Song
0-8217-5844-6 $5.99US/$7.99CAN

Apache Tears
0-8217-6435-7 $5.99US/$7.99CAN

Warrior's Heart
0-8217-7076-4 $5.99US/$7.99CAN

To Tame a Savage
0-8217-7077-2 $5.99US/$7.99CAN

To Tame a Texan
0-8217-7402-6 $5.99US/$7.99CAN

To Tame a Rebel
0-8217-7403-4 $5.99US/$7.99CAN

To Tempt a Texan
0-8217-7705-X $5.99US/$7.99CAN

Available Wherever Books Are Sold!

Visit our website at **www.kensingtonbooks.com**.

More by Bestselling Author

Janet Dailey

Bring the Ring	0-8217-8016-6	$4.99US/$6.99CAN
Calder Promise	0-8217-7541-3	$7.99US/$10.99CAN
Calder Storm	0-8217-7543-X	$7.99US/$10.99CAN
A Capital Holiday	0-8217-7224-4	$6.99US/$8.99CAN
Crazy in Love	1-4201-0303-2	$4.99US/$5.99CAN
Eve's Christmas	0-8217-8017-4	$6.99US/$9.99CAN
Green Calder Grass	0-8217-7222-8	$7.99US/$10.99CAN
Happy Holidays	0-8217-7749-1	$6.99US/$9.99CAN
Let's Be Jolly	0-8217-7919-2	$6.99US/$9.99CAN
Lone Calder Star	0-8217-7542-1	$7.99US/$10.99CAN
Man of Mine	1-4201-0009-2	$4.99US/$6.99CAN
Mistletoe and Molly	1-4201-0041-6	$6.99US/$9.99CAN
Ranch Dressing	0-8217-8014-X	$4.99US/$6.99CAN
Scrooge Wore Spurs	0-8217-7225-2	$6.99US/$9.99CAN
Searching for Santa	1-4201-0306-7	$6.99US/$9.99CAN
Shifting Calder Wind	0-8217-7223-6	$7.99US/$10.99CAN
Something More	0-8217-7544-8	$7.99US/$9.99CAN
Stealing Kisses	1-4201-0304-0	$4.99US/$5.99CAN
Try to Resist Me	0-8217-8015-8	$4.99US/$6.99CAN
Wearing White	1-4201-0011-4	$4.99US/$6.99CAN
With This Kiss	1-4201-0010-6	$4.99US/$6.99CAN
Yes, I Do	1-4201-0305-9	$4.99US/$5.99CAN

Available Wherever Books Are Sold!

Check out our website at **www.kensingtonbooks.com**